Our Nana Was a
NUTCASE

Ranjit Lal has written over thirty books for both adults and children. Some of his books include *Tigers of Taboo Valley*, *The Crow Chronicles*, *The Life and Times of Altu-Faltu*, *Bossman and the Kala Shaitan*, *Birds from my Window*. He has been a winner of the Crossword Best Children's Book Award for *Faces in the Water*.

Our Nana Was a
NUTCASE

Ranjit Lal

RED TURTLE

RUPA

Published in Red Turtle by
Rupa Publications India Pvt. Ltd. 2015
7/16, Ansari Road, Daryaganj
New Delhi 110002

Sales Centres:

Allahabad Bengaluru Chennai
Hyderabad Jaipur Kathmandu
Kolkata Mumbai

ISBN: 978-81-291-3578-0

First impression 2015

10 9 8 7 6 5 4 3 2 1

The moral right of the author has been asserted.

Printed at Repro Knowledgecast Limited, Thane

For Leena and Puni

1

 $\mathcal{T}$hirty thousand feet above the Arabian Sea, the commander of the Empress Noor Jehan, a Boeing 747 heading into Mumbai from London, suddenly cocked his head.

'What the heck is that?' he asked the co-pilot. 'Sounds like a commotion back there…Go and check!' The co-pilot rose and opened the cockpit door. There was an air hostess just outside, her face pale, she had been about to call.

'What the…?' the commander and co-pilot started.

'Dum-lagake haisha! Jor lagake hai-sha! Haisha-haisha-haisha!'

The chant from the passenger cabin filled the cockpit. The voices of 300 passengers were raised in unison.

'Sir…sir…a passenger's having a baby!' the air hostess stuttered. 'The lady's father is with her and he's a doctor and he's doing the delivery—thank god. We've curtained her off from the other passengers. But he's got all the other passengers to yell, to encourage the mother!'

And a little while later, a cheer reverberated through the plane. 'It's a little girl,' the stewardess gushed, smiling. 'And she's yelling her head off too!'

At the end of the flight, the lady's father thanked the commander and is reported to have said: 'Sorry for the uproar, but my daughter had an urgent deliverable to make and thank you for the cooperation!'

Urgent deliverable, I ask you!

Anyway, so that's how I, Avantika 'Jumbo' Singh (better known as 'General Gosling', would you believe it) came into this world, twenty-one years ago. Granted I'm still a little chunky and round in the face but 'jumbo'? No thank you very much. My hair shines and curls attractively around the nape of my neck, and everyone says I have a 'happy person's' face and 'sunflower' smile (with good teeth). I have dark brown eyes, and a figure that makes guys' eyes swivel. And free air tickets for life!

'It was the quickest way to pop you out, Gosling,' Nana always chuckled, winking at me and raising his eyebrows at Mom, who glowered at him. 'Your Mama was so mad at me! She popped you out like a champagne cork!'

Even now, I get embarrassed when I board a plane. But if you'd met Nana, you could well imagine he'd do something like that. He was big and paunchy, ruddy and pink as a smacked bottom, with a round face and three chins, bushy silver eyebrows and hair, and tufts sticking out of his ears. He had this huge smile that made all the stray dogs and cats and donkeys and urchins swarm around him wagging their tails, and a stentorian bellow which sent them scuttling off as fast as they could, giggling helplessly.

Mama and Papa (who were rising stars in the Foreign Service and were being transferred to remote corners of the world like they were on a giddy carousel) dumped me and my three siblings on Nana, one by one, hardly before we were able to walk. Actually, I always thought it was Mama's way of getting her revenge on him. Poor Nani had died when Mama was just a toddler and Nana, a surgeon in the armed forces, was at that time himself being posted all over the place. So he had put her in boarding school at about age six. Now, Mama was returning the compliment because Nana had taken early retirement—just before my birth. He had in fact come to London to fetch Mama, who had patriotically insisted that I be born in India. But of course I had to jump the gun and popped out in the plane. Papa had been attending some major conference at the time and couldn't get leave.

Apart from me (the stable ballast in the family) there's Harshita (alias Duckling), who's now eighteen and has had her nose in a book ever since she was three; she has a wobbly bum and actually runs like a duck. She is always scribbling in her precious diary and loves collecting owls, frogs, turtles and wacky parrots made of crystal, wood, ceramic, metal or anything really—and a lot of other stuff. She's the 'rocket scientist' amongst us, or so she likes to believe. She's also a bit snooty—those uppity eyebrows of hers can put boys off! She can be bitingly sarcastic but tends to get emotional very quickly and is very sensitive.

Then there are the twins, Niharika and Nihal, who are now a terrifying fourteen. They had been christened Dumpling and Dingaling Enterprises Pvt. Ltd. by Nana—and are still called that! Niharika is a bit like a dumpling, but she bullies and still smacks Nihal unmercifully, so he really is a bit of a dingaling too. Both of them have only one ambition in life: to make quick money, by any means possible. As usual, Nana hit the nail on the head with their nicknames. When Duckling discovers that the pair has been rummaging in her 'collections' to find if there's anything they can sell to their notorious friends, they run like rats.

Nana, as I mentioned, was a surgeon in the Army, and after retiring early because he did not want what had happened to Mama to happen to us, settled down in Mahaparbatpur—a small hill-station town in Himachal—in the huge old rambling bungalow his very wealthy ('and fancy-dress princely!') father had left for him. By then he'd pretty much seen it all—bits and pieces of dismembered and blown up human beings, popped out eyeballs, 'crispy' fried ears and sliced off noses, and all the other things a landmine can do when you step on it—the works. After retiring, he worked on an honorary basis, part-time at the local pediatric hospital, which was desperately short of doctors and qualified staff. It's a single-storey whitewashed building with a broad verandah running around it and big windows and wild pink roses climbing the walls and over its red tin roof.

This is also where Shabnam (Shabby) Aunty works and who everyone says would have married Nana long ago if it hadn't been for her gross son Raksha (we called him Rakshas of course!), who when he was just twelve went through the roof like a howitzer shell when he heard the rumour and is said to have chased his mother around the house with a broken Coke bottle!

Shabby Aunty, needless to add, is neat as a pin with not a hair out of place even after she's dealt with screaming brats who have puked all over her like Vesuvius erupting. She must have been about twenty-four or twenty-five when she met Nana. Her marriage was already kaput and she remained fanatically devoted to Nana all his life. She must be around fifty now (though she still looks just about thirty), while Rakshas is around twenty-five but behaves like a two year old. He has serious anger management issues. It's amazing that someone as sweet and gentle as Shabby Aunty could have produced someone as downright violent as Rakshas, but there you have it. They say Shabby Aunty never saw it coming—that she had produced a little Frankenstein who needed drastic obedience training. He was the only thing she had after her husband deserted her when she was barely twenty-two. By the time she did realize it, Rakshas was a hulk who threw food at the walls if he didn't like it. Alas, for the longest time, Shabby Aunty had a blind spot as far as he was concerned and let him get away with stuff that was completely gross. Thankfully, Rakshas got a 'job' in Mumbai, though it seems he's more often between jobs than in one.

Shabby Aunty and Nana were really made for each other (to use a trite cliché) in spite of the yawning difference in ages; they were an 'item' for as long as I remember and it was so clear that they adored each other. It was really too sweet (Duckling rolls her eyes in disbelief even now!). They'd met at the hospital—Nana was then maybe a very distinguished fifty-five and took her under his wing, though soon it seemed to be the other way around. They often operated together, she as the anesthesiologist and I really admired the way they worked as a team in the theatre.

It's something I've always wanted to do too—healing people—and am studying for. It's wonderful to see the smiles on the faces of parents when you've cured their kids. I've got a large collection of photographs of such happy endings. Of course, there's also a terrible flip side too, of which I'm well aware; being a doctor is a lot like doing drugs while being on a roller coaster!

That apart my other great passion is photography. I got hooked ever since the time Nana showed me how pictures were developed in the darkroom. This was the time he still used film, and it seemed like pure magic (understandably, I was only five years old then). Of course now everything's gone digital but I had found my passion. The house is stacked with fat albums of my pictures and even now I prefer printing out pictures and arranging them in albums rather than keeping them on the computer. We have a complete photographic record of all birthday celebrations, holidays, fooling around at home, school, the car rallies we've been taken to, everything we've done really. I rarely step out without my camera. Not all the photographs are brilliant but as Nana put it, 'General, sweetheart, this is a fantastic and valuable photo-record of our family history. Sociologists and anthropologists will be beholden to you one day.'

I've had great practical 'training' in surgery and medicine too (I know that sounds pompous but it's true). Nana took me with him to the hospital regularly ever since I was a toddler (before the Neerameerabais joined us), so I was quite used to the smell of ether and the screaming of kids, and built up a bulletproof immunity against all the infections the kids in the hospital distributed so generously. Some of my earliest memories are of driving to the hospital in the old khaki WW II Willy's Jeep with Nana, bouncing down the mountain road, all huddled up against the early morning chill. Even later, when I was older, I hung around Nana's clinic quite often, helping out largely by cuddling the babies and playing with them. But if I was ever in the vicinity of the hospital and heard the chant, *dum-lagake-haisha, jor-lagake haisha!* emerging from inside, I'd skedaddle double quick. All the nurses knew the story of my birth (Nana and his big mouth) and ragged me unmercifully. He still did that in the delivery room, regardless of the protests of the other doctors. But it made all the mothers-to-be in the ward blush furiously and giggle like schoolgirls, and momentarily forget their pain. His tiny patients and their mothers adored him. The nurses of course, would have died for him!

'Works every time! The babies hear the chant and out they pop like popcorn in the microwave!' Nana said gleefully, winking ferociously. '*This* is what you call genuine chanting!'

Needless to add, Mama made sure he was nowhere near her when she had Duckling and the twins. Nana would look at them mournfully and say, 'I'm so sorry sweethearts, I missed out… Your mom never told me anything…she was very naughty!' But then his eyes would light up. 'Even so, Duckling, you began following me from the moment you laid your eyes on me; first by wriggling on your tummy, then on all fours, then by bouncing on your bottom, which was so well padded, and finally waddling along on two legs! As for you two, I nearly gobbled Dumpling up when I saw her, she looked so delicious, and well Dingaling what can I say—my one and only grandson!'

I'll never forget the day Mama and Papa dropped off the twins. It had been raining and I'd been watching a National Geographic film about an orangutan orphanage in Indonesia. There was a lady with two orphaned baby orangutans in her arms on the screen, and then who do you think walks in with two toddlers under his arms? Nana!

'General Gosling, two babies for you to look after, sweetheart. They're called Dumpling and Dingaling! Call the Major too and meet them!' Both the babies were looking around with wide eyes, their thumbs stuck firmly in their mouths exactly like those orangutan babies.

Behind him Mama and Papa followed, smiling falsely. How could any parent smile at such a time? For a very long time and maybe even now, I never forgave Mama and Papa for what they had done to the twins and us. Of course I don't remember how I had reacted when I had been 'abandoned' in Shadow House with Nana for the first time. I was just about able to walk. I was four when Duckling joined me and remember that she cried a lot and Nana walked around with her on his shoulder for a long time, patting her curls and singing to her in his deep bass 'comfort' voice. Dumpling and Dingaling too were upset when Mama and Papa eventually drove away—they were barely a year old. I was seven at the time, Duckling was four and between us, we tried to pick up and console these two screaming, heartbroken, terrified babies and smothered them with hugs and kisses. Duckling was (and still is) more down-to-earth in her approach to them and thinks I'm a bit of a marshmallow. Thankfully, we had the Neerameerabais who knew what to do to make abandoned toddlers happy.

We've lived in 'Shadow House', this old rambling bungalow, for pretty much as long as I can remember. After the others joined me, we all went to school in Nana's old blue Ford Woody station wagon, collecting half the neighbourhood's kids on the way. It was called the Khatara Neela Bus but was actually in beautiful condition with lovely white-wall tires. Nana's passion was restoring old, rusted, ramshackle cars. One of the most magnificent of his collection (which we call the Emperor's Phroo-Phroo Collection because of the way the horns sounded) was an ancient black Rolls-Royce. You can't imagine what happened when he decided to pick us up from school in it once, wearing a chauffeur's uniform complete with peaked cap. I nearly freaked but prissy missy Duckling stuck her snooty nose and fat bum in the air and waddled down the driveway as though she were Queen Victoria. The two baby brats were plainly thrilled and jumped up and down yelling, 'Yay, we're going home in the Rolls-Royce!' The huge, magnificent old car, polished and gleaming drew up to the gates, Nana blew the 'phroo-phroo' horn so that everyone (including the principal) stared in awe and stood to attention, and the sun dazzled off its chrome headlamps and that noble Grecian radiator. Graciously, he opened the doors for us, doffing his cap and ushered us inside. I could have died! And then…the bloody great Rolls stalled and refused to start.

'Push!' Nana said, his eyes twinkling. 'Get out and push!'

And so the four of us started pushing this monstrous car, a Rolls-Royce at that, getting nowhere, while all the other dumb kids just stood around and laughed and clapped. Suddenly and very mysteriously, after we were bright red with the exertion and embarrassment, it started up again and off we went.

'These old cars are really moody!' Nana commented, shrugging. He stopped a few yards down the road, 'Now go and call all your friends who live on our route!' I knew exactly what he'd been up to. I guess it taught (some of us) a lesson but that's how Nana did things.

You might imagine it was boring and lonely, living in a small back-of-beyond hill-station, but Mahaparbatpur was famous for its 'differently-abled' (that's Nana's description) schools most of which had a very progressive approach to education, and we were rarely short of company or friends. Nana patched up umpteen of those silly boarding school boys at the dispensary, where they would be brought when they did idiotic things like fall out of trees or play with petrol and firecrackers in their dormitories.

'You, my friend, have been exceedingly foolish!' he would roar as yet another fifteen-year-old boy would be driven over with his elbow sticking out at a frightening angle. 'Before you climb a tree to steal walnuts, make sure you have your exit strategy planned for an emergency evacuation in the event the principal comes looking for you. If you jump from twenty feet this is what happens.' Or, 'If you want to become a terrorist, just walk across the border, they have excellent training facilities there, young man!'

The idiots would then invite him to umpire their next cricket match or accompany them on a hike and try to inveigle an invitation to visit his 'workshop' and tinker with his precious cars so that they could catch my and Duckling's eye.

But what bugged us the most about Nana was that he was such a stickler for punctuality and discipline.

'This is like a damn boot camp!' Duckling would often protest tearfully, or when informed that 'Major miss Duckling, the time now is 1934 hours and you are exactly four minutes behind your scheduled bath time. May I kindly have an explanation in writing? You are upsetting the bathing schedules of the good Misses Gosling and Dumpling and Mr Dingaling, which in turn will cause an unacceptable delay in dinner time because the chicken's ETA out of the oven is precisely 2030 hours and it cannot be kept waiting!' The explanation usually was that Miss Duckling had her nose stuck in a book and couldn't take it out.

'That's okay then, sweetheart,' Nana would say, beaming, after Duckling emerged from her (shortened) bath so we could keep to our schedules. 'Reading is okay but try not to do it again at this time!' I think what also bugged us a lot was that there was no way you could really remain mad at him and sulk for very long.

It really was strange; on the one hand he was completely nuts, on the other, an extremely regimented and disciplined ex-Army officer. He didn't run the household alone; he had his two devoted Gurkha batmen (the 'Chakrams') to do most of the running around. He had given them the nicknames Mahavir Chakram and Paramvir Chakram because of the sheer foolhardy courage they had displayed during some terrifying battlefield encounter. They would die for Nana a thousand times over. Their wives, who are sisters, Neerabai and Meerabai (we call them the 'Tragic Neerameerabais') did the cooking and looked after the twins and Duckling. They still unnecessarily interfere in my life. Well, they've looked after all of us since we came to Shadow House and basically brought us up as they would have their own kids, I suppose. And boy, was theirs' a tragic tale: their young kids who were with their grandparents at the time were killed in a monstrous landslide that took the entire village down with it. They never went back because there was nothing to go back to. Numb with grief, they stayed on with us and had sworn never to have children after that. So in essence, we had been raised by them with Nana in overall charge. At least twice or thrice every week Shabby Aunty would drop by and make sure everything was all right. The house ran like clockwork, though I don't think any 'normal' family's routine was just like ours.

Here, for example is what a 'typical' school-day and weekend was like at our house, just before it all started to go crooked and wonky. Compare it to yours:

0600 Hrs: All four of us would rocket out of our beds as the Colonel Bogey March would suddenly blare, accompanied by the tramp of marching feet on the wooden floorboards. Nana would be marching up and down in the corridor outside our 'cubicles', in his military boots, playing his golden trumpet and sounding like a drunken barati band. Occasionally he would mark time (we didn't notice it for a very long time, but gradually he was marking time more than actually marching and his marching steps were becoming smaller and more mincy) and start singing in that stentorian baritone of his: *'Hitler! He only had one ball...! Goering! Had two, but very small...'*

I mean which grandparent in the entire world would do that? Duckling and I would sit up convulsed in giggles and the other two would lustily join in. We liked to believe they hadn't a clue as to what he was on about. Mama would have had a coronary if she heard them! Then we had five minutes to turn down our beds and stand ready for inspection. Till I turned thirteen, we all slept together in the single enormous bedroom (the 'Barracks') on the first floor that stretched across the width of the house. Once I hit thirteen, he had a 'private cubicle' partitioned for me. 'For your privacy and comfort miss, before you start hounding me about it,' he said. He did the same for Duckling when she entered her teens. Now, two of us have our own little rooms— complete with dressing table and built-in-cupboards and knick-knack shelves, and the twins share a bunk bed in the remaining section of the room. They're still too thick as thieves to want their individual spaces.

Once assured that we had been roused, Nana would turn and salute a grinning Meerabai. 'Right, Sergeant-major, the brats are yours, spruce them up with spit and polish!' he would roar even as the twins hurled themselves at him and then made tracks for the bathroom. Neerabai of course would be in the 'mess' getting our breakfast and tiffin ready.

0630 Hrs: Breakfast. If it was Monday, it was cornflakes, bacon and fried eggs sunny side up; if Tuesday, idli, dosa and samosa...Weekends we could choose what we wanted and he would don his chef's cap and looking a bit like a ruddy Pierre in Beau-Peep, swat the air with a ladle, muttering, 'Damn bluebottles, report to the omelet right now. On the double!'

0700 Hrs and we'd all be standing in line on the porch for 'pre-school' inspection. He'd march up and down the row, his eyebrows rising and falling dramatically, swagger stick under his arm, snorting and snuffling like a rodeo horse.

'Major Duckling, retie those ribbons sweetheart!'

'Private Dingaling, stop chewing your tie, you are not a billy-goat, sir and cannot possibly be hungry! You had three eggs for breakfast and downed two litres of full-cream milk, man!'

'General Gosling, you have a hibiscus growing out of your ear, my love! Would you like to place it in a vase? Right then, patloon, march to Mountain View Point!' Dutifully we would troop down to the gazebo at the edge of the promontory in the garden and stand in a row to stare reverently at the great panorama of the Himalayas glittering like great shards of shattered cut-glass across the northern horizon in front of us.

'But Nana, they're there every day!' I had once protested. Often of course, they were shrouded by clouds and fog, but they were still there!

'General Gosling, then you have nothing to worry about, do

you? You need to worry the one sunny morning you get up and see that they're not there! So thank them for their kindness and be grateful that they didn't up and leave in the middle of the night. Now, about turn and into the paddy-wagon on the double hup-two-three-four!'

He did this every blessed day and we still didn't get fed up. Every day while staring at the mountains, we would see something different or new, or he would point it out to us.

'Patloon,' (he knew very well, it was 'platoon' but would insist on saying 'patloon', and very often add, 'patloon dheeli dali'— platoon at ease!' which sent the twins into hysterics.) 'Note that falcon at one o'clock. It is looking for breakfast…if it dives hit the dirt because it can do 320 kmph and doesn't miss!' Or, 'Major Duckling can you describe the exact shade of the sunlight kissing Nanda Devi, right at this moment? Choose one: rose pink, peach vodka, apricot jam, or Duckling's-cheek?' Or, 'Describe in not more than ten words that cloud formation up there! What does it remind you of? Will it rain or hail or snow candy-floss by this evening?' And then of course, inevitably:

'The sky is?'

'Green!' the twins would chorus.

'The grass is?'

'Blue!' He'd nod appreciatively.

'You brush your teeth with?'

'Shampoo!' the twins would roar, and chime on, 'and you wash your face with toothpaste!'

It happened every day and every day we could barely suppress our giggles. Sometimes he'd turn up on the porch in full uniform, but with a scarlet and canary yellow monkey cap with a turquoise blue bobble on his head. He'd roll his eyes.

'So what's so funny?' he'd demand truculently, his eyes

twinkling. 'It's cold this morning!'

I got a lot of priceless pictures.

We'd rattle down the driveway onto the winding road to the first 'stop'. The kids we picked up knew they had to be punctual, or they'd be left behind—no give or take here. The Ford had a perfectly good electric horn, but Nana always used the 'baw-baw' big bulb horn fixed to the door as he approached the 'stops', and which sounded exactly like a drunken donkey's bray. It was a half-hour drive, winding through the forested mountain roads from the high green 'plateau' on which Shadow House squatted. We drove over several nallahs and streams that tumbled down the mountain side, down to the outskirts of Mahaparbatpur, where our school was located. We picked up virtually every kid who went to our school and lived along the road. There must have been around ten kids besides us four stuffed in the car with our bags on the roof, singing raucously. When we reached, Nana would stop outside the gates and yell:

'Right patloon, to battle stations on the double; fix bayonets; chaaaarge! We take no prisoners!'

'Your grandfather is bananas, I love him!' Sahiba, one of my best friends would giggle. 'You're really so lucky.' Most of my girlfriends were in love with him.

No doubt we were lucky; I remember once how trouble brewed en route to school: we would drive past a small cluster of garishly painted houses, outside which invariably, one of the sourpuss teachers of our school would be standing, waiting for her rickshaw or whatever. I would spot her as soon as we came around the bend and quickly look the other way. Duckling and the others were usually too busy yakking and making a racket to notice anything. Ms. Sourpuss did notice. One morning she cornered me, glowering. She was this bad-tempered hag who had probably never smiled in her whole entire life. She caught my arm.

'Avantika Singh, you rudely drive past me in that big blue car every morning while I'm waiting in the rain.'

'Uh…really, ma'am? I haven't noticed…there are so many kids in…'

'And you don't have the courtesy to offer me a lift! Don't you have any manners at all, girl?'

'Uh…sorry ma'am…I'll…um…where do you stand?'

'Don't pretend you don't know! You'd better stop the next time.'

'Sure ma'am, I'll keep a lookout.'

So I told Nana. He nodded. 'No problem, General, we'll pick the hag up!' His eyes twinkled and he whispered conspiratorially. 'Um what time do we drive past the old bat's cave? I think we'll bring forward our departure by ten minutes, eh? Inform the others, but not a word to anyone else. I have a plan…'

The next day, we drove in through the 'old bat's' gates ten minutes before our scheduled time. There was no sign of her. Nana got to work on the 'baw-baw' bulb horn. In the quiet of the early morning it sounded as if a whole convention of demented donkeys was serenading her! Several dogs, lying in the sun, leapt up as if shot and ran off yelping. Windows opened and people stuck out their heads. Nana waved cheerily and continued to work the horn. Scarlet faced, Ms Sourpuss emerged from her house, hastily stuffing the last of a parantha into her mouth and scuttled to the car.

'Good morning, ma'am!' Nana boomed. 'Such a lovely day! Avantika said you'd be waiting…'

'Sorry, sir,' Sourpuss stuttered. 'I was about to come out of the house.'

But the witch was tenacious. Next day *she* came down ten

minutes early and we had to pick her up without doing the donkey cabaret act. Having her in the car for twenty minutes was like turning it into a hearse and driving to a funeral.

'Never fear!' Nana said, unfazed. 'Now we bring out De-Big Bazooka!'

'De-Big Bazooka?' Our eyes lit up. De-Big Bazooka was our huge, over-friendly bhutia dog, who in the car was impossibly licky and drooly—and loud.

'Yes, he'll sit up in front with me and she can sit next to him. You kids pack up the rear pretty tight.'

That was the last time Ms Sourpuss took a lift with us. I sneaked some lovely pictures!

As for the rest of the day: Either Nana or one of the Chakrams would pick us up from school in the afternoon in the Khatara Neela Bus; if it was Nana there was a good chance that we'd go for tea to Madandas's' Backery and Pastrees which had the best lemon tarts and butter biscuits ever. Of course the whole caboodle of about ten kids would accompany us. On the last leg of the drive, after all the other kids had gotten off, we'd brace ourselves.

'Right, Private Dingaling, nineteen times thirteen is?'

Poor Private Dingaling would stutter and mutter and roll his eyes desperately and scrabble in his satchel for his calculator.

'Private Dumpling, thirteen times nineteen is?'

And Private Dumpling would flutter her pretty eyelashes and say innocently, 'The same as nineteen times thirteen, Nana'

'Clever girl!'

'Two hundred and forty seven, Nana!'

'Private Dingaling, did you use your calculator for that?'

'Umm…no…yes sir!'

'Good man! No man should need to calculate that in his head. But if you have to it's easy: thirteen times twenty is two hundred and sixty, minus thirteen is two hundred and forty seven. Now patloon, give me the nineteen times table to twenty!'

He was also a stickler for checking our homework (another 'deliverable'). Fortunately, our school didn't believe in over-burdening us with homework but it had to be done properly. Of course before that, when we'd get home the Neerameerabais would be waiting to pounce on us.

'Right patloon, get washed and changed and report to the War-Room asap.'

The 'War Room' was on the first floor, set perpendicularly to our 'Private Barracks', painted a glowing chrome yellow and dark blue and stretched right across the length of the house. Four solid polished teak desks stood all in a row, facing a widescreen plate glass window through which we could see the mountains. The computer table stood at the far end, and the opposite long wall was lined floor-to-ceiling with crammed bookshelves. A small wooden table with a fat register stood in front of it—this was Duckling's fiercely guarded domain. She had catalogued and organized the books according to category (adventure, biography, sci-fi, humor, 'not for ages 12 and below' etc.) and you had to make an entry in the register every time you took out a book and returned it. It was an unwritten rule—all the children's books that came into the house were common property and belonged to the 'Library'. Two entire shelves, stretching the width of the room, sagged under the weight of my photo-albums, neatly labeled date-wise.

We had to keep our homework ready for inspection and then get on with it. Nana would examine each of our assignments, grunt and then settle down in the huge old easy chair and snooze while we worked.

'Wake me up if you have a problem or after you've finished,' he'd say and promptly start snoring. At his feet De-Big Bazooka would stare at him adoringly and sigh.

While Dumpling and Dingaling would conspire to do their homework 'collectively', they'd also be the first to get fidgety and restless. This could be a nuisance when you were wrestling with equations and stuff. Duckling of course, who was the sharpest of us all, would finish quickly, shut her books or laptop, raise her wretched eyebrows at me and smirk and then settle down with her latest story-book or in front of the computer to play games. I'd just clench my teeth and grind through my work. It did make me mad, but then Nana explained it—very prophetically I now think—this way:

'Sweetheart, Duckling might be a high-performance turbo-charged hi-octane engine that will perform brilliantly on her day. But you're a heavy torque diesel that will just go on and on forever, no matter what the obstacle, at all times. So don't worry!'

So usually, the others would finish before I did and wake Nana for 'post-homework' inspection. He'd check and 'dismiss' them with the 'patloon dheelee dali!' release.

'You are free to go! Report to Sergeant-major Meerabai for baths at 1930 hours!' They'd scuttle off, yelling and giggling with glee and leave me, feeling like a dork at my desk. Nana would come over and drop a kiss on my head.

'You have more responsibility, sweetheart,' he'd say, and settle down again and wait for me to finish. 'You have much tougher and more complex problems and issues to grapple with.'

You bet I did.

Once dismissed the twins would usually race around with De-Big Bazooka or go over to their friends' or to a nearby park for the rest of the evening. Duckling would disappear up a walnut tree in the garden with a book, or lock herself up in her cavernous 'museum' on the second floor, where she hoarded all her, well, collectibles. She also collected matchbox labels, river pebbles, chocolate wrappers, feathers, old clocks, stamps, coins, padlocks—she was crazy. Or she'd have her similarly peculiar friends over and get into serious discussions about whose collection was bigger and better. I would go off on my mountain bike for a ride. Sahiba lived a kilometre or so down the road and loved biking too. So she along with her lanky elder brother Arun Bhaiyya and I would set off to bike the trails, often bumping down to the jade green stream that snaked through the gorge below to (illegally) fish and take photographs. Sahiba and Arun had lost their father many years ago, and Arun—a bit of a stick in the mud—had sort of taken it upon himself to be the great male protector of his family and would chaperone and follow Sahiba everywhere. Irritatingly, he treated us like kids, with a sort of amused disdain that pissed the heck out of us, but he too had once fallen out of a tree and had to get his arm set by Nana, so there. He was always so serious and solemn you wanted to throw a bucket of water over him. Anyway, if I was in a generous mood I would pick up a pebble or two for Duckling. At home Nana would wander off to his 'workshop', to tinker with his cars. We knew we had to 'reconvene' by 1900 hours, no questions asked, no excuses accepted.

Baths and dinner over, we'd repair to the big living room. Usually the curtains would be left open, so we could look into the black velvet night outside and the pinprick lights on the other side of the valley. In the distance, the ever-present mountains would glimmer silver in the starlight and sometimes I would wonder if there was anyone up there on them and what they were thinking right now. If it got chilly, one of the Chakrams would light a log fire.

'Do you know why we leave the curtains open?' Duckling

once whispered evilly to Dumpling and Dingaling. They shook their heads.

'So that any leopard prowling about outside can see who's inside—and they love juicy dumplings and dingalings! Sweet dreams babies! Yum-yum!'

The twins exchanged scornful glances. 'Hah, Didi, I think any leopard would prefer someone with a fat, juicy hamburger bum!' Dumpling replied tartly and exchanged a high five with Dingaling.

'Hamburger bum? You...you, Nana, did you hear what she said?' Sometimes, Dumpling could floor even Duckling.

'She got you there!' I grinned, 'Touché!'

About twice a week, Nana would say, 'Duckling, fire up the Skype, baby, let's talk to your Mama and Papa! They said they would be available at around this time so I made an appointment.'

'Okay Nana, no problem!'

I suppose we ought to have liked talking to Mama and Papa, but really it was strange because after about three minutes, none of us knew what to say to them. I mean they were so completely out of our lives that they wouldn't understand the context of anything we told them. It was the usual, 'How're your studies going? What's the weather like? We hope you've all been studying hard and doing your homework...Be good, don't give Nana any trouble!' sort of eighteenth-century conversation which faltered quickly. Mama would often be all dressed up and Papa pacing impatiently in the background jingling car keys—obviously they had to go to some important function and we had caught them just before they left, even though Nana had made an 'appointment'. Usually it was a relief to shut down and revert back to normal. At that hour this usually meant:

'Patloon to barracks! General Gosling and Major Duckling may read for a further period of forty-five minutes, Privates

Dumpling and Dingaling will have lights out in fifteen minutes, after we have read the next thrilling chapter of *Why the Cannibal Kings Ate Eno Fruit Salts and Threw Up!*'

Nana would come to each of us one by one, kiss our foreheads and say goodnight.

The weekends were completely free; we could do what we liked when we liked for as long as we liked (meal-times remained sacrosanct of course). Nana would absolutely insist that we finish all homework and assignments on Friday evening itself, no matter how long it took, so we could be completely free over the weekend. I usually accompanied him to the hospital on Saturday mornings, where I helped out. They were so short staffed they were grateful for whatever help was forthcoming. It was nice to share some private, 'professional' time with him and Shabby Aunty and watch them work. We would normally get over by three in the afternoon. At home, Duckling would reorganize and re-label and re-arrange her collections, poring lovingly over them, dust the books in the library (and talk to the characters in them) and iron out crushed chocolate wrappers. For a potential rocket scientist this was a peculiar habit.

Dumpling and Dingaling Enterprises Ltd. would get down to serious business. One afternoon, Nana and I got back a little early from the hospital to find a long line of kids standing patiently outside the garages where his cars were. A small table had been set up, behind which Dumpling sat, collecting money and handing out 'tickets'. Dingaling stood by the side entrance at the far end, tearing the tickets of the kids as they filed past him and went inside. A notice next to the desk read: Rare, Brand New, Famus Vintage Car Collectshun and Mashinery—See Rare and Luvly Cars Here and their Completely Nakid Nuts and Bolts! Chevrolet, Rollsroyce, and all! Entrance ₹5/- only! Free nimboo-paani if you buy a ticket! Timings: 11 am to 3.00 pm strictly!'

They were really busy at the time we got there; some sort of argument had broken out as one of the kids had wanted his little brother to be entered free ('He's under four years old and even at the zoo entry is free!') and the twins were contesting the point ('Then go to the zoo, don't come here!') fiercely.

Matters were getting a bit shirty and the twins were finding themselves outnumbered as many of the other kids joined issue. Some spotted Nana who raised his eyebrows and put his fingers on his lips. The twins had their backs to us and didn't seem him. Very quietly he joined the ragged queue which was beginning to re-form.

A compromise had been reached and the under four-year-old kid was allowed to enter for half price. Dumpling shook her head exasperated and resumed her place behind her desk, riffling through her pad of 'tickets' as Dingaling went back to his post. She looked up startled as Nana suddenly loomed in front of her.

'Please can I have a ticket, miss?' he asked.

Never has a business enterprise been shut down with such speed. Dumpling rocketed out of her chair, grabbed the fat pink purse into which she had been stuffing the takings and fled, with Dingaling right behind her.

I got some marvelous photographs of the whole thing, much to the twins' indignation.

But of course, an inquiry had to be conducted.

'Dumpling & Dingaling Enterprises Ltd, to the War Room for Inquiry, now!' Nana barked, after a rather sheepish tea had been taken. Duckling and I grinned. This was going to be good. We followed.

'Sit!'

'Nana...we were just...'

'...collecting for poor people...all those homeless, nangu-pangu people...'

'How much did you make?'

'A hundred and fifty-seven and fifty...'

'Stupid, it was only a hundred and fifteen and fifty...'

'Count it and decide!'

'Yes, Nana!'

Nana stuck out a hand. 'My cut!' he demanded, 'hand it over!' I exchanged glances with Duckling.

'What, Nana?' the twins' eyes goggled.

'They were looking at my cars. So I want fifty per cent. How much is that Miss Dumpling?'

They re-calculated furiously and arrived at ₹125.50 as the grand total, and then counted out Nana's share. He put his big fist over it and nodded. 'Very well, now what you have kept for yourself put it in the charity tin in the hospital. And tomorrow you will invite all those kids for tea and buns at Madandas's Backery and Pastriees.'

'Yay! Nana!'

He grinned wolfishly. 'Yes! And the bill amount will be deducted from your pocket money in easy installments over the next three months.'

'Nana! But they already got free nimbu pani!'

'However, in recognition of your entrepreneural spirit you shall be entitled to entertainment expenditure amounting to the said amount.'

'What?' They looked at each other. Nana ruffled their heads. 'You don't have to pay, you little hoodlums. Now run away and think up some new scam!'

They hugged him and bolted. They didn't have to think of any new scam.

That night, I heard whispering from their cubicle. I sneaked a look. The two crooks were sitting on Dumpling's bed, gleefully counting money.

They'd made considerably more than the ₹125.50 they had declared. Those two were going to go places.

Nana's cars also held a fascination for the schoolboys from the nearby boarding schools, who loafed around during the weekends aiming catapults at birds. Some of them, the matchbox collectors, were Duckling's friends. By about four or five in the evening there would usually be a motley bunch of half a dozen boys loitering near the garages. Nana would emerge, scowling with mock ferocity, his bushy eyebrows knitting over his brow.

'Have you come here to ogle my beautiful granddaughters?' he'd inquire fiercely, wiping his greasy hands on a bit of waste.

'No uncle, sir, we only want to see the cars!'

'Then make yourselves useful!' Nana would bark, tossing them dusters and a tin of wax polish. 'What are you standing around like that for with your hands in your pockets? Get to work on the Chevy Bel-air and then the Rover 3 litre!'

'Yes, sir!'

Afterwards of course, he'd put the roof down on the Chevy and we'd all go for a drive, the boys grinning like idiots as they sat on the folded-back canvas roof. Nana had to fool around; often he would 'lose' his way and take the car down bumpy narrow dead-end tracks, insisting it was a short-cut and then try reversing all the way back. Or he'd drive all the way down to where the road met the main road and say, 'Let's take Delhi now!' or simply drive past the boys' schools while returning in spite of them yelling, 'Uncle stop, please stop!'

'Oh!' he'd say, 'are you sure you get off here?'

Then one morning, he took a 'wrong' turn while dropping us

to school. We'd been making a real racket, clapping our hands and singing and never noticed. Suddenly the car stopped, as Nana peered through the windshield.

'Oops!' he said, 'where are we?' We looked out.

'Nana, you took the wrong fork about ten kilometres back!' I said, quickly getting my bearings. 'We'd better go back quickly, we're going to be late!'

We were late—for the first time ever—and Nana was quite chagrined. He apologized to each of the kids we had picked up. Of course, he had been fooling around as usual; only this time had slightly overshot the mark so to speak and had just gone on driving. Quite possibly he'd been waiting for one of us to raise the alarm, which we hadn't so he had to—and we had come a long way by then...

The next morning, he unfolded a route map and put it in my lap. 'We're here General Gosling,' he said jabbing a point in the map, which had a big red X marked on it, 'and your school is here! Navigate sweetheart!'

That was the first sign, I now realize, and how it all started...

2

Nana would normally hand us our 'allowance' on the first Saturday of every month. This was also when the staff would get their salaries. It was payday for everyone.

'Now let's see how much you can spend by Monday morning,' he'd grin, as we'd count our money and say our thanks. 'You should be broke by then again!' Dumpling and Dingaling Enterprises Pvt. Ltd would quickly count their money and check each other's notes and then start plotting how they could double the amount by Monday morning. Duckling would tie herself in knots and agonize over whether to spend the money on yet another book, or a set of unusual delicate glass frogs she had seen at the weekly bazaar. I would stash my money away and plan a trip to the junk jewelry market with Sahiba or invest it in photo printing paper or cartridges which were cruelly expensive.

One Saturday, in the middle of the month, Nana called the twins to his study that was alongside his bedroom downstairs. I thought they'd been up to mischief again, involved in some underhand business deal as usual. But they emerged brimming and humming with excitement—they had a secret they could barely keep secret. They skipped around Duckling and me, cheesy grins all over their faces.

'So why did Nana summon you to his HQ?' Duckling asked. 'What's he court martialing you for now?'

'Nothing, Didi!' Dumpling said, rapidly blinking her sparkling black eyes.

'As if we're crooks!' Dingaling added indignantly. 'Actually he's...'

He got a quick hard pinch from Dumpling. 'Shut up!' she hissed. 'Do you want...?'

I exchanged glances with Duckling. 'They've been up to something. Well, it'll come out sooner or later...'

'And then we'll have some fun!'

'Hah!' Dumpling snorted, sticking out her tongue. 'As if you know anything and as if we're going to tell you!'

Well we got to know pretty soon what was up. That evening the Neerameerabais came up to me, looking embarrassed.

'Baby, aaj sahib ne phir pagar diya... He paid us our salary again.'

'What?'

'He paid us as usual last Saturday, and now he's paid us again.'

'What? Are you sure?'

'Yes, baby here it is.'

They scrabbled around and produced the money.

'Oh, he must have forgotten.'

'We told him, but he wouldn't listen.'

'Oh!' This was odd, because Nana was quite meticulous in such matters. 'Has he paid the Chakrams again too?' I asked. They shook their heads.

'We don't know,' they admitted with disarming honesty. 'As if they would tell us!'

'Um...okay...I'll speak to him.'

I heard a shuffling sound outside my door and some whispering. I put my fingers to my lips and walked silently to the door as the Neerameerabais watched, amused. I flung it open. Their ears glued to the door, the twins nearly fell in, then leaped back and gave a surprised shriek and fled along the corridor and down the stairs. So they had been eavesdropping!

'Baba-baby bahut badmash hain!' the Neerameerabais said as they emerged from the room. 'They know everything.'

I looked at them and down the now empty corridor. Well, I knew everything now, too! And this could be fun. I pulled Duckling out of the library.

'Want to get the better of those two?' I grinned. Her eyes lit up. Who wouldn't?

I gave the two little villains a charming big sisterly smile at dinner that night. 'So babies, what are you investing your pocket money in this month? Any new business venture being planned? Duckling and I might just be interested.'

They exchanged panic-stricken glances, as Nana looked on benignly. 'Those two are going to outdo even the Ambanis,' he said fondly. 'Just you wait!'

'What business?' Dingaling squeaked. 'We have no businesses.'

'We are not having any auctions anymore,' Dumpling added hastily. They had not too long ago tried auctioning part of Duckling's beloved owl and frog collection without her knowledge. ('Only the duplicates Didi, and we were going to give you half the money anyway so you could buy new frogs and owls.')

'You could try money-lending,' Duckling now suggested seriously. 'Especially if you have a lot of spare cash floating around. Lend it to your friends who have finished their pocket money already and charge them hefty interest.'

'Interest?'

'Ya, you know, if you lend them a hundred bucks, you can charge them twenty bucks extra for every week they keep it for. So after the first week they'll have to pay you ₹120. At the end of the second week, they'll have to pay you ₹140. Then, when they return it you can lend that out to someone else and…'

'Wow!' The twins' eyes were shining.

'But of course, if you've finished your pocket money already then it might be difficult to start the scheme.'

They shook their heads vigorously. 'No, no, we haven't finished. We've…hardly spent anything.'

Nana smiled. 'Dears, even they couldn't have spent it so quickly.'

'Ya, ya,' the twins chorused nodding vigorously. 'We haven't finished it; we still have it, nearly all of it.'

'Good!' I nodded seriously. 'So we'll discuss this further sometime soon, right? So we can set you up for business.'

They looked hunted. 'Yes, Didi.' Then, being who they were, they rallied.

'But we'll have to think about it. You know, some of our friends might not return the money and say we never gave it to them in the first place. What would we do then?'

'Hmm, funny friends you have! You'll have to ask them to give you something of theirs worth that amount before you lend them the money. So that in case they don't return it, you'll still have what they gave you.'

'Wow!' Dingaling's eyes lit up. 'You mean I can ask Aloo to leave his mountain bike with me when he takes the money and I can use it until he returns it? Wow!'

'And the extra twenty rupees,' Dumpling reminded him, 'you shouldn't forget that!'

'Tell you what,' Duckling said sweetly, 'I'll write out the contract and we'll rubber stamp it and seal it so it'll be pucca when you lend out the money.'

'But you do have enough to lend, don't you?'

'Yes, yes.'

'Great!'

'But but we don't have rubber stamps,' said Dingaling. 'What do we do about those? Are they really needed?'

'Oh, yes, everything has to be properly stamped.'

'You want rubber stamps? I have rubber stamps!' Nana boomed. 'Lots of them! I use them on every letter I send to the government. They always work!'

'Right!' Duckling said, rubbing her hands. 'You guys collect Nana's rubber stamps and keep them ready and we'll have a meeting in your cubicle just before lights out time, okay? I'll bring the contract then.'

'Um...okay...Didi!' The two knew something was not quite right with this 'deal', but couldn't quite put their finger on exactly what.

'And then tomorrow you can lend your money to Aloo and ride his bicycle too!' I grinned.

To ratchet up the tension we kept the two crooks waiting till it was nearly their 'lights out' time. Nana had saluted and kissed everyone and said goodnight and gone downstairs. Duckling and I wrapped handkerchiefs around our faces. We crept up to the door of the twins' cubicle.

'But why are they interfering in our business?' Dumpling was whispering indignantly. 'Normally they only do after we've done something. Not before...'

'Do you think they know?'

'Nah! They're too dumb!'

We barged into the room and switched off the lights.

'Put your hands above your heads and stay where you are!' Duckling barked in a muffled hoarse voice. 'Privates Dumpling and Dingaling, you are both under arrest for racketeering!' They screamed.

'Hand over the dough! We have a warrant to search your

room!' I snapped.

'But, but...'

I switched on the lights and took a quick couple of pictures. They were clutching each other and staring at us, pale with fright. Then they saw it was only us and their colour returned.

'Okay, kids, the game's up. Hand it over!'

'Hand what?'

'Dumpling! The money!'

'Didi...but...the deal, you said...' Dumpling's big eyes filled with tears, like that of a thwarted innocent. 'We've even got the rubber stamps like you wanted.' Her voice petered away. Dingaling looked scared.

'Babies, we know what happened. Nana gave you your pocket money for the second time this month by mistake, didn't he? Now either you give it to us, so that we can return it to him, or, better, you hand it over to him with an apology first thing tomorrow morning, under our direct supervision.'

'But...but...'

'No buts!'

Duckling had crossed her arms in front of her chest. 'May I ask why you did not tell him he'd already given you your pocket money last Saturday?' she asked icily, tapping a foot on the floor.

The twins blanched and suddenly (as you sometimes do) I felt sorry for the little devils.

'We...we...tried...but.'

'But...but he wanted us to have it...'

'So, only because of that we took it...'

'Do you know he might have only been testing your honesty?'

'Yes,' Duckling added, flashing me a glance. 'He might not have taken it back yesterday because he wanted to see what you would do with it—whether you would keep it or insist on returning it.

Oh, yes he was testing your honesty big time!'

The twins exchanged glances and looked at the rubber stamps strewn around on the bed. 'You mean he's...'

I nodded. 'Yes, my beautiful, he was just checking up. Who knows, if you fail he may not leave anything for you in his will. The Rolls-Royce, for example.'

'What?' The thought horrified them. 'Okay, we'll give it back first thing tomorrow morning, promise! When he wakes us up!'

'Good!'

'But...then, but then how will we begin our interest business?' Dumpling wailed, looking at the rubber stamps. 'We've got the stamps and all the pocket money he gave us last week is almost finished so we can't use it!'

'Tell you what!' Duckling said, 'Gosling and I will lend you some money to start the business. We'll give you a hundred bucks, which you can lend out.'

'But...' Dumpling frowned and beetled her brows; she was no spring chicken. 'But how much would we have to give you back?'

'For every hundred bucks we lend you you'll have to give us a hundred and fifty back at the end of the week!' Duckling grinned ghoulishly.

'Didi, you only want to rip us off!'

'Okay, we'll discuss this later. Goodnight, babies!'

'Goodnight, Didi.'

I followed Duckling to her cubicle, grinning. It was not often we got the better of those two rascals and it felt good. But there was something pricking the back of my mind, like a piece of apple skin between your teeth.

'You know,' I told Duckling frowning, 'it could well be that Nana was really testing their honesty—or lack of it.'

Duckling grinned. 'Yeah, we'll know tomorrow!'

'But if he was, why did he pay the Neerameerabais twice also? Surely he wasn't testing their honesty? That's beyond all doubt.'

Duckling shrugged as she picked up her book and prepared to get into bed.

'Dunno,' she said absently. 'Maybe he did forget.'

'If he did forget,' I went on like De-Big Bazooka worrying a bone, 'why didn't he give us our pocket money twice also? Why only the twins and the Neerameerabais?'

Duckling shrugged, already engrossed in her book. Then she grinned. 'Dunno,' she said again, and added, 'anyway we could tease him about it! That he loves those two rogues more than he does us and so pays them twice over!'

'Whatever,' I said, 'but it's going to be fun watching those two return their duplicate pocket money tomorrow!'

'Patloon, rise and shine!' The blasts from the plangent trumpet shattered the quiet of the new morning, and we shot out of bed. It was Saturday, and glory be, a very long weekend (with Monday and Tuesday off!) lay ahead. Normally we could sleep as long as we liked, except that we had planned to go on one of our overnight trips to what Nana had christened the Secret Rainbow Villa. On one of his drives with the Chakrams, he had discovered this crumbling abandoned Forest Rest House, built of stone, perched on a narrow mountain ledge, with a rainbow waterfall cascading down near it into a wide pool before it fell over the edge and tumbled into the forested gorge below. Ivy and wild roses crawled all over the forgotten structure and it merged beautifully with the fern-filigreed rock-face and overhang rising just behind it. Like most such rest-houses, the view from its verandah was just spectacular—pine and fir forests crowding down the steep slopes to the valley below and beyond were the mountains, glittering, floating weightlessly in the middle of the sky. It was about a four-hour drive from Shadow House and the last twenty kilometres were pretty hairy, along a single-lane stony track clinging to the edge of the mountain side and even involved crossing a wide and spirited stream that ran through a deep gorge crowned by dangerously poised boulders. This gave way to a pretty little meadow, dancing with wildflowers, after which the track, burrowing between high-shouldered cliff faces, spiraled steeply to the plinth where the villa was built.

Nana had promptly 'taken control of the territory' and spruced it up with the Chakrams. He'd got the rooms cleaned and whitewashed, and even oiled the door hinges. He'd brought over a gas cylinder so that the kitchen was functional. Sheets, towels and mattresses, crockery and cutlery had been stocked and stored too. And he had been smart: When we left, he locked the front door with an enormous iron padlock and sealed it with official looking red sealing wax to keep nosy hikers out. We went there three or four times a year and Nana always insisted we set off at the crack of dawn. On this occasion, we'd be picking up Shabby Aunty and Sahiba and Arun en route, so I was really looking forward to the trip.

Now as we stood sleepily outside our cubicles for the usual inspection, the twins stepped forward, each holding an envelope. Both envelopes were liberally daubed with purple and red rubber stamp markings.

'Nana, sir!' Dumpling said, holding forth her envelope. 'You gave us our pocket money twice, by mistake! Here's the second one!'

Dingaling did likewise.

Nana stopped in front of them and frowned. 'What? You got paid twice?'

'Nana,' I said stepping forward, 'you also paid the

Neerameerabais twice—they've returned the extra amount too!'
I had an envelope too.

'What? Must be a computer error! Major Duckling, will you please check my laptop sweetheart?'

'Sure, Nana!'

'Here it is, Nana,' Dumpling said, reluctantly proffering her envelope.

'Thank you!' He took their envelopes, put them in his tunic pocket, stood back and saluted the twins.

'Dismiss! Re-convene in mess for breakfast in thirty minutes. We leave straight after!'

He turned on his heel and then at the top of the steps stopped and swiveled around.

'Privates Dingaling and Dumpling!' he roared.

They tumbled out of their room.

'Reporting, sir!' The two stood to attention, half smiling, half nervous.

'In view of the sterling honesty you have displayed—you may keep this as a bonus!' He took out the envelopes and returned them to the twins, drawing them to him and giving them a couple of smacking kisses. Then he shot a meaningful glance at Duckling and me before turning on his heel.

'Did you see that?' Duckling snorted indignantly after he had stomped down the stairs. 'He obviously believes that he paid us twice too, and that we haven't returned our double share!'

The twins emerged from their cubicle smiling triumphantly.

'Didis, thank you for your offer but we've now got enough to start our own interest business so we don't want your hundred bucks!'

Duckling and I glared at them. 'Well good luck to you. Now get ready pronto!'

Nana liked our trips to be 'mass family affairs', which meant he would try and gather up as many people—family, friends, acquaintances and even strangers he might have offered a lift—as possible. We always took two cars—the good old Ford Woody and the sturdy World War II leftover Willy's jeep, complete with spade and winch ('in case we get stuck in the stream'). Both the Chakrams and the Neerameerabais would accompany us as would De-Big Bazooka, bouncing in the jeep along with the baskets of food and drink. Any normal family, reaching such a place, would simply open up the rooms, dust a bit and settle down happily. With Nana, it was nothing like that.

First, he would order the convoy to halt a good two or three hundred meters from the house, just after we had crossed the stream, in the flowery little meadow. He'd rake the area with his binoculars and nod grimly as the twins looked on expectantly. Then to their utter delight, he'd take out a piece of charcoal and begin rubbing it on their faces, in order to 'camouflage' them.

'Privates Dumpling and Dingaling, we are now in enemy territory and have to annex the property. Will you reconnoiter and report back? Break the seal and clear the rooms. Here is the key—guard it with your life! Take the walkie-talkie. We take no prisoners! Over!'

The twins, grossly thrilled would get down on their stomachs and proceed to crawl up the slope towards the house as the Neerameerabais and Shabby Aunty would shake their heads in despair. De-Big Bazooka would rush to and fro madly, wagging his tail, his tongue hanging out half a mile.

'Really, you are as bad as they are!' Shabby Aunty would protest as the twins went through the reconnoiter ritual. With her short, silver-grey hair and neat baseball cap, and T-shirt and jeans, Shabby Aunty always looked dead cool. Her grey eyes twinkled.

Nana leaned against the warm bonnet of the Ford. Embarrassed, Duckling and I would roll our eyes at Sahiba and Arun, who would shamelessly grin and watch the wriggling twins.

'Right, now secure the area!' Nana would bark into the walkie-talkie. The twins would 'break' the seal, 'search' the rooms and radio back.

'Clear, Nana! Over!'

'Clear!'

We loved coming here, primarily because of the waterfall that cascaded down into a wide, shallow pool where we could paddle. The water was clear as gin, and we could see the fish dart around near the sandy bottom. Jewel-like dragonflies and damselflies would dance low over the water, sometimes kissing the surface in order to lay their eggs. Duckling of course, would begin a feverish search for unusual pebbles that looked like precious stones and pieces of driftwood licked smooth and sculpted finely by the water.

I loved the place too because it was fabulous for photography. The light could be soft and mellow as a silken caress, or hard and brittle as a broken beer bottle. I never got tired of taking photographs here.

'Right, patloon!' Nana barked after we'd had our huge lunch. 'Ten hun!' We stood all in a row, Duckling and I raising our eyebrows in despair.

'Your Nana is just too cute!' Sahiba gushed. 'I love him!'

'Yeah it's okay for you, we go through this stuff six times a day!' I grumbled. As usual Nana marched up and down the line.

'Patloon, we are here on a Secret Mission!'

The twins' eyes brimmed with excitement. Nana reached into his tunic pocket and took out a grubby piece of paper.

'This,' he said, 'is a secret map I obtained at considerable risk to my life! It is an ancient map of this area, which is why I've brought you all here. Now, even as we speak, the enemy may be watching my every move—and they want that map!'

'Nana! Then don't wave it around like that!' Dumpling cried, horrified. 'They can see it…hide it, hide it!'

'Ah,' Nana said, his eyes gleaming. 'But Private Dumpling I *want* them to think that I have it here! You see, this is a TSWGC map!' He lowered his voice. Dumpling raised her hand.

'What's TSWGC, Nana?'

'Top Secret Wild Goose Chase, of course! As I was saying, this is a TSWGC map, the real map is…in the seat pocket of the Woody where all the other maps are!'

'Oh.'

'Now listen very carefully because I will say this only once.'

'What Nana?'

'One of you will go to the car and take the map from the seat pocket. It looks just like this one, but has official Utterly Top Secret Government of India rubber stamps on it. You will take it and then all of you will pretend you're going for a nature walk or bird-watching. The Chakrams and Neerameerabais and De-Big Bazooka will go along with you. Shabby Aunty and I will remain here and pretend to sleep. I shall put the dummy map in a place where if anyone is watching us now, will be able to see. You all follow the instructions on the real map and find the treasure. The map has directions to the first clue, and every clue will have directions to the next one, which you will plot on the map till it takes you to the treasure.'

'Treasure?'

'What treasure?'

'Not another treasure hunt!'

Nana's eyes flashed. 'There has to be treasure at the end of any map, otherwise it's a useless map. Anyway, what you might find may not be gold or silver; it may be secret plans for secret weapons that can do your homework for you.'

'Yay, let's go, let's go!'

'Your Nana is nuts!' Sahiba giggled as the twins rushed off to the Woody. I exchanged glances with Duckling and she grinned. Both of us knew what was up. Nana just wanted a little bit of 'privacy' with Shabby Aunty. You could hardly blame him, but trust him to set up this complicated rigmarole. And he did this every time we came here, which meant he had driven all the way here a day or two earlier to set up the whole thing. He really was nuts.

Sure enough, there was another grubby map in the Woody, which the twins nearly tore in half in their excitement, each one clutching at it. It was covered with a lot of official looking rubber stamps, which said things like: 'Top Secret and Most Utterly Stupid!' 'Leaks For The Eyes of TV News Channels' Fools Only!' 'Govmant of Idiots!' 'Ministry of Morons and Blithering Dunderheads!' 'Go Take a Hike!' (Nana had actually used some of these in official correspondence and apparently no one had noticed!)

We giggled helplessly, but the twins were thrilled to bits.

'Gosling Didi, come on help us with the clues!' they cried.

'I think this is more Duckling's line,' I said, 'she's always got her nose in books and stuff!'

Good-naturedly, Duckling sat the excited pair beside her and frowned over the map. 'Okay, the first clue says, "Fried tree with forked tongue. Beneath whose bleeding bosom is hung!"'

'Didi, you said bosom!'

'That's what the map says. What do you think it means?'

The twins frowned. They looked around. The pines swayed secretively all around us, the breeze cool and refreshing. We all looked around. Nana's treasure hunts had a way of getting to you.

Suddenly Sahiba pointed. 'Look, that half dead pine, it's been struck by lightning and is split in half. It looks like a snake's forked tongue.' Sure enough, there it was clear as daylight, about two hundred meters away.

Already the twins had raced up to it and we followed.

'Look, it does have a bleeding bosom,' I said. Like many of the pine trees in the region it had been recently (by the Chakrams I suspected, because no one else really came here) tapped for raw turpentine and a trickle of sticky honey-colored resin oozed down the split in its trunk. Just under the little conical cup, affixed to collect the resin, was a small brown envelope tacked to the trunk.

From there on, the clues led us one by one along the path of the twinkling, gurgling stream, through the gorge. The twins charged ahead eager as terriers, while we struggled to keep up.

'I can't believe it!' Sahiba said, shaking her head. 'Your grandfather actually comes all the way here to set up a treasure hunt for us! To think he goes through all the trouble!'

I shrugged. 'Well he loves going for long drives in his cars—that's how he discovers places like this... It's a sort of passion, I guess.'

There was a treasure at the end of the hunt—an ex-cigar box of chocolate 'gold coins', very tightly sealed with tape so the ants couldn't get at it, hidden behind a big 'bulls-eye striped' rock. Thrilled, the twins raced back to show Nana, closely followed by us.

'We found it, we found it!' they cried, struggling to get the sticky tape off it.

'Good show!' Nana barked, as Shabby Aunty grinned. 'Good show, troops. Good show!'

That was the last time we had a proper treasure hunt. Three months later, when we went to the Rainbow Villa again and Nana sent us off treasure hunting, we were foxed good and proper. The clues were all in the wrong order as if they'd been mixed up: like when you get map directions that say, 'Turn right five kilometres before you reach the crossroads.' How the heck do you know when you're five kilometres *before* you've reached somewhere? Well, for the first time the poor twins gave up and then Nana pretended to forget where he had buried the treasure. Luckily, Paramvir who had come with him the previous day to set it up remembered, so all was well.

'Now shall we have some lunch?' Nana said, sounding quite relieved.

'Tea, Nana, tea!' the twins corrected him. 'We've had lunch!' His shaggy eyebrows interlocked and he shrugged.

'Well, if you all want to have tea we'll have tea,' he said, 'but I really would like to have lunch! We normally have lunch before tea, but if you want to have it the other way around that's okay, though how you can have tea not having had lunch first...'

'He's just so droll!' Sahiba moaned. 'He's one in a million! This is like the mad tea party!'

Duckling nudged me and pointed towards Shabby Aunty. She was staring at Nana, her head cocked slightly to one side as if trying to figure out what Nana had just said. She looked as if she couldn't believe her ears.

3

$\mathcal{I}$t was soon after the messed up treasure hunt trip that I began to hope Shabby Aunty might just ask Nana to marry her, and the hell with Rakshas. She suddenly seemed to...well...how can I put it...fall in love with him all over again! To the twins' consternation she now visited the house nearly every day (and made them tidy up their 'cave'), and Nana and she went for long walks and drives by themselves.

'Just look at them!' Duckling snorted. 'Hand in hand, arms around each other! And she's taking the lead! That's the sort of thing you and I should be doing with boyfriends—not them!'

'Big deal!'

'Really! The other day Meerabai came scurrying out of Nana's study, her face scarlet. I managed to peek in before the door shut—they were in a clinch! I tell you!'

'Well, good for them, I suppose,' I said with a faint tinge of envy. 'Nana is a handsome dude and Shabby Aunty is pretty striking and they get on like a house on fire in spite of the difference in their ages. So what's wrong?'

'Can you imagine what would have happened if the twins had spotted them?'

I grinned. 'Knowing that pair, they would have begun a blackmailing racket.'

What followed was even more unexpected—and shocking some might say.

We had just sat down for lunch one Sunday while a tail-end monsoon thunderstorm rumbled and roared outside. We were having puri-aloo with imli-chutney and chhole followed by halwa. Shabby Aunty was lunching with us as usual, sitting at one end of the table, with Nana at the other. Before the puris started rolling up she tapped her spoon against her glass and smiled as we looked up questioningly.

'Children, I...er...we have something to tell you,' she said as Nana beamed but said nothing.

'What, what, what?' the twins chorused.

'I'll be moving in here this week and will be staying here with you all from now on.'

We stared at her, mouths open. She was smiling, but a shadow of immense sadness flitted across her face momentarily, which made my throat clench. I swallowed and then glanced at Duckling, whose eyebrows had rocketed into her brow. *Living together?* At their age? Wow! Cool! Then I grinned as I thought how shocked the teachers would be at school when they learnt about this. They would know soon as Mahaparbatpur was a small place. It would be a scandal!

'But...but where will you sleep, Aunty?' Dumpling asked, batting her eyelashes innocently.

'In the guest bedroom downstairs, sweetheart!'

'Oooooo...' Dumpling's eyes were like dinner plates, but she had the grace to blush.

'Yay!' Dingaling said, 'Wow!'

The guest bedroom was just across from Nana's bedroom. I exchanged meaningful glances with Duckling who grinned into her napkin.

'Are you going to marry Nana?' Dumpling asked, getting to the nub of things as usual.

'Then we'll have to call you step-Nani—that sounds funny,' Dingaling said, working things out in his head.

'Not at the moment,' Shabby Aunty smiled, looking at Nana, who had gone crimson. 'We'll have to see about that.'

'Oh,' I gulped. 'Aunty, have you told Raksha?'

For a moment her faced closed up. She shook her head and then smiled fondly at me.

'I think we should let Raksha know what he needs to know,' she said. 'Nothing more. And he really doesn't need to know this at the moment.'

This was getting better and better.

'But won't he find out?' Duckling asked.

'Sweetie, we'll cross that bridge when we come to it. Now let's get on with lunch, shall we?'

'So what do you think?' I asked Duckling after lunch, when we had gone to our Barracks. It was still pouring, so we had to remain indoors. 'Why do you think she's moved in after all these years? What's changed?'

'Simple,' Duckling said calmly and giggled. 'They've fallen in love again. And for once Shabby Aunty can't care two hoots what Rakshas might think. High time too. It's just too romantic!'

'Umm, but it's going to change things for us too with her around all the time.' I wasn't quite sure how I'd like that. Duckling's eyebrows wiggled.

'You mean Nana won't have so much time for us as he has now?'

'Yes, that and she'll be poking her nose into our affairs,' I didn't mean to be as brutal as that sounded but I was pretty happy with the arrangements as they were and here was an outsider staking her claim on Nana, who really, while at home was exclusively *our* property. It was beginning to rankle a bit.

'Well, we know her pretty well, so we know what to expect,' Duckling said philosophically, polishing a lovely glass owl with a soft piece of muslin.

'I guess.' But I still wasn't too convinced.

The twins too had been discussing the developments.

'Gosling Didi, will Nana still wake us up with the Colonel Bogey March every morning?' Dingaling asked me worriedly. 'He plays so loudly, he'll wake up Shabby Aunty too.'

'Well maybe he won't! That would be a blessing, wouldn't it?'

Dingaling shook his head vigorously. 'No, I *like* being woken up by the Colonel Bogey March every morning!'

I winked at Duckling. 'Well, maybe he'll play the tune but probably won't sing the words.'

'But now we'll have to clean up our room every day,' Dumpling grumbled. 'That Shabby Aunty really gets after us.'

'I wonder what Mama and Papa will think,' I said to Duckling. 'I wonder if they've been told, or like Raksha are on a need to know basis!'

'Mama'll freak!' Duckling giggled. She mimicked Mama perfectly: 'Living in sin! At their age! With our innocent children living in the same house! What kind of example is she setting? Just what will everyone say? Our good name will be mud! What are they thinking?'

'Say, this is going to be fun,' I said lightening up, thinking of the eventualities. 'This is going to be really interesting.'

That evening, when we gathered in the drawing room just before dinner, Nana glanced at us still looking slightly bemused. One of the Chakrams was driving Shabby Aunty home, and it was just us. I was reading, Duckling was rearranging her collection of frogs on the sideboard and the twins were as usual discussing some business deal in whispers. The rain had thinned; it was misty and raindrops still tadpoled down the large plate-glass windows looking like silver tears.

'Well patloon, what do you think?' Nana asked us at last.

'About what, Nana?' I asked.

'Shabby Aunty living here with us. Are you okay with it?' Bit late to ask, I thought sourly, now that it was fait accompli.

'Oh that! I think it's great!' I said.

'Nana, will you still wake us up with Colonel Bogey?'

His eyes twinkled and he ruffled Dingaling's hair. 'You bet I will, Private!'

'Will you wake Shabby Aunty that way too?' Dumpling asked innocently. She was a real sharpie. 'You have to!'

Nana frowned. 'I'll give it a shot.' He grinned suddenly. 'Let's see what happens!'

'For how long will she be staying with us?' Dingaling asked.

'For as long as she wants to,' Nana replied.

'Oh...'

'But why does she want to stay with us now?' Dumpling asked frowning. She looked worried and exchanged glances with Dingaling. 'And will you give her all your money and the Rolls Royce and Packard?' she asked.

Nana went up and kissed her.

'Don't you worry about the Rolls. One day that will be yours and Dingaling's. I don't think she's interested in the cars, but you could ask her.' He grinned at the thought. 'But maybe she just wants to spend more time with us,' he went on, 'to see how nice we really are. And it's easier to do that staying here with us than driving up and down the mountain all the time.'

'Nana, have you told Mama and Papa?' Duckling asked perceptively.

The twins looked on expectantly. Nana took a deep breath.

'Come here, you two mercenaries,' he said drawing them to him. He lowered his voice to a hoarse whisper. 'Actually Shabby Aunty is moving here to work on a Top Secret Assignment! So, no one outside, and I mean no one, must be told! Not until I give the all clear! Got it?'

Thrilled, the twins nodded, their eyes shining.

'Roger, copy that!'

'Our lips are sealed!'

'Good, now say goodnight and run along!'

I exchanged glances with Duckling. Obviously he didn't want Mama and Papa to know just yet. Mama would really throw the kitchen sink at him!

But I have to say, he was still looking a bit bemused. Bemused by his good fortune? Or bemused because he too, didn't really know what had changed?

As for us, at the time we hadn't a clue why Shabby Aunty had really made her move.

Whatever, it was an exciting move in several ways. Shabby Aunty spent her first night at our house that Wednesday, after most of her things had been brought in the Woody from her rooms in the hospital staff quarters. The Neerameerabais cooked up a fantastic tandoori-chicken dinner to welcome her. They seemed quite happy that she was shifting too, which also surprised me a bit, because no doubt, Shabby Aunty would now be in command of the household and not them. That Saturday, when I went to the hospital, I was sure it would be roiling with gossip. Everyone there knew that Shabby Aunty had shifted to our house. But surprisingly, none of the nurses or doctors or even the orderlies mentioned anything. It was business as usual, as if nothing had happened. Of course, the news filtered into school. Sahiba accosted me just a couple of days later, grinning.

'So, I hear your Nana's girlfriend has moved in with you guys?' she said her eyes sparkling. 'I tell you, he's quite the dude. You have no idea how many of the chicks here—teachers included—have the hots for him!'

I shrugged nonchalantly. 'Well something like that—they have separate bedrooms of course!'

'Of course!' Her eyes shone mischievously. 'Babe, you should be happy; he's setting up a perfect precedent.'

'What do you mean?'

'Well, he can hardly say no if you decide to move in with someone, can he?'

'Don't be so idiotic!'

Actually it was amazing how quickly Shabby Aunty settled into the routine of our house. Probably, she had spent so much time with us and she knew us and our ways so well, there was very little adjustment she needed to make. That first Wednesday night it was strange having both Nana and her come up to say goodnight to us—and I have to admit I did feel, with a pang, that we would now have to 'share' him with her. But I think they realized that too and they came up separately to say goodnight, first Shabby Aunty and then Nana.

I was reading when she came into my cubicle and sat down on my bed. I thought she was looking radiantly happy, but of course that could really have been my imagination working overtime.

'Hi Aunty,' I said, book-marking my page.

She smiled. 'Well, this might seem strange to you...'

'It's great to have you, Aunty.'

'Thank you, darling. It's lovely being here.' She leaned forward and kissed my cheek. 'Goodnight, Gosling!' She drew back, her grey eyes twinkling. 'Now I have three more goodnights to say!'

I heard her say goodnight to the others and then five minutes later Nana clomped up. I knew he'd first say goodnight to the others and then come to me. True to form, he followed the routine and I looked up as he knocked and then entered. He stood at the end of my bed; in the dim golden pool of the reading lamp, he looked knockout handsome.

'Well Gosling, what do you think?'

'About what?' I asked, batting my eyelashes like Dumpling would have.

'About the new…arrangement.'

'I think it's great! She's such fun to have around.'

He nodded, and then a puzzled look came over his face momentarily. 'Yes…yes,' he said at last. 'Er…General…there may be talk…just ignore it or tell me who's been gossiping and I'll run them over in the Woody.'

'Sure!' I grinned. 'Actually you just have to yell and they'll be out of here like bats out of hell.'

He smiled and squeezed my hand. 'Do you know what those two little rascals asked me to do?' he said.

'Dumpling and Dingaling?'

'Yes. They want me to wake Shabby Aunty up the same way I wake you guys up.'

'So are you going to?'

He nodded dolefully. 'They made me promise.'

'You could always pretend…'

He shook his head. 'They want to be there when I do it! They want to see what happens.'

'Shabby Aunty will probably whack you over the head with the trumpet and move back to the hospital.'

'I know! Any ideas General Gosling?' The old mischievous grin was back.

'You'll have to warn Shabby Aunty,' I said, 'or you'll probably give her a heart attack. She had better wear industrial strength ear plugs too.'

He nodded and leant over. 'Actually,' he whispered, 'I thought of a plan. This is what I thought we'd do...'

I have to say, Shabby Aunty was a hell of a sport about the whole thing. Early the next morning I was awoken not by Nana but by the twins, shaking my shoulders vigorously. It was just 5.45 a.m. fifteen minutes before our usual wake-up call.

'Gosling Didi, wake up!' Dumpling said urgently. 'We have to go down and wake up Shabby Aunty! Nana's going to play the Colonel Bogey for her.'

'Uh...what?'

'Wake up, wake up!' Dumpling pushed Dingaling. 'Go and wake up Duckling Didi,' she ordered. 'Hurry!'

We got into the spirit of the thing and went downstairs, just as Nana emerged from his room in full uniform, with his trumpet. He grinned and squinted at the twins and winked and then saluted them smartly. They were simply agog. We gathered outside Shabby Aunty's bedroom. Very quietly Nana twisted the door knob and pushed the door open. Like all the doors in the house, the hinges were oiled, so it opened soundlessly. Breathless with excitement the twins peeped inside the dim bedroom. They saw the figure huddled under the bedclothes, emitting faint snores.

Nana marched in and put the trumpet to his lips. His cheeks puffed and he blew...

In a second all hell broke loose. As the first blaring notes of 'Colonel Bogey' blasted out, an ethereal white figure rose out of the bed, its arms wide, screeching:

'Aaaaaarghhh bhook lagee hain—I'm hungry!'

Nana dropped the trumpet with a clatter. 'Troops retreat!' he yelled, turning on his heel as the bed-sheet covered apparition exploded out of the bed and came after him. 'Run!' The twins squealed and turned and fled. And Duckling and I were left rolling about on the wooden floor in hysterics.

'Shabby Aunty 1; Twins 0!' I spluttered as Shabby Aunty emerged from under the bedclothes grinning. 'Aunty you're too much!'

'Oh my god!' Duckling groaned. 'Now we have two adult nutcases to deal with!'

The twins had gathered in a quivering mass in the drawing room, sitting on Nana's lap, trying to comfort him and being comforted at the same time.

'I told you,' he gabbled, kissing them turn by turn and squinting wildly. 'She turns into a monster at night. Better to let her sleep as long as she likes babies or she'll eat us.'

'Nana, she was just fooling,' Dumpling said as Dingaling cast a doubtful look at Shabby Aunty who had transmogrified back into her usual sweet self.

'Good morning, Privates,' she said blithely, kissing the twins and then Duckling and myself.

Nana stood up. 'Right patloon, back to Barracks for morning drill. On the double, hup, two, three, four!'

Two Saturdays later, something odd happened at the hospital. I was helping Nana in the OPD that morning when a child was brought in. The little girl had fallen down and cut her forehead nastily on a rusted tin can. As I held the screaming child and tried to soothe her, Nana skillfully stitched up the cut, singing softly to her in his deep baritone, which magically calmed down the kids. While the girl's mother watched anxiously, he bandaged her wound, and stood back and primed a tetanus shot.

'Just a little prick,' he murmured even as the poor child's eyes widened in horror. He was done even before she realized it.

'Wow, you're a brave little thing aren't you?' he said admiringly, as I stroked the girl's cheek and wiped away her tears. 'You should command my battalion!' He turned to the mother.

'She'll be fine, ji,' he assured her. 'But let her stay here for a couple of hours. She hit her head and I'd like to be sure she's all right before sending her home.' I gave the child a couple of dolls to play with and followed Nana to his next patient. Shabby Aunty was in the theatre operating with another doctor. Nana saw a few more patients and then turned to me.

'Gosling, sweetheart we better give that little girl her tetanus shot before we send her home,' he said, striding off towards the little girl's bed. She was sitting up happily playing with her dolls as her mother sat beside her.

'But...but Nana you already gave her that shot.'

'But of course not! Come on, dear.'

'But...but...'

'Get me the tray, please,' he told a nurse.

Within minutes he had primed the syringe, much to the child's complete horror. Her mother just looked on, thinking the little girl needed another shot.

'Nana, you gave her the tetanus shot just after you bandaged her up.'

'Eh? But of course not. Come on now, Gosling. It's okay baby, just a little prick.'

Thankfully, I had made a note on the child's card—that was part of my 'duty'—I would make the entry of the medication and the time it was given and the doctor (Nana or maybe Shabby Aunty) would check and initial it. I was very meticulous about it, writing clearly in all caps. 'See Nana, you gave her the shot at 10.46 a.m.'

He glanced at it, his brows furrowed.

'Oh...so I did,' he murmured. 'Just as well we checked, otherwise we would have given the poor thing a double dose!'

He put down the syringe with a clatter, patted the traumatized little girl on the head, examined her briefly and told her mother she could take her home.

'Don't let the bandage get wet and bring her back tomorrow for dressing,' he instructed.

I might have let it go as a bit of absent-mindedness except that an hour after they had left, Nana sat back in his chair in his room and said, 'Gosling, will you go out and call that little girl and her mother in? I'd like to check her again and then she can go home.'

'But Nana, you already sent her home,' I said, not knowing what to make of it. He puckered his eyebrows.

'What? She's gone home? Oh well, then tell her mother to bring her tomorrow for dressing and not to get it wet.'

'Sure Nana.' I shrugged. Maybe it was just one of his 'days', like the one when he 'lost' his way to school or got the treasure hunt all mixed up at Rainbow Villa.

'Guess what happened at the hospital?' I told Duckling that afternoon. We were sitting on her bed and she was showing me a set of delicate frogs made of dark green, yellow, blue and red glass that she had acquired. I have to admit they were kind of beautiful—like those brilliant arrow poison frogs.

'What?' she asked, lovingly admiring her caché.

'Nana was at his absent-minded best! He nearly took out a kid's liver instead of the appendix!'

'Don't bullshit!'

'No, but he tried giving a poor little girl two tetanus shots instead of one. I had to show him the child's card.'

'What?'

'And he forgot that he had discharged her. He asked to see her after he'd sent her home.'

'Oh!' Duckling's eyes narrowed. 'What if he had been operating and actually made that mix-up?' she asked suddenly. 'What if he did remove a kid's liver instead of appendix?'

'Shabby Aunty would have stopped him,' I said airily. 'She's always with him in the theatre when he operates.'

But suddenly what Duckling was driving at became ominously clear to me too. 'Oh, you mean...'

'I think you'd better tell Shabby Aunty what happened. She'll know how to deal with it.'

I didn't like the idea one bit. It would be like telling tales on Nana—that was gross. At the same time, it could become a very serious matter. But I really needn't have worried, because here's what happened at dinner that night:

The twins had been more fidgety and restless than usual, all evening. They were continually giving Duckling and me meaningful looks and then whispering into each other's ears. Duckling did a quick inventory check to ensure none of her collections had been touched and I wondered what the two little devils were cooking up now. We had just settled down when Dumpling launched her first missile.

'Nana, Gosling Didi said that you removed some little girl's liver instead of appendix today!' she said, batting those infernal eyelashes of hers. 'Is that so? Did you put it back in later on? Did it fit?'

'Eh?' Nana looked startled, and Shabby Aunty suddenly became all alert.

'Dumpling, don't talk rubbish!' I spluttered, feeling my face turn red. The little squirts had been eavesdropping again.

'And she said you wanted to give a child an injection twice

over,' Dingaling looked martyred. 'And you forgot you had sent her home. We heard her!'

'Rubbish!' I'd gone scarlet. 'Aunty, Nana it's all rubbish. They've been eavesdropping again hearing bits and pieces and making up everything else,' I blustered, my ears all hot. 'Just wait you two, till we get back to the Barracks!'

'But we heard you!' Dumpling insisted petulantly.

Duckling—bless her—came to my rescue. 'Nana,' she said, 'which cars are you thinking of entering in this year's Classic and Vintage Car Rally in Delhi?'

'Thanks,' I whispered, nudging her.

'Cars?' Nana's puzzled look suddenly cleared. 'I thought we'd enter the Golden Hawk in the Classic Car category and um… maybe the Packard in the Best of the Show category.'

'Wow!' The Studebaker Golden Hawk was a 1957 classic in gold and maroon (which always gave carburetor trouble), and the Packard, a really rare 1934 1108 Dietrich Convertible Victoria. Only three had been accounted for until ours turned up, discovered by Duckling and I, rusting away and forgotten in an ex-maharaja's stable. It was a leviathan of a car, now jewel-like in stainless-steel silver and midnight blue. Both cars had been lovingly and painstakingly restored and refurbished and looked like a million bucks (and were worth considerably more).

'Wow, we'll run away with all the prizes for sure!' I said enthusiastically. Fortunately, the rest of the dinnertime conversation revolved around the cars and no one said anything more about the incident at the hospital.

'Thanks, Duck,' I said as we prepared for bed later that night. 'It was becoming embarrassing. Really, we ought to be careful—those two brats need their big ears pulled off. They're always eavesdropping.'

Duckling grinned. 'Yeah.' Then she sobered down. 'You know, but maybe you should tell Shabby Aunty about what exactly happened. It could have been just a moment's absent-mindedness but it did involve medication.'

'Yes, I know. It's just that I'd feel like I'll be squealing on Nana.'

I needn't have worried. When Shabby Aunty came to say goodnight, she sat down on my bed and looked at me.

'Gosling dear, exactly what happened at the hospital this morning?'

'Um…um…'

'It's all right dear but you need to tell me.'

So I did. Her face closed up a bit and she went pale and held my hand.

'Thank you,' she said softly at last. 'I'm so glad you told me this.'

'Aunty is…is everything all right?'

She pursed her lips. 'Well dear, you do realize Nana is getting on a bit. So he will tend to forget now and then, like he did with that treasure hunt at the waterfalls. The trouble is that he can't afford to do that while working at the hospital.'

'So?'

She just shook her head gently, leant forward and kissed me.

'Goodnight, Gosling,' she said softly.

There were tears glimmering in her eyes.

The next morning, Nana woke us up as usual, with his trumpet. The last notes of Colonel Bogey were still reverberating in our ears when we heard a crash followed by a clanging sound. Nana had suddenly dropped the trumpet and crumpled to the ground.

'Look!' Dingaling cried as we rushed up. 'Nana's been shot! Arrghhh…!'

4

*T*hankfully, Meerabai, who had been standing by as usual, somehow managed to break his fall and shrieked for the Chakrams. They were up in a trice, and hoisted Nana up by the armpits and put him in a chair. Shabby Aunty had also run up by now and was firmly patting his cheeks. Neerabai fetched a glass of water.

We watched, paralyzed with horror. Nana was pale and grey, and then thankfully opened his eyes. But they were glazed and sort of silvery, like those of a dead fish, and he looked as if he didn't understand where he was or what had happened. He was clearly dazed.

Shabby Aunty had run down and returned with her stethoscope and blood-pressure machine.

'Wh...wha what you're doing?' Nana mumbled. Then his eyes cleared and the colour started returning to his cheeks.

'You fainted, dear,' she said, and then put the stethoscope to her ears, and began pumping the bulb of the machine.

'Non...nonsense!' He was beginning to bluster.

Shabby Aunty disconnected the blood pressure machine and slung her stethoscope around her neck.

'Was it okay?' I hardly dared to ask. Duckling clutched my hand and the twins huddled together beside me.

'A bit low, but it's okay now. It must have dropped suddenly, which is what made him faint.' She turned to him. 'How're you feeling, dear?'

Nana made as if to stand up. 'Nothing wrong with me!'

'But Nana, you *fainted!*' Dumpling said accusingly as Dingaling nodded.

He stood to attention, wobbled a bit, and saluted. 'Nothing of the sort! Just checking your reflexes, Privates!' he said, and shuffled off downstairs, flanked by the Chakrams.

'Shabby Aunty, is he really all right?' Duckling asked.

'He's okay, but we'll do a few tests at the hospital today. I think he overdoes it sometimes and forgets his age.'

Thankfully it did seem to be just that. To our surprise that afternoon, Nana and Shabby Aunty picked us up from school in the Woody and took us to Madandas's Backery for tea. The only difference was that Shabby Aunty was driving instead of Nana.

'How're you feeling, Nana?' the twins asked, flanking him and holding his hands as we walked into the café.

'Top of the pops, Privates!' he boomed, ruffling their hair. 'Nothing wrong with me!'

'So did he have the tests?' I asked Shabby Aunty softly. She nodded.

'His heart is fine. It does seem to be a momentary fall in his blood pressure, that's all.' But she didn't quite meet my eye as she said that. 'I've made him take a week's leave from the hospital.'

'Oh.'

'He can tinker around with his cars. The Chakrams will keep an eye on him.'

'He agreed?'

She smiled. 'Not without a fight! But I won! I told him that the Studebaker's carburetor needs cleaning and the Packard too needs a change of plugs and oil, so he's going to be busy doing that. He was on the Internet the whole afternoon, trying to access plugs for the Packard. He's been e-mailing some guy in Indore who may have a set.'

'Good. He looks okay now.'

Indeed he did. And he was back in form. A bunch of morons from one of the boarding schools were at the next table, ogling me and Duckling and whispering, winking and snorting in their usual gross way. Occasionally a wolf whistle would rent the air accompanied by coarse laughter. Suddenly Nana stood up. He marched over to the boys' table.

'Good evening, gentlemen!' he said pleasantly.

'Oh oh!' I groaned as Duckling put her face in her hands, red with embarrassment.

'Good evening, uncleji!' one of the boys cheekily replied and winked as the others laughed.

'Good evening SIR!' Nana barked suddenly and snapped to attention. 'And STAND TO ATTENTION when you're speaking to me, you little nitwit!'

Wow! The boys shot to their feet stuttering.

Nana stalked around their table, eyeballing them fiercely, his moustache and even his eyebrows bristling. 'Now, if you want to meet the two lovely ladies at the next table, you may introduce yourselves in the proper civilized manner of gentlemen and not as if you have just fallen out of the trees yesterday and don't know where to park your tails. Tuck your shirts into your pants and straighten your ties! NOW!'

'Yy...yessir...no ss...sir,' they mumbled confused.

'But first,' Nana went on with a malicious gleam in his eye, 'you will have to ask my permission and I will ask them if they wish to talk to you, which I gravely doubt!'

'Oh my god!' Duckling groaned. 'He's going on like some character in Jane Austen.'

'Yy...yyes sir, it's okay sir...sorry sir...'

'Very well. DISMISS!'

Hastily the boys got up, paid their bill and fled.

Nana returned and grinned and saluted. 'Action taken—enemy routed!' he reported.

'Nana, that was so embarrassing!' Duckling groaned.

'Baby, they were winking lewdly at you,' Nana said, taking Duckling's hand. 'And no one, NO ONE does that to my Major Duckling. They were lucky to get away alive.'

'Nana, they were just idiots!'

'And they'd remain idiots all their lives if they weren't disciplined. What this country needs is a good caning.'

'Nana, you were great!' Dumpling said. She whispered something to Dingaling, who nodded. 'Nana,' she went on, 'when we have to make our dangerous business deals, you can be our bodyguard. Some children don't like paying us when they have to and start to fight.'

Nana grinned and nodded. 'And how much will you pay me, eh?'

Shabby Aunty smiled. 'You're all the same!' she said, 'One worse than the other!'

By nightfall, we had all but forgotten about Nana's fainting spell that morning. It was a lovely clear night and he took us out to the gazebo to stargaze through the telescope.

'Can you imagine,' he told the twins, his voice deep and rapturous, as they listened enthralled, 'that just as we're peering through the telescope at the stars, there may be living creatures somewhere out there peering through their telescopes at us at this very moment? They must be wondering about us as we wonder about them.'

Duckling grinned and joined in (she loved complicating things). 'And even better, if they're a hundred light years away from us, it means it's taken light one hundred years to get to us from them, so we're seeing them as they were one hundred years ago and likewise for them, they're seeing us as we were a hundred years ago. Imagine that.'

Dingaling was more interested in the shooting stars that suddenly pulsed, sketched a silver line across the dark night sky and vanished.

'Look!' Nana whispered hoarsely. 'That bright star up there, it seems to be winking in Morse code. Get a pencil and take it down as I spell it out! Hurry! "H E L L O D U M P L I N G A N D D I N G A L I N G E A R T H L I N G S S T O P G R E E T I N G S F R O M L A- L A L A N D," he dictated slowly.

'La-La land! Nana as if! Stop fooling!'

'Baby, if you knew Morse code you would be able to decipher the message yourself!'

'As if they would know it.'

Nana drew himself up. 'Morse is the Universe's language,' he declared. 'Everyone in space knows it.' He glanced at his watch. 'And now I know it's bedtime, troops. Back to Barracks, hup two three four!'

When Shabby Aunty came up to say goodnight, I asked her again.

'Aunty, you're sure Nana is all right?'

She took my hand. 'Well, he was in good form this evening, wasn't he? But Gosling, he will probably have to stop going to the hospital.'

'Oh, that will upset him.'

She nodded. 'It's going to be very difficult to break it to him,' she sighed. 'He's so headstrong. But we can't take that risk. He's had a couple of memory lapses and another one in the hospital can be dangerous. I can't be around him all the time to check on him. He would hate that and it would be demeaning. At least he's agreed to take leave for a week, I'll have to speak to the director and see how we can work this out—maybe they could extend his leave period.' Then she smiled at me. 'You don't worry about it! It'll work out. It always does.'

I hoped it would. Maybe we were just making a mountain out of a molehill. Everyone had memory lapses: I forgot where I'd put my stuff, so many times. Even Duckling was constantly misplacing her precious curios and then getting into a flap. So maybe there was nothing to worry about and things would work out with Nana. Maybe it was just a momentary lapse and he'd be fine.

In the event it turned out to be much easier than we anticipated. By the end of the week, Nana was so involved in getting the Silver Hawk and Packard shipshape that he readily agreed to extend his leave period indefinitely. We never knew whether he too had realized what had happened and what could happen if he had a memory lapse, say in the middle of a surgery, but we (and especially Shabby Aunty) were grateful. He was a doctor after all.

Sometimes, on Saturday afternoons we would all go to town when the weekly bazaar was held. Villagers from the surrounding mountain villages disgorged from smoky diesel buses and pickups early in the morning, bringing handicrafts, livestock, herbs and medicinal plants, fresh eggs, vegetables, fruit, pickles and murrabas, honey and other such local produce to sell. With the proceeds they would stock up on groceries, food and bright plastic items. This was Duckling's happy hunting ground, for there would be stalls selling artifacts from old bungalows that had been torn down (for yet another garish tourist resort), and she was an expert bargainer.

The twins rushed up and down the crowded, kaleidoscopic aisles and usually came to a halt in front of the stall selling candy-floss. I would stalk through in a more dignified manner, slyly eyeing some of the lovely junk (and sometimes genuine) silver jewelry on sale, taking photographs galore. Nana and Shabby Aunty would take a quick look around and wait at 'Madandas's Backery and Pastrees,' which overlooked the bazaar, and from where they could watch the market's hurly-burly while sipping their green tea in comfort.

On this particular Saturday, Shabby Aunty got a call from the hospital early in the afternoon and had to leave Nana alone at Madandas's. Before leaving, she found me and Duckling and asked us to keep a discreet eye on him and join him when we were through. I was busy taking photographs and Duckling was trying to wangle a deal for some pretty nifty (but tarnished) silver animals. I found a convenient spot which gave me a good view of the market and from where I could keep an eye on Nana too. He was sitting on Madandas's verandah under a huge purple and pink striped awning. Then I saw the twins rush up to him excitedly. They took him by his hands and dragged him off to a stall selling violently hued boiled sweets and packets of psychedelic sugar-coated fennel.

Duckling drifted up to me after feigning disinterest in the little silver animals she was lusting after—all part of her elaborate bargaining strategy.

'That fellow will come around in about fifteen minutes,' she murmured. She glanced at me. 'What's up?'

'Dumpling and Dingaling Enterprises are working over Nana,' I grinned. 'They've just made him buy a huge amount of toffees, sweets and sugared saunf… Shabby Aunty is out of the way.'

Duckling grinned. 'They don't miss a shot do they?'

They didn't. They escorted Nana back to his table at

Madandas's and vanished in the bazaar. About fifteen minutes later, I glanced towards Nana again. He was smiling benignly at passers-by—and then what do you think happens? Messrs Dumpling and Dingaling approach him again, smiling sweetly and ingratiatingly. They chat briefly and then take him by the hand and lead him to another sweet vendor...and buy another load of sickly looking stuff. Then they escort him back, and disappear into the bazaar again. Instinctively, I photographed them. They were up to something.

Twenty minutes later they were back. They sat at Nana's table while he got them a mango juice. They slurped it up, chatting away and then nodded and got up. Dumpling very sweetly took Nana by the hand and Dingaling looked on as if butter wouldn't melt in his mealy little mouth.

'Gottim!' Duckling suddenly said in my ear and I jumped.

'Wha...?' She held out a little cloth bag. 'I bought the lot for what one single one ought to have cost,' she grinned.

Then she noticed the twins and Nana. 'They're back...'

'Third time. They're up to some hanky-panky again.' I followed them in the viewfinder. Sure enough they went to another sweet vendor and bought up a whole lot of chocolate and chikki and stuff.

'But...but...?'

'We have to get to the bottom of this,' I said, lowering the camera as they returned to their table. The twins were now stashing away their loot in their knapsacks, which had begun to bulge. They looked very pleased with themselves and headed for the Woody, where they carefully deposited the contents of their knapsack into a big bag as Mahavir grinned at them and patted their wicked heads. Then they headed back to Nana.

'I don't believe it! Are they doing him for another round? Just what the heck are they up to? And what is with Nana—indulging them like that?'

We waited ten minutes as the twins angelically finished off the lemon tarts Nana had ordered and looked around, dangling their legs under the table. They said something to Nana, who nodded benignly and pushed back his chair.

'Not again!' I was aghast.

'Okay, let's round them up,' Duckling grinned. 'Time we unraveled the mystery.'

We ambushed them at the sweet stall. They'd gone back to the first one, and the shameless fellow was grinning all over his face as he weighed out the selection the twins had pointed out.

'Hi babies, having a good time?'

They jumped nearly a foot in the air. 'Hi Gosling Didi, Duckling Didi, did you get some nice photos?' Dumpling blinked her pretty eyes.

'Lovely ones of you! By the way, what are you guys buying? The whole shop?'

'Just a little bit. You know we don't get these sweets at Madandas's Pastrees. They're home-made and with natural goodness and all with pure jaggery and windblown, wildflower honey made by wildbees so very healthy.'

'Yes, Miss Willie Wonka.'

The twins exchanged glances and then looked at us, clearly trying to assess how much we knew.

'Nana's very nice, he insisted he would buy all this for us.'

Nana beamed benignly. 'An army marches on its stomach!' he boomed, 'and a sweet army like one here, marches on sweeties!'

I took Nana by the arm. 'Nana, you've been buying them sweets all afternoon,' I whispered.

His eyebrows knotted. 'Nonsense my dear—it's just this lot, just a little secret indulgence, while the dragon lady is away. Makes life worth living for them.'

The twins stood primly by his side, hands folded in front of them, halos shimmering bright. I exchanged glances with Duckling, whose eyes had widened as she grappled with the meaning of what Nana had just said. I took her by the arm.

'Right you two,' I said briskly. 'We meet in my room before lights out tonight, savvy? We have things to discuss!'

'You want to help us with another business again?' Dingaling asked, and promptly got his foot trodden upon by Dumpling.

'Sure!'

Of course the little hoodlums didn't show up. When I went to their room, they were both ostensibly fast asleep in their bunks.

'Up!' I said and unceremoniously hauled the blankets off them. 'Come on, don't pretend!'

'Ummm,' they moaned and yawned and flopped back to sleep.

'Tired,' Dumpling murmured, her eyelashes fluttering.

'Up in three or we're going to tickle you!'

'Mmm...'

'One...two...' I lifted Dumpling's pajama top and wriggled my fingers over her well-padded ribs and tummy. She sat up with a squeal, as did Dingaling in the bunk above.

'Didi!'

'Okay, this won't take long. Why did you make Nana buy you sweets four times this afternoon? And how come he agreed?'

'We didn't! He only bought us once when you came,' Dumpling could fib without batting an eyelid. I took a deep breath.

'He forgot!' Dingaling blurted as Dumpling shot him a poisonous look.

'You know, I took photographs,' I said, holding up my camera. 'Want to see?' Dumpling paled but stuck out a stubborn jaw.

'Didi, these days with Photoshop you can do anything.'

'And at the moment I'm about to spank your fat fanny! Try and Photoshop that!'

Duckling, standing by so far, helpfully picked up a table tennis bat lying nearby. 'Here,' she offered. I took it and smacked it against my hand.

'Out with the truth now! You made Nana buy you enough sweets to start your own wholesale business. You put them all in that bag in the Woody.'

Dumpling folded. 'We…we just wanted to buy stuff for our own stall, for the school fete on Monday.' The tears (all humbug) had begun to glimmer. 'It's for the poor and destituted people who have never eaten a sweetie in their lives. We didn't want to deny them. We want to put some sweetness in their lives…why should they…'

'Okay, baby that's enough.'

'How come Nana agreed? He would have bought you all you wanted the first time but not again and again.'

'He just forgot,' Dumpling reiterated, and my heart sank. 'We were just fooling when we asked him the second time, but he had forgotten that he'd already bought us stuff. So then we tried again and again.' Her eyes brightened, 'And it worked!'

'Hello, what's going on here? A midnight conference?'

'Oh hi Shabby Aunty. When did you get back?'

'A little while ago, dear. The hospital was in such a state. Another bus accident. So what's going on here?'

We told her. 'I see,' she said quietly and sat down. She looked tired. I turned to the twins and steamed on.

'Now listen, you two unscrupulous hoodlums, you know Nana sometimes has problems remembering things, right?'

They nodded solemnly.

'That is not something you take advantage of. Got it? It's

despicable to do that!'

Shabby Aunty nodded as Duckling paced up and down, looking as if she were fuming.

'Yes, sweeties, you probably didn't realize it, but it's not a nice thing to do,' Shabby Aunty said.

They hung their heads (humbug style).

'We're sorry,' they mumbled, 'we won't do it again.'

'You'll be in real trouble if you do!' Duckling suddenly barked, doing her bad cop thing. 'You'll be grounded for six months!'

'We said we're sorry,' Dumpling said petulantly as Dingaling nodded. 'What more do you want us to do?' She snuffled and wiped her eyes against her sleeve—two waifs standing by their bunks, persecuted by three cruel people.

I looked at them and melted and drew them to me. 'It's okay,' I said, kissing them. 'Just don't do it again?'

They nodded and smiled up at me beatifically. 'Okay Didi!' they whispered.

'Huh!' Duckling snorted, stomping up and down. 'Huh!'

Shabby Aunty smiled tiredly. We put the twins to bed and retreated.

Duckling grinned. 'Hopefully that should teach them. How I love doing the bad cop!' She eyed me. 'But you need to be tougher. You're a marshmallow.'

I shook my head. 'They're incorrigible!'

Shabby Aunty had her arms around our waists. She looked tired and I suddenly realized, sad.

'I think we need to talk a little about Nana,' she said softly, and I felt a sudden chill—and that boulder of dread shift uncomfortably in the pit of my stomach. I could see much the same thing had happened to Duckling.

'Okay Aunty.'

We settled down in my room, Duckling and I sitting on my bed and Shabby Aunty in the blue armchair I use for reading. She looked at us.

'It looks as if Nana might have started suffering from...'

We heard shuffling footfalls on the wooden floor in the corridor outside and looked up. Nana appeared in the doorway. But it didn't matter, because the blood had drained out of my face as I realized what Shabby Aunty had been about to say. 'Suffering from...' And I knew what. Everything suddenly fell into place—a truly horrible place. We'd been studying about this in Psychology class and so far I had been too blind to see the dreadful truth hiding in plain sight all along, under my nose! For a moment I swayed dizzily and then gripped the edge of my bed.

'Good evening troops! What's going on here? You look like you're plotting a coup d'etat! Those two little villains are already asleep.' Nana glanced at his watch—by now, Shabby Aunty ought to have said her goodnights and gone back downstairs. It was his turn.

He sat down next to Duckling.

'They must have got tired out running up and down the bazaar all afternoon,' Shabby Aunty said. 'And I think we should say goodnight to the girls now. I'm tired too.'

I got into bed and Nana kissed me and snapped to attention.

'Goodnight, General. You may read for a further period of thirty minutes as per protocol.'

I grinned and flicked him a salute back. 'Goodnight Nana, sir!'

A little while after I had switched off my light, Duckling crept into my room.

'Are you awake, Gos?'

'Ya.'

She shut the door and switched on the reading light. She

was looking as if she had been crying.

'What's the matter?'

'Gos, what do you think is wrong with Nana? Why does he keep forgetting like this? What was Shabby Aunty trying to say?'

It was a place I didn't want to go to—a word I didn't want to say. I gulped.

'I hope I'm wrong,' I said in a strange hollow voice. 'But it looks like Nana's getting, or has got, dementia or something like that.' My voice dropped to a whisper. 'Maybe even Alzheimer's. We were studying about it in class. It all it all fits in...'

Duckling eyed me incredulously. 'No way,' she said in a strangled voice. 'No way! He can't possibly have that.' She took a deep breath. 'We won't *allow* him to have that, will we, Gos?'

I shook my head, but the boulder in the pit of my stomach didn't budge.

The next morning at about eleven, we suddenly realized that there was an unusual bustle outside our front gate. There seemed to be an awful lot of kids from the boarding schools hanging around and making a ruckus. Perhaps there had been an accident, or there was an injured animal or bird lying on the road. There was no sign of the twins and Nana and Shabby Aunty had gone off to 'test drive' the Studebaker. Duckling and I went out to take a look.

A large colourful 'stall' had been set up just outside our gate. Two trestle tables (Nana's work tables) were groaning under the weight of sweet packets and boxes that the twins had made Nana buy at the market yesterday. The large sweet packets had been divided into several smaller ones, most attractively tied up with colourful satin hair ribbons and gift wrapping paper. Dumpling and Dingaling Enterprises Pvt. Ltd. was doing a roaring business. Paramvir and De-Big Bazooka had been hired as security.

'Hello kids,' I greeted the pair as they looked up completely unfazed and unashamed. 'I thought these were for the class fete tomorrow.'

'Didi, it's been cancelled, what to do!' Dingaling said to a rare approving nod from his twin.

'And ants would get these and spoil them so we thought we'd sell them today itself.' She clicked her tongue sympathetically and indicated the clientele. 'These poor children weren't able to come to the market yesterday, so they've come here instead.'

I glanced at the prices. 'Whew, that's quite a premium.'

'What?'

'You're charging much more than what it cost Nana.'

'But of course. Otherwise what's the use?'

'Are you donating the money to a good cause?'

They grinned and nodded. 'Us!' they said candidly. 'We want to buy that cool remote control helicopter and fly it across the valley with a video camera attached.'

'We'll call it the Helicam!'

'Good luck!'

'Thanks Didi, we love you!'

'Huh!' Duckling snorted, 'Huh! Little crooks!'

In the sparkling clear light of day, the dementia devils of last night seemed to have retreated—besides it was only a suspicion I had had—no doctor had actually said that. Everything seemed back to normal. I was setting out for a bike ride, Duckling was going back to croon over her latest acquisitions, Dumpling and Dingaling Enterprises were back in business, Nana and Shabby Aunty were driving the Studebaker in the mountains, possibly scouting for another treasure hunt location.

But that afternoon, while Nana was resting, Shabby Aunty came up to the War Room and told us...

5

'I've suspected it for a while,' she said quietly, taking our hands and looking at us in that frank direct manner of hers. 'We had a scan done and it appears that Nana has had several tiny brain strokes over a period of time—they're called mini-strokes.'

Duckling and I went very white.

'They're very small and won't cause paralysis,' Shabby Aunty added hastily, squeezing our hands. 'They're caused by the formation of plaques in the brain, which sort of fuse the circuits there, preventing messages and instructions from getting through. That is why he has these short-term memory lapses and loses his way while driving. It also explains why he has begun walking the way he has with those short shuffling steps. Messages and instructions from the brain don't get transmitted to where they're supposed to go.'

'Is...is...it dementia...Alzheimer's?' I whispered. 'Will he forget who we are? Will he continue to recognize us?'

'Darling, there's no point worrying about what it may be. It's best to take things day by day. We've started his medication and this may make a difference. I've got in touch with a well-known neurologist in Delhi too.'

'Does he know?' Duckling asked brutally. Shabby Aunty sighed.

'I think he does. He is a doctor, after all and would have recognized the symptoms but we can't be sure because it is so easy to delude and fool yourself into believing otherwise.' She looked at us. 'And when it's to do with the mind, you really don't know what the truth is and what is not because everything seems like the truth when you're thinking of it, but later, might not. Complicated, isn't it?'

'So what does this mean…for…' My voice went into a squeak. 'For us and everybody?'

'At the moment nothing changes. We just have to keep an eye on him. I've instructed Paramvir and Mahavir to ensure he doesn't drive away in any of the cars on his own. It's going to be difficult to get him to stop driving himself, but we'll have to see how to do that eventually. Meanwhile, you guys carry on with him as usual. Okay?' She smiled.

'Okay!' And suddenly I was angry. 'Do Mama and Papa know?' Where the heck were they when they were needed? Really this was their problem, not Shabby Aunty's or ours. Nana was *Mama's* father for crying out loud and Papa called him 'Papa' too—what the hell for when they were eternally AWOL from their family? Shabby Aunty nodded and sighed.

'Yes, I told them.' She shrugged. 'Your Mama didn't really believe me I think, until I quoted the doctor's report. Then she said they might come to visit sometime, maybe within the next six months or so. At the moment they're very busy because some important international conference is due to be held in Washington, for which they have to do a lot of backroom negotiations so that everything can be ready to be signed and sealed.' She smiled wanly. 'Your Mama said that if it goes off well and they can pull off a major political deal, then both she and Papa would probably get a huge promotion and be made ambassadors.'

'Great! So then one will be sitting in Japan and the other in Canada making the world a better place,' Duckling remarked bitterly, 'How nice for everyone!'

'Duckling, they're very busy and very important people,' Shabby Aunty said hugging her.

She left us shortly afterwards, kissing us goodnight. Minutes after she'd gone, both Duckling and I were down in the War Room firing up the computer, googling 'dementia' and 'Alzheimer's'. An hour later both of us reached the same conclusion.

'Nah! No way!' Duckling said shaking her head in horror. 'He doesn't have this! He still knows who we are. He's not depressed or unpredictable or confused. He doesn't repeat himself...too much at least. He still feeds himself.'

'It's just not possible,' I agreed with a shudder as we shut down the wretched machine. 'It's gross, this disease—eating away your brain, making you forget who you are or how to be a person; Nana will never forget us.'

'We won't give him a chance!' Duckling said fiercely, wiping her eyes. There were tears running down both our cheeks.

We didn't say it aloud but we were both thinking he had bought the twins a whole lot of sweets four times in the space of a single afternoon and hadn't remembered...

But to our great relief it really did seem that he didn't have this terrible affliction after all. The next few months rolled by more or less normally. Nana got completely involved in renovating the cars; he'd had the Silver Hawk re-sprayed (twice, because he had forgotten it had been done once, but it didn't matter because it looked all the glossier for it!) After he had dropped us to school (with Shabby Aunty usually driving) they'd return home and the Chakrams would tell him what needed to be done to what car that day. They kept a sharp eye when he used the tools, especially the power tools. Shabby Aunty too encouraged him to work with his hands and to think of innovative ways to get around seemingly intractable problems. Often, they had to fabricate parts of the cars in the tool-shed or at the local mechanic's garage after poring over engineering drawings and sketches from manuals and hammering out the part or machining it on the lathe.

Oh yes, he did tend to forget, though sometimes that could be useful. On Saturday mornings now, since he had stopped going to the hospital, he roped the entire lot of us to wash and wax all the ten cars including the ones not taking part in the rally.

'They mustn't feel neglected,' he said, tossing us the chamois leathers. 'Spruce 'em up, patloon. I will not have sad, dusty cars in my garage!'

As always, a bunch of uncouth boys from one of the boarding schools (not Duckling's peculiar friends on this occasion) turned up, offering to 'help Nana uncle sir' with the washing and waxing.

'Sure! The more the merrier!' he boomed, as they stood in a row, grinning like idiots, when they came to ask permission. 'As long as you have not come here to ogle my beautiful granddaughters!' He rolled his eyes, 'If you have, I have given orders to De-Big Bazooka to eat you!'

'Thank you uncle, sir!' They gave him exaggerated salutes and snapped to attention, which he loved.

'Good men! Now take a bucket and washcloth and get to work!'

The problem was that those idiots *had* actually come to ogle me and Duckling. Both of us invariably would be in shorts and noodle-strap tops (because we'd be soaking wet by the end of the washing session) and all those boys wanted to do was look down our shirts. They'd do cheap things like kick their cloths under the cars and ask us to please pick them up. Or spray us 'accidentally' with the hose. Or ask us to pose near the cars so they could take pictures. It was disgusting. Before we could complain, Nana solved the problem in his own way.

One Saturday, the boys had just finished working on the buttercup yellow Sunbeam (that he had promised to give me when I turned eighteen) and the big silver '53 Mercedes 300S and stood ready for inspection. Nana walked down the line, eyeing them and the cars.

'Well fellows, what are you waiting for? Get to work!' He jerked his jaw towards the Sunbeam and Mercedes.

'B...but...uncle...sir we've finished...'

'If...if you like we can help Gos and Duck with the Thunderbird...'

'Nonsense! Look at these! They haven't been cleaned. So get on with it!'

That day, he made those fellows wash and wax the two cars four times over. And every time they finished, and stood ready to have their work 'inspected' he'd eye them and jerk his jaw towards the gleaming cars.

'Well men, what are you waiting for? Get to work!'

That really zapped them and they were completely pooped by the end of it, because if anything, Nana was a stickler for detail and every square inch of the cars had to be glossy and gleaming, and absolutely spotless from the inside too. What made it worse was that he would shuffle around the cars as they worked, shouting instructions and pointing.

'That door handle man, I can see fingerprints on it! Make it sparkle. And just look at that bumper, use some elbow grease men! The rear bumper...the rear bumper...!' And then, at the end of it all he ordered them to start all over again as if they had just got here and had done nothing for the past three hours.

Duckling and I stood by the Ford Thunderbird we had polished and grinned at them. Then we got bored and went in.

Those fellows never returned after that session.

Duckling and I never knew whether Nana had just tripped up over his short-term memory again that day, or if it had been a deliberate ploy on his part to get rid of the boys.

Early that November, we were to drive all the way down to Delhi for the Vintage and Classic Car Rally. Nana was a member of one of Delhi's top clubs and had booked one of their residential cottages for us to stay in. We'd be leaving early Wednesday morning, reaching by Thursday afternoon. The rally was on Sunday and we'd be starting for home on the following Tuesday to reach back by Thursday—a week's expedition. Shabby Aunty had got an appointment with one of Delhi's top neurologists— Dr Shareef—for 11 a.m. on Tuesday morning in spite of Nana's protests. We would set off for Chandigarh, our overnight stop on the way back home, right after that.

Apart from the Studebaker and Packard, we'd be taking Shabby Aunty's Innova, pulling a trailer that would contain all the spare parts that might be needed. The twins of course, were hugely excited and so were Duckling and I. We'd planned massive shopping expeditions to Janpath and Dilli Haat and all those glittering malls.

Nana too was very excited. 'Just you see,' he told the twins, who were jumping up and down. 'The Packard is going to be the belle of the ball. Her sister won the big prize at Pebble Beach this year!'

The problem was that he wanted to drive the Packard down personally, and it was one hell of a monster to wrestle up and down steep and twisty mountain roads. Sometimes you had to do a three point turn to get around the bends and backing it up or down on a narrow mountain road was the stuff of nightmares.

'He insists!' Shabby Aunty told us, 'but it should be all

right. One of the boys will be with him—the other will drive the Studebaker and I'll drive the Innova.'

With great glee, the Chakrams had fitted the Innova with a siren to clear the way ahead for us. It would be leading our grand cavalcade with the Packard following and the Studebaker bringing up the rear. Needless to add, the twins would be riding with Shabby Aunty and taking turns at switching on the siren when required.

One of the 'bonuses' of the Delhi trip was that Mama and Papa would be flying down on a whistle stop trip and we'd get to meet them: very briefly, they informed us, as they'd be tied up in meetings all day.

'So what's new?' Duckling had remarked acidly and turned away, as I compressed my lips and said nothing. I knew exactly how she felt. There was anger deep inside me too, like a glowing red coal, but I tried to quench it every time it began to burn.

'Sahib...sahib...theek ho? Sahib...sahib...are you all right?'

Lounging comfortably in the back of the Packard I awoke with a start. Beside me, Duckling sprawled, her head lolling on my shoulder also fast asleep. Up front, Paramvir was looking urgently at Nana, and had put his hands on the giant steering wheel and was guiding the car. Nana's head had dropped to his chin and his eyes were closed. Thankfully we were in the plains, and the road was straight. Somehow Paramvir slowed the huge car down and steered it to the side of the road and then brought it to a squealing halt. The weather was balmy but he was sweating.

'Wha...what happened?' I asked groggily, rubbing the sleep from my eyes. We had left the previous morning and were now on the last leg of our cross-country journey, just about 150 km from Delhi. The Packard, drop-dead gorgeous in midnight blue and stainless-steel silver had behaved magnificently and even the Studebaker had not hiccupped even once. As we drove through small towns and villages, children laughed and cheered us on, running beside the cars and Nana blew the 'phroo-phroo' horn. Duckling lounged in the back and waved languidly like a maharani tossing toffees out of the window. Up front in the Innova, the twins happily turned on the siren, clearing the way. But now we were well in the country, surrounded by fields. Behind us, the Studebaker slowed and stopped and up ahead the Innova suddenly braked as Shabby Aunty checked her rear-view mirror.

'Sahib fainted,' Paramvir said, sprinkling water from a thermos on Nana's face. By the time Shabby Aunty had reversed and joined us, Nana's eyes were flickering open and he had that same frightening dead fish expression that he'd had when he'd fallen at home.

'Wha...' He looked at us blankly as if not recognizing us. But he recovered quickly, though now we made him lie down in the back of the Packard. Paramvir took the wheel and Duckling sat up front, while I sat next to Nana keeping a hawk-eye on him.

'His salt level must be low—we'll have a blood test done in Delhi,' Shabby Aunty said. We pressed on and entered Delhi's mad traffic by three that afternoon.

'How're you feeling, Nana?' I asked.

'Top of the pops, General Gos, top of the pops!' he replied, but he sounded a bit slurred and seemed listless.

'Great!'

'Nana you fainted while driving!' Poor Duckling still hadn't recovered from the shock.

'Nonsense, Major poppet—that car runs so silkily I just nodded off for a few seconds. Her engine is like Irish-cream and honey.'

The club, a sprawling whitewashed colonial style building was located in Central Delhi amidst enormous tree-shrouded grounds. We settled into the sparkling little cottage that Nana had booked. The Chakrams dusted down the cars and looked under the hoods to check for oil leaks and other potential problems. Nana sat in one of the comfortable cane chairs in the bougainvillea-filigreed verandah and barked instructions at them. Shabby Aunty got hold of a diagnostic lab which sent a fellow over to take a blood sample from Nana.

'What's this for?' Nana demanded truculently. 'Why have you called a bloodsucker?'

'We need to know exactly what happened back there on the road, dear, that's all! Now give him your arm.'

Grumbling, he obeyed. 'You women! Always making such a fuss over nothing! Oww! Has this idiot ever done this before? He just bit me! Leech, sir!' He rolled his eyes at Dumpling and Dingaling who were watching with avid interest as the blood went up the syringe.

'Privates, do something! He's sucking me dry! I'll be just a husk blowing in the wind...Stop him! Save me! Aaargh!'

'Nana, be brave!'

'He has to be cruel to be kind!'

They had been rather quiet during the episode on the road, but by now had recovered their spirits and set about exploring the old colonial club house and grounds.

They were back in minutes and tackled Nana.

'Nana, what's our membership number?' Dumpling asked innocently. 'They won't give us ice-creams or anything otherwise. We have to sign for them and write down the number. Better if you give us the card, then no one will bother us.' Nana's eyes twinkled as he ruffled their hair.

'You know, I forgot my membership number and the card at home,' he said worriedly. He lowered his voice. 'Don't tell anyone—this is top secret. If they know, they'll throw us out in the middle of the night.'

'Nana, stop fooling!'

'You signed in when we got here and took your card out, remember?'

By the evening Nana was in full form.

'Patloon, we'll have dinner in the dining hall,' he declared. 'So you sweeties better dress up! Inspection at 1930 hours! We have to be there by eight and out by nine-thirty. They eat children after that.'

But we were happy, for he seemed to have gotten over his episode on the road completely and was back to being his 'normal' self.

We were really surprised at how many people came up to our table at dinner to vociferously greet Nana. Most were ex-colleagues from the armed forces, and some—the ones who were really warm—he had operated upon and saved their lives in some godforsaken battlefield and they hadn't forgotten. But he embarrassed the hell out of us. The exchanges went something like this: a ruddy faced gentleman would walk up to our table, the greetings would boom back and forth like gunfire, Nana and the gentleman would shake hands and embrace. Then Nana would point towards us.

'Meet my patloon, sir. That lovely lady is General Gosling, she was born in the first class cabin of the Empress Noor Jehan. Her lovely sister beside her is Major Duckling—she maintains a library of 5,000 books at home and has read every one of them at least three times and knows them by heart. Those two are Privates Dingaling and Dumpling who are shortly going to make mincemeat of the Ambani brothers!' And finally, more gently, 'And this is my good friend, Shabnamji who is Commander-in-Chief of the patloon!'

The visitor would grin good-naturedly, and sometimes sit down and join Nana for a beer. Duckling and I would go purple with embarrassment and have to introduce ourselves by our proper names.

'Nana just fools around,' I would explain, smiling inanely as the visitor would nod.

'Don't worry about that, my dear,' one friend told us, 'in the Army, he gave names to everyone—including Field-Marshal Sam Manekshaw! So you're in good company!'

Not one of his friends ever mentioned Mama and Papa or asked about them.

While Nana and the Chakrams messed about with the cars the next day—they had to go for 'scrutineering' that afternoon—Shabby Aunty took us shopping, with firm instructions to the Chakrams to ring if anything untoward happened. But Nana seemed just fine and was really looking forward to the rally. Mama and Papa had landed in Delhi early that morning but rang to say that they could only meet up with us late that evening. They would see us at the club. It had been over two years since we had last met them, and we were a bit nervous.

That evening, we had been sitting in the verandah, bathed and changed, chewing our nails, waiting for them when they rang to cancel. Apparently they had just received a call to go to the PM's residence for an 'important meeting' and they were sure we'd understand. They'd call again and fix up another time.

'Oh sure, we understand!' Duckling snorted. 'So what's new?'

Shabby Aunty looked troubled and hugged Duckling. 'It's all right, baby,' she said softly, wiping a runaway tear that had rolled down Duckling's cheek.

'I think they must really hate us!' Duckling suddenly choked, as Shabby Aunty hugged her tightly. 'Why did they bother to have us?'

'Shh… it's all right, they're just very busy people,'

We looked up as headlight beams cleaved through the mauve twilight accompanied by the purr of the Packard's giant V12. The two cars were back—and both had passed without any problems.

'India Gate at 0800 hours for flag-off, troops!' Nana boomed jovially. 'We should run away with all the prizes. Competition's a collection of moth-eaten, rust-buckets! We rise and shine at 0600 and depart from here by 0700!'

'Nana, Mama and Papa cancelled their meeting with us,' Duckling complained.

'Oh? They're in town?' Nana looked genuinely puzzled. 'I didn't know that. Have they been posted here? Oh well.' He shrugged and dismissed them.

The rally was enormous fun; noisy, colourful, confusing and tiring. I got really lovely pictures of some great cars and very eccentric owners! We had to drive all the way to a resort in Gurgaon and back via a route that took us up and down a twisty hilly road through the Ridge and then up a steep slope full of hairpin bends. But we—and our cars—were used to steep slopes and hairpin bends. The Packard really was the belle of the ball and was surrounded by admirers and photographers. Nana was in his elements and we basked in reflected glory too. Nana had dressed up like a maharaja, in a gold raw-silk sherwani complete with a magnificent pugree with a peacock feather pinned to it with a gigantic (fake) diamond and wore a (fake again) necklace glittering with rubies, diamonds, emeralds and pearls around his throat. We wore shimmering silk ghagras—pink and gold, or purple and gold with ruby-red and emerald-green glass bangles and ropes of 'pearls'. The twins, also in 'royal' fancy dress, simply hitched up their costumes and just went grimly about their business of procuring as many gift hampers as they could from the sponsors. A freebie was a freebie and they weren't going to miss out. Nana glided the gleaming Packard regally past the flag-off point (he'd once removed a bullet from the butt of the Chief Guest, the ex-Chief of Army Staff, 'so he owes me one!'), and the Studebaker followed, piloted by Mahavir. All four of us and Paramvir were in the Packard and poor Shabby Aunty was alone in the Innova, which she had insisted on bringing along as a 'backup' car.

We came away with three huge glittering trophies. The Packard won the 'Best Car in the Show ('Concours d'elegance')' and 'Best Performing Car' awards and the Studebaker got the award for the 'Best Post-War Classic'. That, and armfuls of gifts and hampers from various sponsors, all claimed by the twins, who no doubt would sell the contents to the hungry boarding school kids back home. Both cars had run flawlessly and we really felt for those poor souls who had to get out of their tinpot contraptions and push.

Tired and dusty and surrounded by balloons, confetti and trophies we reached the club at around 7.30 that evening. The Chakrams immediately got about wiping down and vacuuming the cars. We'd lowered the Packard's roof and she had collected an incredible amount of dust inside. A little while after we'd returned, Mama and Papa called to say they'd be reaching in ten minutes.

'What?' Nana said, relaxing in one of the ancient tea-planter's chairs and sipping his beer. 'They're in town? I didn't know that!'

It's really odd and difficult, meeting parents you hardly know and I don't think too many kids have had to experience this. They'd be gone again tomorrow morning and you wouldn't see them for another two years maybe, so it would be silly to fall all over them, and anyway you couldn't really do that because you felt you didn't know them well enough in the first place.

'What are we going to say to them?' Duckling asked. 'How does one start a conversation with them? I mean face to face?'

Of course they had brought us gifts—and very expensive ones at that. Tablets and iPads and iPods and Play Station games and Belgian chocolates and what have you. But this is how they met us and we met them:

We heard their cars, and went out into the verandah, Duckling and I exchanging nervous glances, and the twins holding each other's hands (normally something they did when they were facing a court martial). A Gypsy and a white Ambassador, both with flashing red lights drew up and a posse of Black Cat commandoes leapt out and (as Nana would have put it) 'secured the perimeter' in hilarious filmy style. Mama got out of the car; she was wearing an elegant gold and blue silk sari and a thick pearl necklace. She had obviously had her hair and face done (they were probably on their way to a reception or party after this). She looked at us and smiled and extended her arms—half-way.

'Sweeties, we've missed you!'

'Liar!' Duckling hissed in my ear.

I pushed the twins forward. 'Go to her!' They went, slowly at first but running the last few steps. She hugged them—gingerly as though she might catch something—and air kissed their cheeks.

'How you've grown!' Duckling muttered sotto voce under her breath and sure enough...

'How you've both grown!' Mama said and let off a brittle little tinkle. In the meanwhile Papa emerged from the other side, clutching bags of gifts. He was in a black bandh-galla with a maroon carnation in his buttonhole, his hair slicked back with brilliantine.

'Hello my dears, these are for you. Hope you like them...or we can get them exchanged...' He walked over and handed over the bags to me and Duckling. 'My, my,' he said as an afterthought, 'what pretty girls you've become.'

'No thanks to you!' Duckling muttered evilly.

'Papa!' Mama screamed as Nana—in baggy long shorts and a greasy sports shirt—emerged, followed by Shabby Aunty smiling uncertainly. Nana's eyebrows rose quizzically and he cocked his head to one side.

'And you are? Have we met before?'

For a moment there was a deathly silence as we all looked at him. He had to be joking! I felt the terror stir again because Nana genuinely looked baffled. Then Shabby Aunty whispered something to him and nudged him.

'Oh,' he said, still looking puzzled. 'If you're sure. I thought she was in Ottawa or somewhere.' He smiled vaguely.

'Hello my dear,' he said as Mama went up to him a little nervously. Serves her right, I thought uncharitably.

'Getting a dose of her own medicine, isn't she?' Duckling whispered cruelly.

'Hey, take it easy Duck.'

Papa had merely patted the twins and us on our heads as we headed into the drawing room.

'So how are your studies going?' Papa asked no one in particular and smiling generically as Mama took out her compact and checked her lipstick.

'Gosling's done really well this year,' Shabby Aunty said, 'and Duckling's topped her class as usual.' She smiled, 'As for the other two—I think their returns on investment have been higher this year than ever.'

'Aunty, what's returns on investment?' Dingaling asked immediately.

'Profits, dear.'

'Oh, that's okay.' And after a moment: 'Is that why you say happy returns of the day on your birthday?'

Really, I thought suddenly with a stab of bitterness, it was weird; this conversation ought to have been happening the other way around: *Shabby Aunty* ought to be asking those questions about us and Mama and Papa should have been answering them proudly.

'Oh,' Papa said, and smiled vaguely, stealing a glance at his Rolex. 'That's good.'

'Do you think they know that Shabby Aunty's shifted in with us?' Duckling suddenly whispered in my ear.

'Probably not,' I nudged her and smiled. 'Mama would have had a cow!'

'So how are you, Papa?' Mama asked. 'You're looking so well, touch wood.'

Nana eyed her keenly. 'I know I've seen you before somewhere,' he said, beetling his brows. I tell you it was funny and scary at the same time, because we had no way of knowing if Nana genuinely had not recognized Mama or was just pulling her (and our) legs, which was equally possible.

'Dear, really!' Shabby Aunty chided, putting an arm on him. 'Don't go on like that!'

'You haven't changed,' Mama tinkled. Nana's brow cleared.

'*Dum lagake haisha!*' he suddenly said, wagging a forefinger at Mama.

'Papa, you're incorrigible!'

And then he fired his Exocet. 'You better ask them if they remember who you are,' he said, jerking his head towards Duckling and me and putting an arm around the twins.

There was an embarrassing silence.

'Papa, really don't be silly, now. Of course they know!'

'Baby, you should never have had children,' Nana went on, letting loose his second missile, 'but I'm glad you did for my sake.'

'Papa!'

Mama smiled at us in a brittle sort of way and shook her head. 'He's probably tired and rambling,' she tried rationalizing.

'So how has your visit been so far?' Shabby Aunty asked, changing the subject.

'Good, very productive,' Papa said, looking at his watch again. 'Excellent. We're due at Rashtrapati Bhavan after this for a reception.'

'Not exactly bonding with *us* are they?' Duckling whispered laconically. 'But the PM and President are so lucky!'

It was odd, and it made me feel guilty that I didn't really *feel* anything for Mama and Papa, except perhaps that slow burn of anger and resentment. There was genuinely no bond, let alone bonding; they were strangers. Mama and Papa had deposited us with Nana and the Neerameerabais one by one barely as soon as we could walk, and had more or less disappeared from our lives. 'What are you thinking about, sweetheart?' Nana suddenly asked me gently. I shook my head and smiled.

But it was just so weird. Mama and Papa and their posse of strutting Black Cats departed for Rashtrapati Bhavan twenty minutes later and everyone (including them, I suspect) heaved a sigh of relief and reverted to normal.

'They're like those parents you read about in the old English books,' Duckling said as we got ready for bed. 'You know, the kind who used to come to India and send their five-year-olds to boarding school in England and hardly saw them again...'

'At least we have Nana,' I said, brushing out my tangles.

Duckling glanced at me, her eyes filling up and I knew what she was thinking.

We had Nana...but for how long?

And what would Dr Shareef say on Tuesday after seeing him?

6

Shabby Aunty had tentatively suggested that the four of us should drive straight on to Chandigarh (our overnight stopover) in the Packard and Studebaker with the Chakrams, while she would take Nana to the hospital for his appointment and follow us later in the Innova.

She faced an immediate mutiny.

'No way! Aunty, we want to come to the hospital too!' the twins chorused, sticking out their jaws.

Duckling and I (for once) agreed wholeheartedly with them. We all loved Shabby Aunty very much and knew she was very fond of Nana, but he was *our* nutcase Nana and we had to be with him and...well...frankly we had no one else. We just had to be there.

'We'll come too, Aunty,' Duckling said. 'We can't ditch you.' There was that too—we couldn't leave her alone to face whatever diagnosis Dr Shareef arrived at. Shabby Aunty's perfect eyebrows rose and her eyes narrowed; the ghost of a smile broke out. Then she nodded.

'All right,' she said, and gently ruffled Duckling's head. 'If that's what you want. It's very sweet of you.'

'Yay!' the twins yelled happily. Shabby Aunty beckoned us over.

'Come here, all of you... See, we might have to wait for a while in the OPD, so you'd better take your games or a book or something along to amuse yourselves.' Then she took a deep breath and looked at the twins. 'And Privates, the people who come to this waiting room are often not well—in the head...'

'You mean they're crackpots?' Dingaling asked. 'Bonkers?'

'Not crackpots—ill. So they might behave peculiarly and some may even shout or shriek but that's only because they're not well and may be in pain. They don't know what they're doing or what's happening to them. They are not happy people.'

'Will Nana become like that?' Dumpling asked, her eyes wide.

'No, sweetheart. Nana has something different.'

'Besides,' Dingaling added in a rare flash of brilliance, 'he can't become like that because he's already a nutcase! A real fruitcake!'

'Dingaling, really!' But Shabby Aunty could barely suppress her smile.

Duckling's eyes sparkled. 'Actually, the patients may be like you both—often you don't know what you're doing!'

'Haha, very funny Didi, we know exactly what we're doing!' Dumpling retorted. 'Besides sometimes even you don't know what we've done!'

'Like...' Dingaling chimed in and promptly got his toes trodden on by his twin.

Next morning, when we waited in the neurological department's OPD, it was hell of a reality check, not only for the twins but for Duckling and me as well. The twins took one look at the vacant-eyed, blank faced, twitching, drooling and mumbling collection of patients-adults and horrifyingly, children too—accompanied by their worried relatives or attendants and quickly held hands and sat down quietly. I looked around, equally shocked; what kind of lives did these poor people live—and what kind of lives did their loved ones live? Shabby Aunty completed the formalities, even as Nana continued to grumble and say we ought to have been on the road by now. Shabby Aunty came up to us.

'Half an hour at least,' she said, 'Gos and Duck, why don't you take those two to the gift shop and cafeteria and buy them an ice-cream? They're looking a little shell-shocked.'

'Come on kiddos,' Duckling said kindly, taking the twins by the hands. 'We have shopping to do!'

We ushered the two out and immediately they reverted to normal.

'It's awful,' I told Duckling, 'in that room…' I shuddered, 'and here, it's like everything's normal, as if that horrible room doesn't exist.'

We wandered back in after twenty-five minutes, just as Nana's name was being called. The twins, followed by Duckling and I rushed up as Shabby Aunty and Nana headed towards the doctor's room.

'Children, why don't you wait outside?' Shabby Aunty suggested, as Nana shuffled purposefully towards the doctor's door.

'Aunty, we're coming inside!' Dumpling insisted.

'Yes, we want to come!' I said and Duckling nodded. I was curious about how the doctor would examine Nana. If I were to become a doctor, this would be valuable 'experience' for me.

Nana walked into the doctor's room escorted by Shabby Aunty and followed by the whole caboodle. The doctor rose from his chair. He was of medium height, had thick black wavy hair graying at the temples and a tilt of the head that made him look as if he were assessing you sardonically. His cheeks were round and ruddy, his eyes black with the hint of a humorous glint in them, I thought. He smiled, and didn't seem at all fazed by the invasion—probably he was used to this sort of 'family invasion' of his clinic.

'Good morning, Doctor!' Nana boomed, standing to attention and saluting. 'Let me introduce you to my patloon!'

Shabby Aunty—who knew Dr Shareef from before—smiled apologetically. The doctor bade us stand at the far end of the room as Nana and Shabby Aunty settled in the chairs in front of his immaculate table. He went through Nana's medical papers and MRI scan and nodded.

'Very good, sir,' He looked at Nana sharply. 'A hundred minus seven is?' he asked suddenly. Nana frowned.

'Eh?'

The twins' eyes popped.

'Seven minus from a hundred is?'

'Ninety-three, sir!'

'Seven taken from ninety-three is?'

'Eighty-six.'

This went on for a bit, and I noticed the twins' lips twitching as they did the sums mentally. Duckling and I grabbed their hands and shook our heads when Nana hesitated once or twice; we knew they were dying to prompt him.

'What did you have for breakfast this morning?' the doctor suddenly asked.

'Eh? I guess the usual,' Nana frowned.

'Which is?'

'Egg…um maybe a boiled egg with toast.'

'Very good, sir. And for dinner last night? What did you eat for dinner?'

'Dinner? Some kind of chicken curry and dal, chapatti and rice, the usual.'

'What is your address? Where do you live?'

'At home, sir!'

'Yes, but what's your address?'

Nana rattled that off verbatim.

'And your phone number?'

'Uh, let me give you a missed call,' Nana said, taking out his mobile. 'Then you'll have it.' The doctor smiled.

'Do you remember the number?'

'Why should I?' Nana asked blankly. 'I don't call myself.' He pressed a button. 'Here,' he said, squinting as the number came up on his screen. 'Here it is. 0981...'

'Okay, thank you, sir. Now what is today's date and day?'

'Didi, why is he asking Nana such silly questions?' Dumpling whispered to me. 'Next he'll ask Nana his own name!'

'Shh...'

'Dumpy,' Dingaling suddenly hissed, clutching her. 'We can...' he leant over and whispered something in her ear. She nodded, her eyes glinting with mischief.

Meanwhile, the interrogation continued.

'Sir what car do you drive?'

Duckling and I exchanged glances.

'Eh?' Nana shook his head and pointed at Shabby Aunty. 'The Commander in Chief won't allow me to drive back,' he said. 'But otherwise I drive the Packard and the Studebaker and the Ford Woody and the Sunbeam and the Thunderbird and the Rolls and the Rover 3 litre and the Mercedes.'

The doctor's eyebrows nearly disappeared into his hair. He nodded.

'Yes, yes,' he said hastily, quickly making a note.

Shabby Aunty smiled. 'He does actually, doctor,' she said. 'He's got quite a collection of classic and vintage cars.'

'Oh, I see. Very good. Now sir, would you walk across the room for me please, and then back again?'

Nana stood up and walked stiffly up to us, did an about turn and shuffled back.

'Can you take bigger steps, sir?' the doctor asked.

'You mean goose steps?'

'If you like!'

Nana demonstrated a couple and then reverted to his shuffle.

'Very well.' The doctor pulled out a pad and took out his pen. Then he said something to Shabby Aunty, who turned to us.

'Children, could you wait outside please?'

'It's okay,' I said loftily as we left. 'Patient-doctor confidentiality has to be respected.'

'What's that?' Dumpling asked curiously.

'What the doctor tells the patient must remain secret between them.'

'But Shabby Aunty is still there.'

'Well, she is almost his wife so it's okay I guess.'

'Never mind,' Dumpling said tossing her head. 'We'll get it out of Nana, won't we?'

Dingaling nodded.

'Get what out?' Duckling asked.

'Oh, the secrets that the doctor tells him.' She smiled sweetly. 'You see Nana is sure to forget that the doctor would have told him to keep it a secret so we'll just ask him and he'll tell us.'

'But,' Duckling grinned triumphantly, 'Nana will probably also forget what the doctor told him in the first place!'

The twins made a face.

We all piled into the Packard for the trip back, after the appointment. Shabby Aunty drove, while the Chakrams followed in the Studebaker and Innova. The twins settled themselves one on either side of Nana, at the back.

'Nana, a hundred minus seven is?' Dingaling suddenly barked.

'Eh? Ninety-three.'

'Ninety-three minus seven is?'

'Eh, what's this? Now don't you start this nonsense!'

'Nana you better practice—so that the next time the doctor takes your test you get a hundred out of a hundred!'

Dr Shareef had prescribed medication—salt tablets and big blue pills called Levipil, amongst others—and said he would like to see Nana again in three or four months, which basically meant after the winter. He said that Nana should walk as much as he could and exercise too and continue to work on the cars—under supervision.

We were glad when the Packard finally purred through the gates of Shadow House the following evening, and were greeted joyously by De-Big Bazooka and welcomed by the Neerameerabais. It had been a great trip, not without its hairy—and uncomfortable—moments though.

'You're going to need a new trophy cupboard, my dear,' Shabby Aunty remarked, pointing at the glass-fronted cabinet that glittered with the silverware the cars had won over the years. She made room for the new entries.

'Yes,' Nana said, 'the next rally is in March, in Chandigarh. I think we'll enter the Rover 3 litre and the Rolls-Royce for that.'

We got back to our 'normal' lives: the school run continued as usual, with Shabby Aunty or one of the Chakrams driving the Woody, and Nana alongside. The only difference was that now often the twins would suddenly bark out, 'a hundred minus seven is?' at Nana on the way back—before he could ask us the nineteen times table! And instead of roaring back at them, he would just ruffle their hair and shake his head. He still insisted on driving the cars, but one of the Chakrams always accompanied him. Shabby Aunty had given them control of the car keys, so

Nana couldn't sneak off solo. His walking too had become a bit worse, and he had starting using a stick. He'd also got a bit quieter and no longer roared out suddenly as he used to.

We kept Mama and Papa informed about his condition—though they still seemed skeptical, as if they didn't really believe it. And they still didn't know that Shabby Aunty had shifted in with us.

'Keep in touch,' Mama would say, 'and let me know how he is. The Chakrams know how to take care of him. Avantika (Mama never called me Gosling), you make sure he takes his medication. Call Shabnam Aunty if there's a problem. We'll see what arrangements can be made when we visit next.'

Then came that morning in early December, when our rise and shine routine changed forever. Nana failed to come up. Instead, at about a quarter past six I was woken up by Shabby Aunty gently shaking my shoulder.

'Baby…Gos…' she said softly. 'Wake up dear and wake the others up.'

'Wha…but Nana?'

'He fell again, in the bathroom. Paramvir caught him in time.'

'Oh…oh…'

'He's all right. He's having his tea now in the patio.'

She leant down and picked up Nana's trumpet from beside my bed where she had put it before waking me up. She smiled.

'He insisted that I play this and wake you up like always. He said how will the patloon rise and shine otherwise?'

'Do you know the Colonel Bogey March?'

'I can try!'

But alas, her discordant blasts did not impress either me or Duckling or the twins or Nana. Later the twins came to the rescue.

'It's all right Nana' they told him. 'We've made a recording of you marching and playing the trumpet and singing the Colonel Bogey. We'll play that at 6 o'clock and wake ourselves up. You can rest and have bed-tea.'

'You made a recording?' Duckling asked, her eyes narrowing suspiciously. 'Why did you do that?'

'Just like that!'

'Hmm...'

She was right to be suspicious. A few days later, Sahiba came up to me giggling. 'You know what happened at Arun's school yesterday?' she asked. 'Your little twin racketeers created a furore!'

'What? But they don't go to...they're here with us...'

'Apparently they burnt a CD of your Nana singing a rather rude version of the Colonel Bogey March and playing the trumpet and sold it to one of their friends who put it on the school's PA system just before Assembly. The kid's lying low, but Arun recognized your Nana's voice and did some detective work thereafter. He's seen the boy and his friends hanging around with the twins.'

'Oh shoot!'

Duckling paled. 'Gos—they wouldn't have burnt just one CD. They must have burnt several.'

'So...'

She started giggling. 'All the schools in Mahaparbatpur are going to march to Nana's version of the Colonel Bogey March. The twins must have made a killing!'

Anyway, so now instead of Nana marching up the stairs and giving us the rise and shine, we got ready and marched down and presented ourselves for inspection in the greenhouse outside his bedroom. The mornings had turned frosty and brittle, the cold sharp and tingling but not clammy, the skies a burnished blue. Usually Nana would be having his tea there with Shabby

Aunty and would nod appreciatively as we marched up and stood at attention in a row before him. He'd stand up, give us a somewhat shaky salute and nod and say, 'on your way troops, take no prisoners!' If it wasn't too freezing, he and Shabby Aunty would accompany us. It was astonishing how warm it remained in the greenhouse, though Nana would often be wrapped up in a greatcoat and muffler and wearing that ridiculous rainbow-coloured monkey cap of his. We did our homework by ourselves now, in the War Room, but had to show it to him in his study, to save him the effort of climbing the stairs unnecessarily. He'd look at our work perfunctorily, and nod and say, 'Very good… very good, soldier, darling' and dismiss us. The one thing he still insisted on doing was to come upstairs to the Barracks and say goodnight to us. He took a bit of time on the stairs, and one of the Chakrams would follow close behind him, ready with a helping hand; we could hear him clomp his way up slowly. As always, he'd first say goodnight to the twins and then Duckling and me.

Mostly he would just smile fondly at us, kiss our foreheads and then briskly salute us and say 'goodnight soldier!' in his usual brisk, no nonsense way, as if nothing had changed at all, and shuffle out. But sometimes he would talk, and that could be scary.

'Well, General Gos,' he told me one night, stroking my hair and sitting down on the bed. 'This old General is fading away, so you'll be in command soon, eh! Take good care of the Major and the Privates, sweetheart. Of course Shabby Aunty will look after you but ultimately they're your responsibility!' And appallingly, he never once mentioned Mama and Papa when he said such things.

'Nana, don't say things like that!'

He looked puzzled. 'Damn legs!' he said explosively, 'They refuse to march any more. They've obeyed orders their whole lives!'

'Maybe it's just the cold.'

And always, I wondered, how much did he know about what he had and what could be lying in wait for him?

The winters could become ferociously cold. It was eye-poppingly bracing when the skies were clear and the sun was out, but when it fogged over and began to rain or hail, the chill tunneled into your very bones and seized you up. It did snow, perhaps once or twice during the season, which was the highlight for the twins, but otherwise it could be pretty miserable outside. Driving and cycling was hazardous, what with black ice lurking under trees, and poor visibility. The boarding schools shut down and most of our friends went home, (the ones who lived here often took off to the plains too) so it could get pretty lonely sometimes—and the twins' business deals shrank. The occasional storm would bring down power lines and mobile phone networks and there'd be reports of roads blocked by avalanches and landslides. But we kept warm as toast because at home there were pine-scented log-fires blazing in every room, virtually round the clock! All through the year, the Chakrams would collect fallen wood they found in the surrounding forests—branches, twigs, even uprooted trees, or those shattered by lightning, cut them into logs and store them in the shed at the end of the garden. We never had to buy or cut a single log and were kept fragrantly warm all winter.

But it could be stark and beautiful too; the mountains looked like jagged wedges of chocolate cake covered with soft dollops of vanilla ice-cream. The firs and pines tall and dark and proud as guardsmen creaked under their thick quilts of snow; occasionally a branch would give way with a resounding crack that echoed like a rifle-shot, startling the pahari crows—black as witches—into the sky.

That winter, for the first time the cars that were being restored and renovated were put into 'hibernation', wrapped up in tarpaulin, because the garages were too cold for Nana to work in, even if he stood right next to the big red-eyed coal 'angeethi' that was kept there. The metal got so cold it could take the skin off your fingers and oil became like treacle. In the past, Nana had somehow managed with mittens and mufflers and balaclava and a lot of colourful language, but not any longer. He fretted over this.

'The Golden Hawk's carburetor needs cleaning again,' he grumbled. Then Shabby Aunty hit on a part-solution. One of the Chakrams took the carburetor out of the car and brought it into Nana's study. Here, he could happily dismantle it and put it back together again and not get pneumonia in the process.

'It'll be good for him too,' Shabby Aunty said. 'Keep his mind occupied. Like doing a jigsaw puzzle.'

'Be careful Aunty,' Duckling grinned, 'next he'll ask the Chakrams to bring in the Packard's gearbox, so he can dismantle that and put it together again!'

But really, as Shabby Aunty put it, the winter was 'as good or bad as you made of it.'

Actually, in the beginning at least, it wasn't so bad for me personally. Sahiba and Arun Bhaiyya hadn't gone down to the plains and so were over virtually every day of the holidays. Arun Bhaiyya helped me 'service' my bike—to my horror he took it to pieces and then told me to put it back together again—as if I had the same problem as Nana!

'You broke it Bhaiyya, so you fix it!' I said hotly, hands on my hips. 'Oh my god, look what you've done to it!' He looked at me totally seriously, his lower lip sticking out just a bit.

'Anyone can break something, but not anyone can fix it. So you need to know how to do it.'

'Oh, but I didn't break it.'

'I told you, it doesn't matter who broke it, but you should

know how to fix it. You must be self-reliant!'

Who the heck did he think he was? Mahatma Gandhi?

'Thanks,' I said sarcastically, picking up a spanner.

'Not that one… you better start off like this…'

Sahiba and Duckling were giggling away. Then Nana shambled into the room.

'Good morning, sir! Morning, General! Ah, so you're re-building your bike…splendid.' He glanced at Arun Bhaiyya. 'You keen on my grand-daughter, eh?' he asked straight out. 'You've come to ask me if you can take her out, eh?' I went purple, and Arun Bhaiyya deflated like a punctured tire and started to stutter as Duckling and Sahiba became hysterical. Then the twins walked in and eyed the wreckage of the bike.

'Gosling Didi, did you have an accident again?' Dingaling asked.

'That bike is totaled!' Dumpling decided. 'Didi, if you like we could sell it to Ramu the kabaadiwalla and give you half of what we get.'

'You will do no…'

'So sir, are you keen on my grand-daughter?' Nana asked Arun again, eyeing him belligerently.

'No no, sir not at all. Her bike needed overhauling—all the gears were not engaging. I'm teaching her self-reliance.'

'You want to get engaged to her, eh?' Nana's eyebrows knitted together. 'Aren't you a little young?'

'No no, sir, of course not. I mean the bike's gears were not engaging properly. She must know how to fix it!'

'Good man!' Nana roared. 'Never give someone a fish, teach them how to!'

'Yes sir.'

'You interested in my Gosling, sir?' he asked again as poor

Arun went crimson. Serve him right for taking my bike to pieces.

Nana grunted and settled down in his armchair, staring outside at the grey winter sky and closed his eyes.

'Nana's hibernating now,' Dumpling informed Sahiba and Arun, 'he'll sleep till lunch time.'

Of course Arun helped me put my bike back together again and rather pompously pointed out the tools I needed to use. Sometimes he'd show me what to do then undo it and make me do it myself again.

'Pay attention!' he snapped once, when I'd been staring out of the window and missed a crucial maneuver. 'The bike is here, not outside the window!' Pay attention? Excuse me! Just who the heck did he think he was? Duckling and Sahiba quickly got bored of watching and went off to the library and the twins too disappeared. I glanced at Nana, stretched out in his armchair, asleep, with De-Big Bazooka at his feet, cocking an occasional ear. Arun Bhaiyya watched hawk-like, waiting for me to make a mistake, so he could pounce again. 'That's the trouble with you girls,' he said suddenly, distracting me from my work again. 'You always want other people to fix things for you. You must learn to fend for yourselves and be independent but you prefer being helpless and having males do things for you all the time.'

Brother!

Arun and Sahiba stayed on for lunch. Mealtimes now could be embarrassing if we had guests because Nana—who had always gobbled his food rather than eaten it—had a tendency to choke. There was something wrong with his swallowing reflex, though privately I thought it was because he was just so impatient he couldn't wait to finish chewing properly before taking the next mouthful. It was scary too and we had learnt to keep a hawk's eye on him while he ate. Most times of course, Nana would cough for a while, go purple in the face and eventually recover and we, while keeping an eye on him would go on eating. Sure enough, it happened that day, giving Arun and Sahiba the fright of their lives, I think.

'Oh-oh!' Duckling suddenly said, flicking a glance at me and then Nana. He had stopped chewing and was looking thoughtful. His face turned red and his eyes started bulging. 'Nana... are you...'

An explosion of coughing and hacking broke out and Nana's dentures suddenly flew out of his mouth on to his plate. Sahiba gave a stifled scream, went white and looked like she might faint— though I couldn't tell if out of fright or disgust. The rest of us kept an eye on him, while continuing to eat, and Arun Bhaiyya looked on completely appalled by our apparent casualness. For once, he didn't know what to do about it himself. Shabby Aunty and Paramvir were at Nana's side thumping him on the back, as the coughing continued in paroxysms.

'Nana sometimes tries to chew his food outside his mouth instead of inside,' Dingaling explained, nodding at poor Sahiba and pointing at the dentures.

'And he forgets,' Dumpling added sagely, 'that he needs to chew before he tries to swallow.'

Paramvir took the plate away, rescued the stranded dentures, washed them and brought them back, wrapped in a napkin, along with a fresh plate. Nana finally stopped coughing, drank some water, slipped the dentures back in and tackled his kheer with vigour.

'Sorry about that dear,' Shabby Aunty smiled at Sahiba and Arun, 'Nana has problems swallowing sometimes.'

'Aunty taught us the Himmler maneuver,' Dingaling informed our friends proudly. 'Do you know it?'

'That's Heimlich, sweetie...'

'Whatever. It's a life saving act. We can teach it to you for ₹250 a lesson. The course is for four lessons. So, for only a thousand rupees you will be able to save a life.'

'That's not much. You can recover it the first time you rescue someone.'

'Excuse me?' Arun Bhaiyya looked puzzled and shocked. I groaned inwardly. Nana spooned up his kheer.

'If we find someone choking, we ask them for ₹1000 first and then rescue them,' Dingaling explained matter-of-factly.

'What? How will the person give you money while he or she is choking?'

'They'll find ways,' Dumpling said airily. 'Especially if they're choking.'

'How many er customers have you had so far?'

'Um, none really but we've only just opened for business. Let school start...'

'Especially with those Bong kids who keep having fish curry for lunch; it's full of bones and they always choke. We'll make a killing out of them.'

'They really are a pair of little cut-throats, aren't they?' Duckling grinned.

'Nothing personal just business.' Dingaling shrugged coolly.

Sahiba recovered. 'So, now you'll charge ₹1000 from your Nana? He got okay on his own, so you could say he rescued himself or well, Shabby Aunty and Paramvir did.'

The twins shook their head. 'No, family gets a discount. Besides we didn't rescue him—Shabby Aunty and Paramvir did.'

'Babies we're proud of you,' Duckling grinned, 'that you can be so honest in a crisis!'

'How can we take money for something we have not done?' Dingaling exclaimed. 'That's not ethical.'

'So do you know how to do the Heimlich maneuver?' I asked Arun, raising my eyebrows.

He shook his head and mumbled something.

'Hah…then I must teach you.' I smiled charmingly, 'For free, unless of course you'd like to pay them a thousand bucks and learn it from them!'

Touché!

Later, as Arun helped me polish my bike (it was sparkling) I teased him some more. 'You really must know the Heimlich. Shabby Aunty says you never know when it can come in useful.'

He grunted and asked me in all seriousness. 'But does that happen at every meal?'

I nodded. 'More or less.'

'Doesn't it put you off your meal?'

I shrugged. 'It did earlier on, but not anymore. We just make sure his food is cut up properly or mashed, so there's less of a chance of his choking, though even that's no guarantee.'

'It must be tough.'

'What?'

'I mean with your Nana and all. The way he is…' He coloured and corrected himself hastily before I could pounce and bite his head off. 'Sorry, I'm sorry I didn't mean it like that. Just that with his forgetting and choking and falling and all…'

I swallowed the retort that had sprung up.

'He's perfectly all right. His short term memory is a bit… bad. He is getting on, you know.'

He wrapped a muffler around his neck. 'Come on, we should go for a test ride,' he said. 'I want to make sure that you've tightened all the nuts and bolts properly and nothing falls off.'

We called Sahiba (who was still closeted with Duckling) and set off. Sahiba went straight home and then Arun and I had a glorious ride (in complete silence needless to add) up and down the deserted forest roads. It was grey and dismal and smoky and our breath blew out in clouds, but it was beautiful. In the gorge below, the river gurgled, jade green, lace white and gunmetal-silver as dippers flitted in an out between the rocks. I was rosy-cheeked and exhilarated when he dropped me home—it was beginning to get dark now and the temperature had plummeted.

'That was great!' I said. 'Thanks.'

'I'm glad you enjoyed it.' He glanced around at the gathering dusk. 'You did a good job with the bike. Bye.'

'Bye!' I said weakly, watching him pedal off. Had he just paid me a compliment?

I wheeled the bike to its shed and entered the brightly lit house my heart flickering happily like the flames of the fire in the hearth.

And then they flickered out soon enough: Just before dinner that night Shabby Aunty's phone rang. It was the police, from New Delhi.

Her son Rakshas had come to New Delhi on a 'business trip' and had gone on quite a different kind of trip. He had fought with his 'girlfriend', taken a huge fistful of pills along with alcohol and then bashed her up before passing out himself. He was in hospital, (so was she, poor thing) under police guard.

'You have to go, Aunty,' I said, trying to sound much older than seventeen and feeling terrible for her.

'But...but your Nana? And you all?'

'Nana will be fine. So will we,' I said more bravely than I felt. 'We'll manage!'

'Call Mama!' Duckling said. 'Ring her up—right now Aunty!'

'Have you told Nana?' I asked.

She shook her head. 'I will,' she said, twisting a handkerchief in her hands.

We stood by as she went up to Nana, now dozing in his armchair, at peace with the world.

Shabby Aunty put her hand on his arm. He opened his eyes and looked at her and smiled contentedly.

'Dear,' she said, 'I have to go to Delhi tomorrow. Raksha had...had an accident.'

'Raksha? Oh.' He digested the news. 'An accident? Has he killed someone?'

I blinked: 'Had he killed someone?' Not, 'Is he hurt?' In some ways Nana's brain was as sharp as ever.

'No, but he's in hospital.'

'He was drunk?'

'That's what the police say.'

'Useless bugger—let him rot!'

'Dear...'

'He's only brought pain and misery to you.'

'Please, it's all right, but I have to go.'

He nodded. 'I guess you have to.' Suddenly he looked alarmed. 'But you'll come back, won't you?'

'Of course.' Shabby Aunty smiled and pointed to us, standing in a semi-circle nearby. 'Besides, the kids are here, your patloon.'

He glanced at us and smiled. 'Yes, my patloon. They won't go anywhere, will you, eh?'

I clutched Duckling's hand. 'No Nana, we won't go anywhere; we'll always be here.'

Nana, who had spent most of his life taking care of us, bringing us up, protecting us from uncouth schoolboys in his gung-ho, hugely embarrassing, 'armed forces' style, was now afraid of being left alone.

We couldn't tell Mama and Papa about the situation because

well they still didn't know that Shabby Aunty had been living with us and had been in charge. They had assumed that we and the Chakrams and Neerameeabais and Nana were managing as we always had done, with Shabby Aunty scandalously popping her head around now and then. And they thought nothing drastic had really happened to Nana. As far as Mama and Papa were concerned, nothing had changed. For us, everything had.

Shabby Aunty left for Delhi in her Innova early the next morning.

7

'Baby, sahib ne Studebaker ka carburetor ko bilkul ulta-pulta kar diya,' Paramvir grinned apologetically and held up the carburetor, which even I could see looked like it had been put together by a monkey with a wrench.

'Oh, can you fix it?'

'Yes, I'll try, but earlier he could take it apart and put it back together with his eyes closed.' Paramvir's deep set eyes were sad as he regarded the mangled carburetor.

It had been a month since Shabby Aunty had left for Delhi and she had still not returned. Rakshas had needed serious detoxifying, long-term treatment and counseling and did not seem very keen on helping himself. Fortunately for him his battered 'girlfriend' had not pressed charges, but had quite naturally dumped him. So now, poor Shabby Aunty had to look after his rehabilitation, no easy task. Her absence at Shadow House was being sorely felt by all of us—especially by Nana.

'Do you think she'll ever come back, General?' he asked me sadly, about twenty times a day.

'Yes Nana, she will. It's that stupid Rakshas who's causing all the problems.'

'Useless bugger! She should have dumped him on a garbage heap. I hope she does. Do you think she'll come back again?'

We spoke to Shabby Aunty every day. Of course, Nana's questions to her were the same, repeated ad nauseam.

'When are you coming back? We're missing you...'

But I had other things on my mind. The Board exams were looming large and I had to spend a lot of time in the War Room, swotting. Occasionally Sahiba would come over with Arun Bhaiyya, who would pompously 'tutor' us in maths and physics (in which, needless to add, he was brilliant), or I would go over to their house. Nana rarely if ever came upstairs now (except to say goodnight) and I missed his company while I sat with my books. As the winter progressed, he really did seem to go into hibernation, stretched out in his armchair all day, smack in front of the fire, occasionally ringing his call bell for one of the Chakrams.

'He's become like a big pink teddy bear!' Dumpling would say. She'd sneak up to Nana and giggling, tickle his ribs.

'Nana wakey-wakey!' she'd tease in a sing-song voice, poised to flee. He'd awake like a surfacing walrus. 'Hey you, naughty girl, run away now!' he'd roar with a bit of his old spirit as Dumpling would scuttle off, giggling, and then along with Dingaling stand to attention and cheekily salute him. He'd flick them a sleepy salute and then settle back to sleep.

We had another big scare one night when he was coming up to say goodnight to us. Halfway up the stairs, his legs sort of folded up under him. In the Barracks, we were startled out of our beds by the sound of Paramvir yelling urgently:

'Mahavir, *kursi lao!*'

We gathered at the top of the stairs and stared in horror. Paramvir was holding Nana up from the armpits and struggling to maintain his own balance and not topple over backwards down the steps. Nana was a solid, heavy man, nearly 200 lbs. and he was a dead weight. There was nothing we could do but hope Paramvir did not lose his balance. Thankfully, Mahavir shot up the stairs from downstairs with an aluminum chair and they somehow eased Nana down into it and then carried him up. He had that same terrifying blank glaze in his eyes, and grey pallor on his cheeks. His monkey cap was all askew, the bobble falling ludicrously over one ear.

'Are you all right?' I asked, wishing Shabby Aunty had been here and in half a mind to ring her up. (Then I thought, bitterly, it should be Mama and Papa I ought to be wanting to ring up.)

'Nana? Nana? Do you read me?' Duckling called urgently, rubbing his hands. 'He's so cold!'

'Didi, will he be all right?' The twins were holding hands again. 'I guess...'

'We'll let him lie down and raise his legs,' Paramvir said, nodding to his brother. They took him to my room, lifted him to his feet and laid him down on my bed, putting a bolster under his feet.

'He'll have to sleep here tonight,' I decided.

'You can bunk with me,' Duckling offered.

But half an hour later, Nana was awake and alert and asking (somewhat slurrily albeit) what the hell he was doing in my bedroom and demanding to be taken to his room.

'Nana, you came to say goodnight and your legs gave way and you fainted. Stay here for the night, I can sleep in Duckling's room.'

'Nonsense, I'm fine. I'll go down. Call the boys.'

He could barely stand, so they took him to the top of the stairs in the chair. And then, as we held our breath, they held him from under the arms, one on either side of him and step by step descended the stairs. At the bottom, the Neerameerabais, looking up anxiously, positioned another chair into which they sat him. Ten minutes later Paramvir came up again and knocked discreetly at my door.

'Sahib is calling you to say goodnight.'

After that, we went down to his bedroom every night to say goodnight. When I told Shabby Aunty the next day what had happened she said, 'Darling, go to the hospital tomorrow and ask them to order a walker and a wheelchair for him.'

'Aunty, he's going to hate that. He'll never use them.'

'I know, he'll make a fuss, but maybe he will.' Then she actually chortled as I frowned in disbelief. 'Sweetie, you can tell the boys to customize his wheelchair.'

'Customize?'

'Yes, they can fix one of those bulb horns and maybe a couple of chrome headlights and fix on motoring club badges and an exhaust that makes farty noises. And yes, get one which has pneumatic tires, the boys can maybe put in springs and shockers. And a customized leather seat too—wheelchair seats can be very uncomfortable.'

'Shabby Aunty, he'll freak!'

'He'll love it!'

'He'll demand they put in a muscle car V8 and 7 speed gearbox too!'

She laughed. 'But he won't have a wheelchair driver's license!'

'We'll have to make him an "L" plate then!' Now I was getting the giggles and Duckling was looking at me as though I were nuts.

'What?' she asked, 'what's so funny?'

'We got to get Nana a hotrod wheelchair tomorrow,' I said. 'Racing specs!'

'Oh,' she said. Her face fell and then she grinned.

'How's Raksha?' I asked Shabby Aunty, though frankly, I couldn't give a damn.

'Feeling sorry for himself as usual.' Shabby Aunty sounded exasperated. 'Not helping himself at all.'

'Oh Aunty, we miss you.'

'I miss you all too, but what to do?'

Nana too would speak to her every day, insisting that I call up first thing in the morning, after we had gone down for the 'wake up' call. (The twins called this the 'already woken up call'.) I would usher the others out of the room as I handed him the phone and he would ring the call bell when he had finished speaking to her—usually in about three minutes! Invariably, he'd look at me and shake his head sadly.

'Did she tell you when she was coming back?' he'd ask, but with no great sense of hope and I would have to shake my head.

'Nana, she'll come back when she feels she can leave Rakshas.'

'Useless bugger. Bloody good-for-nothing!'

One Sunday morning, I went down to say good morning to Nana and this is what I saw: He was already out there, in the greenhouse-patio, fresh and pink as a baby, sitting in his straight-backed cane chair, wrapped up in his charcoal grey greatcoat. The pale winter sun, slanting through the mullioned glass had gilded him tangerine-gold, setting his silver hair ablaze. He was looking quizzically at the twins who were standing in front of him. I walked into the bedroom and suddenly on a hunch, hid behind the curtains and watched. The French windows were open. Dumpling stepped forward and saluted smartly.

'Good morning Nana, sir!' she barked. 'Can you tell me my name, rank and serial number, sir?'

Nana looked at her and smiled benignly. 'Eh? What is that baby?'

'My name rank and serial number, sir!' Dumpling snapped to attention and clicked her heels. Two steps behind her, Dingaling automatically followed suit.

'Your name, rank and serial number? You've forgotten it?'

Dumpling shook her curls exasperatedly. 'Nana, do you know

who I am?'

'Baby!' he smiled, 'You're my little baby!'

'My name, Nana, what's my name?'

'Dumpling of course, I've forgotten that other name your mother gave you...'

Dingaling, looking nervous, stepped forward.

'And me? Who am I?'

'Nana you get five out of ten. You forgot my real name. I am your grand-daughter, Niharika.'

'And I'm your only grandson, Nihal,' Dingaling said quickly, obviously anxious not to be forgotten.

'Of course you are. Now get me the phone and ring up Shabby Aunty for me.'

I picked up the phone and walked into the patio. The twins looked startled.

'Good morning Nana!' I kissed him and handed him the phone. 'Okay, you two let's go inside. And hang on, I want to talk to you.'

'What, Didi?' Dumpling said, one hand on the door handle, ready to flee.

'What was that about? Asking Nana who you were?'

She looked at the carpet and exchanged glances with Dingaling. 'We read on the Internet that people with dementions forget their near and dear ones. So we were just checking.'

'And reminding him who we were in case he did forget.'

'We try and remind him every day.'

'Once in the morning and once in the evening.'

'Like his medicine.'

'Babies, who on earth could forget you two? Nana doesn't have a chance. He won't be able to forget you if he wants to!'

'But we read that sometimes such people don't even know

who they are even when they look in the mirror,' Dumpling said in a small voice.

'So sometimes we take him a mirror and show it to him and ask, "Who is that, Nana?"'

There was no beating around the bush with these two; they read too much.

'Come here,' I said and bade them sit beside me. They looked at me anxiously. 'Listen, even if Nana does forget who you—or we—are it's not as if he doesn't love us anymore. (I was also trying to convince myself.) It's just that some memory part of his brain has blown a fuse—like a bulb.'

'Like when a computer crashes?' Dingaling asked.

'Yes, something like that! And there's another thing,' I gulped. 'Sometimes, this thing that Nana has might make him very sad and quiet.'

'He's already like that—he just sits in his chair all day and stares grumpily at the mountains. He doesn't even work on the cars anymore.'

'He's quiet probably because he's missing Shabby Aunty.' Dumpling pursed her lips and made a kissing sound and arched her eyebrows knowingly.

'So anyway, when he's like that maybe you two can try to make him laugh.'

'How?'

'By just being yourselves, I guess!'

'As if we're clowns!' Dumpling was outraged. Then her eyes brightened. 'But we can behave like clowns if you pay us.'

'You little mercenaries! You want money to make Nana happy!'

'Not Nana—we'll make Nana happy for free. We'll charge money only from you and Duckling because even you'll be happy if Nana is happy.' She looked at me coyly. 'Won't you?'

'You, my little sweetie, are a born huckster.'

But the little sweetie's huckster brain was ticking furiously on; her brow puckered. 'Didi,' she asked, her voice scared again, 'if...if Nana does forget who we are, will that be like forever? Will he never know who we are again?'

I swallowed and then nodded, hugging them both. 'That can happen,' I admitted. 'It's a horrible disease. Let's hope it doesn't and there's no point worrying about that now.'

'But if it does,' Dumpling went on like a little bulldog, 'we'll all be like strangers to him, won't we? He won't know who we are.'

'I suppose we'll just have to make friends with him all over again then, won't we?' I said softly, gulping. What else could we do?

'We're quite good at making friends,' Dingaling averred, 'we've got lots of them.'

'So we can easily make friends again with Nana.' Dumpling glanced out of the window. 'Sometimes, even now when Nana looks at us, he doesn't seem to know who we are,' she said sadly. 'He looks like we are strangers. It scares me, but then he remembers and smiles like a baby!'

Duckling barged into the room. 'Oh so here you are!' she exclaimed. She glanced at the twins and then me. 'What've they done now?' Then her eyes narrowed. 'Hey, Gos everything all right?' She glanced out into the patio and then at me. Nana had put the phone down and was staring at the mountains again. 'Why are you crying?' she asked me softly.

That was not the only 'memory retaining therapy' (Duckling's definition) the twins had lined up for Nana. Now every morning, when we would present ourselves for 'inspection' in the greenhouse-patio where he had his tea, they would place his walker in front of him, help him stand up and walk with him carefully down the paved path to the gazebo at the edge of the garden, one twin on either side, with one of the Chakrams bringing up the rear. Nana would sit down on a tall straight-backed wrought iron chair there and then they (and Duckling and I, smiling sheepishly) would stand rigidly beside him and rake the mountains and forests with our steely gaze for something interesting to see.

'Look!' Dumpling would exclaim. 'Falcon at two o'clock! Looks like it's hunting, Nana, get ready to duck!'

Nana would gaze up at the tiny speck and smile benignly at Dumpling.

'You see,' Dumpling explained earnestly to us, 'if we do it every day—like he made us do—he won't be able to forget. We'll be reminding him every day.'

Then both of them would chorus: 'Nana, the sky is? The grass is? You wash your face with? And brush your teeth with?'

Nana would just smile benignly at them and ask for Shabby Aunty.

But of course, we had to inform Mama and Papa about his condition.

'They ought to bloody well know!' Duckling said fiercely, 'wining and dining in Paris and New York and Rio and all. We have to tell them.'

Telling them proved to be a terrible double-edged sword and it sliced down on us ruthlessly one Friday evening, when I Skyped Mama. Nana was dozing as usual in the drawing room and I was in the War Room upstairs, along with the others. I didn't like at all talking about him behind his back to Mama, but I didn't want him to feel bad either. Mama appeared on the screen, perfectly coiffured as usual, pearls around her throat.

'Hello Avantika darling.' She waved as the others crowded around me and waved back.

'Hi Mama...'

'You look well…'

'Yeah, we're good. Mama—Nana collapsed on the stairs the other day—Paramvir caught him but he now stays downstairs mostly.'

'Ah yes, dear—Shabby Aunty informed me of his condition.' She lowered her voice. 'Um, is he in the room with you right now?'

'No, he's downstairs in the living room.'

'Good, now listen. We've been in touch with a home for old people with special needs like his. It's located a little outside Delhi.'

'A what?' My voice dropped to a whisper. Duckling had gone ashen.

'A home where they look after old people with his condition; I've checked its website and done a bit of research and it looks very comfortable. It's air-conditioned of course, with a pool, spa, putting green, clinic, 24-hour medical help on call, hospital, theatre, full service and so on. He should be very happy there. He'll have lots of company of his own kind. I've seen the brochure—it seems quite beautiful.'

'Who should be happy there?' I whispered.

'Nana, of course!' Mama said a trifle impatiently.

'You want…you want to put Nana in a *home*?'

'But who will look after us then?' Duckling blurted.

'Harshita, he's hardly able to look after himself now, let alone you.'

'But you can't put him in a home. This is his home—Shadow House.'

'We think it will be the best for everyone,' Mama went on, as usual not hearing what she did not want to hear.

'But what will happen to all of us?' the twins suddenly wailed together. 'Where will we go?'

Mama nodded. 'We'll have to discuss that, but here's what

Papa and I have decided will be best: Nihal and Niharika and Harshita still have school years left, so a boarding school could be an option—there are so many in Mahaparbatpur—in fact your current school also takes boarders so they should accommodate them easily. As for Avantika, she'll be finishing school by March next year, so could be with us until she gets admission to university. Where she gets admission will depend on her results of course.'

'Why can't we stay on here, in Shadow House?' I asked ashen faced, trying to come to terms with the speed at which all our lives were being turned upside down.

'Don't be silly. You can't run a house.'

'But Paramvir and Mahavir and the Neerameerabais are doing that already.'

'They may not be after Nana shifts. We won't really need them anymore.'

'Don't need them anymore… but…but…they've always been with us, since we were little.'

'We're thinking of selling Shadow House. A multinational hotel chain has shown keen interest in developing the property. We're thinking of buying a house in London.'

'Selling Shadow House?'

'And Nana's cars?' Dingaling squeaked, 'The Packard and the Rolls Royce and all the others?'

'We'll sell them of course. The hotel people will probably be glad to take them as well.'

'You only want to dump us all!' Dumpling suddenly wailed. 'You don't love us at all. You just want to dump us on a garbage heap and have parties in Paris! We hate you!' She choked off sobbing uncontrollably as Dingaling's face began crumpling up too.

'Niharika, of course we love you darling, don't be silly. This seems all very upsetting at first but everything will be all right—

you'll see. You'll settle down in no time at all, it will be such fun, coming for holidays to a new house in London with new friends and all the places to see. Now stop all this natak!'

Everything will be all right I thought hollowly, as Duckling put her arms around the twins and hugged them. Sure. You've just destroyed our home and family in thirty seconds flat and you say everything will be all right. You've just condemned Nana to death—he would certainly never be able to come to London (to see the wretched Queen and King and the rest of us), and I doubt we or Mama and Papa would go to his godforsaken home too often to visit. They'd as good as deserted him on an uninhabited island. He would just wither and die in no time at all. The flame of anger began to burn again. Meanwhile Mama just went on inexorably in her usual bulldozer mode:

'Avantika, Papa and I are coming to India in April for ten days—that's when we'll sort things out properly. You will have finished with your exams and the others will have their holidays too.'

I took a deep breath.

'Mama, it's okay really. We're managing fine—everything's normal. There's no need to put Nana in a home, he'll only be miserable.'

I could hear her sharp intake of breath and a shadow flickered over her face on the screen. Then she smiled what I called her 'fake, LED PR smile'.

'Avantika darling, listen to me, Nana may seem all right now—you're managing fine, but things are going to get worse—much worse. He might get violent, he may not recognize you all, he may be bedridden, he may wander off and fall off a ridge—you can't deal with all that. We can't put you through all that, it's not good for you, especially the twins, they're too young.' She looked at us placatingly, but we would not be placated.

'Mama we're fine!' Dumpling hiccupped. 'If Nana forgets who we are we'll just remind him!' She shrugged. 'We're already doing that.'

'Like once he forgot he gave us pocket money and gave it again,' Dingaling began and got his foot trodden upon again.

'There's no way you can deal with this,' Mama repeated. 'We can't put you through this. It won't be right.'

'Then why don't you and Papa come back?' I said brokenly. 'Why don't you come back and look after him instead of sending him to a home full of mad strangers and buying houses in stupid London?'

'Darling, you know that's not possible with our jobs.'

Duckling took a deep breath, her face scarlet with anger. 'Sure it's not possible Mama—you and Papa have to save the world from annihilation as you've been doing all along, and the hell with everyone else, especially your family.' She shook her head witheringly. 'You have to make noble *sacrifices* for the cause of Bharat Mata, Mama! You have to be bum chums with the PM and President and never let them down!'

'Harshita apologize at once! That's disrespectful! You will not use that tone of voice with me.' Mama was looking angry now, her mouth drawn into a thin crimson slit, curving down at the edges.

'Go to hell!' Duckling sobbed explosively as the twins looked at her aghast. 'I hate you both.'

'Harshita, how dare you? Apologize at once!'

'Will not!' Then Duckling simply made a rude face and disconnected, sobbing heart-brokenly. White-faced, I put my arms around her waiting for her sobs to subside, saying nothing.

We all knew it had spun way, way out of control.

'She'll ring up again,' I said softly at last.

'Disconnect it or don't pick it up!'

But to our surprise, Mama didn't Skype or ring back or contact us by e-mail. Not immediately, not the next day or week. 'She's waiting for us to call and me to say sorry,' Duckling said mutinously, 'or using this as a cooling off period—like I suppose they do when India and Pakistan have a tiff.'

That night, when I went down to say goodnight to Nana he looked at me and asked straight out:

'Why has Major Duckling been crying, General sweetheart? Have you been fighting?'

'Duckling? Crying? She never does that. No, we didn't have a fight or anything.'

'She has been. Do you know what's upset her? She seems very upset.'

I shrugged and looked around his bedroom to escape his gaze: at the two small, carved silver cannons standing on either side of his mantelpiece, the copper-plated ashtrays made out of gear-wheels on the glass-topped coffee table, various souvenir bits and pieces of shells and shrapnel and bullets he had extracted from army bigwigs' bodies in a glass-topped cabinet (with rude labels under them like 'removed from the hippo-ass of Major-General..., Srinagar'). The curtains were still open (he loved them that way) and through the large French windows that opened into his greenhouse-patio, I could see the range of mountains shimmering under their soft quilts of snow in the distance. As always there were arrangements of dried leaves and ferns—orange, gold and fiery scarlet—that the Neerameerabais made in the pair of tall jade vases, and the silver-framed pictures of us and of Nani and Mama on his chest of drawers. This was where he lived, where he belonged, not some cold-storage sterile 'home' with a collection of discarded loonies. (Poor souls; all of them whoever they were.) I stared particularly hard at Nani and Mama's pictures. We had never known Nani and Nana rarely spoke of her. Had she too been like Mama, I wondered. She'd probably died too soon for even Mama to know her. Nana had been hugely proud of Mama, who had topped the Indian Foreign Service exams and then had met Papa and got caught in the 'razzle-dazzle whirligig' of the 'diplomatic wine-sniffing circus', as Nana put it (which was probably why she was so outraged when Nana did his down-to-earth *dum lagake haisha* act on the plane when I was being born!)

But it was also true that as roving, trouble-shooting national ambassadors and negotiators they were an unbeatable, brilliant team that had defused many international crises. 'They both know how to say exactly the right thing to the right people at the right time—and yet make and prove their point, which is why they've been so successful,' Nana had told us when we had complained to him yet again over their eternal absence from our lives.

And now, Mama and Papa wanted to destroy our 'family life' with him, because it didn't quite fit into their scheme of things—into the brilliance of their lives. How could Mama even think of selling Shadow House? It was her home too.

Ah, but was it? Nana had been forced to put Mama in boarding school after Nani died, because he was being transferred all over the country. During her holidays, she would join him wherever he happened to be posted at that time often living quite rough in remote outposts. Very rarely had they spent time together in Shadow House and that too, only for a few days at a time, so in some sense it had never really been her home. And that, I thought, explained why she loved traipsing around the world all the time and had no feelings for the place—why she was so unconcerned about selling it now. She had no roots. For the four of us and Nana, (and Shabby Aunty too) Shadow House had been the only home we had known and loved.

'General Gosling?' Nana said now, smiling, his eyes brimming with affection. 'Do you copy?' He tapped my head with a finger. 'Sweetheart? Anyone home?'

I started. 'Oh, sorry—I was just daydreaming.'

'Ah yes. When are your exams, darling?'

'In March.'

'Preparations on at full steam in the War Room?'

'Yes, Nana.'

'Good girl.' He looked at me. 'Why has Duckling been crying?'

'I…I don't know. I'll ask her, but you know what she's like.'

'Has she got a boyfriend?' His eyebrows shot up and he winked.

'She has several boyfriends Nana, not just a boyfriend! They swap matchbox labels and coins.'

'Why was she crying? Ask her what the matter is, okay?'

'Sure.' I leant forward and kissed him. 'Umm…prickly!' I screwed up my face. 'Goodnight, Nana!'

'Goodnight, General!' he barked crisply, saluting me sharply and I blanched. In that instant, in the way he said that, there seemed absolutely nothing wrong with him: it was like a momentary flashback to the time when he would wake us up with that scandalous rendition of the Colonel Bogey March on his trumpet and drive us to school in the Khatara Neela Bus and roar, 'Patloon chaaarge!'

As I walked slowly up the stairs to the Barracks that night, the first glimmerings of a plan came to my mind. A plan— hugely audacious, even dangerous, devious—a plan, which I now realize, only a sixteen or seventeen year old would have dared contemplate. Every little detail would have to be clearly and completely thought through. A plan that would mean we could not even tell Shabby Aunty what had transpired. (Mama and Shabby Aunty rarely talked, because Mama had never really approved of the relationship.) But it was a plan that would show Mama and Papa in no uncertain terms just exactly where they got off and that they couldn't mess around with our lives just in order to suit theirs.

'You're mad!' Duckling said staring at me appalled, when I told her. 'You're supposed to be the sane, stable member of the family, remember? I can't believe you thought of this. Have you been drinking?'

'Shut up. But do you think it will work?'

'Work—it'll be like exploding a nuclear device in their faces if it works.' Her eyes gleamed. 'But I love it! It has got to work!'

'We'll need to plan it carefully. Every detail…'

'Ten days. We have to account for only ten days. Probably even less.'

Duckling shook her head. 'We'd better prepare for twenty.'

'Okay.'

'What do you think will happen afterwards?'

'Hopefully Mama and Papa will see sense and will have learned their lesson.'

'Yes. How much do we tell the twins?'

I frowned. 'Only as much as they need to know; just as we do Nana…'

'So they won't know the real reason?'

'They don't need to know that.'

'And the Chakrams and the Neerameerabais?'

'Simple: we just tell them that we're acting under doctor's orders. They can't argue with that.'

Duckling looked thoughtful. 'Hmm…it's a good thing Shabby Aunty is away, it wouldn't be possible otherwise.' She grinned. 'I never thought we'd be thankful to Rakshas about anything but here's to him!'

'Yeah, good on him, the loser.'

'We still have time to think this through properly.'

'I have to think of my stupid exams!'

'Don't worry. I'll start making notes and lists. Everything we might need—this has to be the most exciting, crazy thing we've ever done.'

'Yeah,' I grinned getting infected by the madness of the plan. 'And Nana won't need a hotrod wheelchair now; he'll need a 4 by 4 one!'

About ten days after the 'Total Breakdown of the Skype Talks' (as Duckling headlined it) with Mama and Papa, Nana (who didn't know about it) asked us to Skype them again.

'Ring them up, Duckling, we haven't spoken to them for a long time, sweetheart.'

Duckling looked trapped. I knew she had been feeling bad about being rude to Mama, but she had (you would agree) justifiable cause to be very upset. But now, she would have no option but to apologize. Mama, we knew, would refuse to speak to any of us (excepting Nana) until Duckling apologized—and we certainly didn't want Nana to know about the dust-up. She took a deep breath and dialed them up.

'Hi Mama, it's me your daughter Duckling, I mean Harshita. I'm sorry about last time and here's Nana and he wants to talk to you,'she gabbled. Breathlessly she handed the mike to a rather bemused looking Nana. On the screen Mama smiled brilliantly, her lipstick gleaming waxy red.

'Hello Papa, how're you doing?' She shook her head deprecatingly.'Did you listen to that girl: "your daughter Harshita!" she says! Kids these days! So how are you Papa?'

'I'm doing all right.'

'You look great!'

'Here, speak to the children.' He handed the mike over to me.

'Hi Mama!' I said guardedly. I saw Mama indicate that I should use the earphones.

I put them on.

'Is Nana in the room?' she asked softly. I nodded.

'Very well, don't tell him. Our India dates have been finalized. We'll be reaching Mahaparbatpur on April 15 and will be there till the 25th. We'll be taking him to see the home on the 26th—he will shift soon thereafter. You all will stay on at Shadow House until the end of the holidays, with the servants. We've got admission for the twins and Harshita as boarders at the same school you all are going to now, so there's no change there. I've taken some leave towards the end of June when we'll be packing up and shutting up the house so the hotel people can move in. You will be with us in Washington until you get admission to university.'

'Is…is the deal with the hotel people through?' I whispered, looking at Nana. He seemed to have dozed off as usual.

'All the preliminaries are done. They'll do the physical verification when we come down in April—Papa will show them around Shadow House while I take Nana to see the home so he won't be unnecessarily upset. We'll be signing the final deal at the end of June when I return and hand over the keys.'

I felt faint. Mama moved fast and ruthlessly. She was diabolical.

And now god willing we were going to throw an almighty big, clanging spanner into the works! I just hoped it was big enough.

8

The latter part of the winter was most harrowing for Duckling and me. While I buttoned down to cram for the exams, Duckling took on the responsibility of drawing out an 'Action Plan' for my great idea.

'Secrecy of intent is crucial!' she said, pacing up and down the War Room during one of our frequent before lights-out meetings. (We made absolutely sure the twins were not eavesdropping.) 'We have to let the concerned people know, just exactly what they need to know, at exactly the right time.'

Like the twins and the Chakrams and Neerameerabais.

The right time, we decided, would be a week before we actually put the plan into action. I would be free by then, and able to take command. Also, there would be enough time to make preparations. We had to be very careful about what we told Mama and Papa when we contacted them on Skype. Nana remained much the same—he really felt the cold that winter, but otherwise was well physically. He still fretted about his legs, though the wheelchair that Paramvir and Mahavir were building for him excited him no end. 'Dekh lo! Cadillac SUV banayega!' Mahavir told me grinning as they took the 'stock' wheelchair we had bought to pieces and began redesigning it. Nana was happily 'walking' around the garden and to the garages quite confidently with the help of his walker. But he still spent a lot of time dozing and napping.

'What car is that?' he asked me once, pointing to the Sunbeam. 'I've forgotten its name.'

'It's the Sunbeam...remember?'

'Ah yes. If you say so, sweetheart.'

'You promised I could learn to drive in it and to give it to me,' I went on. (He had.)

'And that's the Rolls-Royce and that's the Packard, which won the prize in Delhi,' Dumpling pointed out. 'They're all our cars.'

'When is Shabby Aunty coming back?' he would ask inevitably and somewhat plaintively. The news on that front alas, was not too good. Rakshas had been detoxified and had then deliberately gone and got himself stoned again. Shabby Aunty was having a rough time and was getting pretty fed up.

'He's the one who needs to be locked up in a loony bin, not Nana!' Duckling said acidly. 'Always whining and feeling sorry for himself.'

Mama and Papa too had steamrollered on with their diabolical plan.

'Please don't let anyone else know about this,' Mama cautioned me. 'You know how people gossip. They just like to talk and distort things. Once things are done, they're done and it doesn't matter and people forget very quickly.'

Yes, I thought, once things are done, hopefully they are done— and you will be able to do nothing about them.

And then at last the exams (always a nightmare) were over. Nana and the others picked me up from my centre after the last paper and we drove straight to Madandass' Backery for pastries and lemon tarts to celebrate. Arun Bhaiyya and Sahiba came along too.

'How was the paper?' Arun asked us, frowning.

'Good, masterji,' I replied cheekily. 'And thank you for the tuitions.'

'Humph—we'll know when the results are out.'

'Uff lighten up Bhaiyya, will you?' Sahiba said. 'We've just finished our exams for god's sake.'

'Your entire futures may depend on your results. You do realize that, don't you?'

Sahiba grinned cheekily. 'Maybe you should simply get me married off to some hunky armywallah—then you'll be free and so will Mama. And maybe you can also get Gos married off too.'

'But but you must learn to be independent first, to stand on your own two feet!' he spluttered outraged. Then he realized he was being teased. Poor stick in the mud was not amused at all. He glowered at us and stomped off ahead, while we giggled behind his back.

'So what are you doing in the holidays?' he asked me, as we settled down at our table.

'Dunno, haven't thought,' I mumbled. 'Just relax a bit at first. Mess around...' I looked dreamily at the sky, 'write poetry maybe.' But then my mood darkened as I realized what really lay ahead for me—and the others.

He looked at me doubtfully. 'That's good,' he said. 'I could critique some of the stuff you write, if you like.'

'She said she'll write poetry Bhaiyya,' Sahiba said, 'not stuff!'

'Thanks,' I said. 'I'll let you know.'

Our countdown would begin soon. Duckling and I had to start putting the plan into action. Our deadline was April 15. Mama and Papa would land in Delhi early the day before and begin their overnight drive to Mahaparbatpur. They should reach Shadow House by lunch on the 15th. By which time...

'Don't let anyone know—especially Nana!' Mama tinkled secretively yet again that evening when she called. 'We would like this to be a surprise for him!'

'Okay...um...where will you sleep?' I foolishly asked (still exam-stunned).

'Silly girl, in the guest bedroom of course! Have the Neerameerabais get it ready.'

Oh shoot! 'Yes, of course, sorry Mama. My exams got over today, so I'm still a bit zapped!'

She had even forgotten to ask about that. 'Oh yes, of course, how did they go?'

'Okay, so-so, some papers were good some could have gone better.'

I put down the phone and cornered Duckling. 'They want to use the guest bedroom,' I said. 'Shabby Aunty's things are there! What the heck do we do? We never told them she'd shifted.'

'Calm down Gos and sit down. Now think: Do you think they're going to fuss about who's been sleeping in which room when they get here and our great nuclear device goes off in their faces? I should hope not! Anyway, we'll move Shabby Aunty's stuff into the lofts.'

'You don't know Mama!'

'Well frankly I couldn't care less what she might think. Now let's get cracking.'

We tackled the Chakrams and Neerameerabais first. The 'doctor sahib's orders', spiel worked a charm. Duckling handed them a list and set of instructions. 'We'll get everything ready,' they said, 'don't worry!'

'Get anything else you think is required,' she told them.

They got busy right away. Doctor's orders were doctor's orders.

Then we tackled the twins. They of course were thrilled. They couldn't care less on whose orders we were acting.

'This is a top secret assignment!' Duckling hissed furtively 'One squeak, one tiny peep from you to anyone, anyone mind you and...' she made a fearsome throat-cutting gesture and rolled her eyes.

Thankfully, Nana remained dozing in his study or the patio and didn't notice the hectic comings and goings in the house as we made preparations.

Finally on the evening before we were to actually swing into action, we told Nana.

'What?' he said, raising his eyebrows doubtfully and looking around his room. 'That's what Dr Shareef said? Are you sure? Here, let me speak to Shabby Aunty to check.'

'Nana, we'd better not disturb Shabby Aunty. That stupid Raksha has been throwing tantrums again and she's got her hands full keeping him out of jail.'

'Oh, very well then. Useless bugger!' He dozed off for a bit. Then he suddenly awoke.

'Gosling, dial Dr Shareef for me will you, sweetheart?'

I exchanged panic-stricken glances with Duckling.

'Um...he's gone abroad to...to Calgary for a medical conference,' I stammered. 'Shabby Aunty spoke to him just yesterday, before he left.'

'Oh well, never mind. Ring him when he gets back.'

D-Day, April 15 dawned steel cool, bright and beautiful. By six a.m., we were out in the driveway helping the Chakrams. Nana sat in his 'Cadillac Super-Deluxe 4×4 SUV' wheelchair, bathed and fresh and pink and watched.

'Good idea patloon!' he agreed, catching the excitement, and we felt thrilled. 'It'll be a good change.'

In the driveway, the Ford Woody and the Willy's jeep stood loaded up to the rafters. The Jeep was pulling a trailer too, piled high with stuff. I had no idea we'd need to cart along so much stuff for a ten-day trip—but then we had to take virtually everything: food, drink, fuel, extra linen, kitchen stuff, washing powder, toiletries, medication. De-Big Bazooka, who was coming along of course, ran excitedly up and down jumping in and out of the Jeep.

My plan was simple:

We would leave Shadow House and spend the next ten days (at least) at Rainbow Villa—the existence and location of which only we knew of, cocking a snook at Mama and Papa.

'We'll just batten down there!' I said fiercely, as I outlined my plan to Duckling. 'When Mama and Papa find that we've flown the coop the shit will really hit the fan. But there's no way we're giving up Nana to them without a fight. There will be a huge hoo-hah—they'll think we've been kidnapped, the cops and the media will make a meal of it, and be running all over the place... and they'll either have to stay on to sort out the mess or go back to saving the world and leave us in peace.'

'They'll never forgive us!'

'Who wants their forgiveness?' I retorted. 'We'll just sit there till as long as it takes for them to come to their senses and they promise to change their plan.'

'Do we inform them where we are?'

'Are you nuts? They'll send their commandoes over to fetch us. So no contact—no telephone calls, nothing. Just silence! Let them stew!'

'They're bound to find us. They'll have search parties and helicopters flying around all over the mountains.'

'The Villa is pretty well concealed under that rocky overhang and the trees in front of it. It can't really be seen from above. We'll just have to be careful—monitor the news on the radio maybe and lie low while they're searching in the area and confiscate and switch off everyone's phones. In any case it's so difficult to get a proper signal from there...'

'But...but, we will have to go back ultimately.'

'Yes, but think of all the negative publicity they'd have got by then. The press will be all over the story. And we'll tell them that we did it because they're abandoning a grand old man, a famous diplomat's father and renowned ex-Army surgeon in a home and are throwing his grand kids into boarding school against their will, and selling off the family's magnificent old mansion and vintage cars to a multinational hotelier. Wow! The media will make a dog's dinner of this! Especially all those gossipy glossies that Mama laps up. They'll be the scandal of the town. They'll be socially ostracized, serves them right, no one will invite them to parties anymore!'

Duckling grinned. 'And it won't do their careers much good. Hopefully they'll be grounded in India after that. It'll be a black mark.'

'Whatever. But we have to do this: For our sake and for Nana's sake. He's done everything for us.'

At 6.25 a.m. we piled into the cars and drove out of the gates of Shadow House.

And that's when a mighty big spanner clunked smack in the middle of our works, as it were.

Two bicycles actually. They skidded to a halt in front of the slow-moving Woody as we stared at them in dismay, and at the two familiar figures dismounting from them.

'Hi there, Gosling!' Sahiba yelled, trying not to sound astonished. 'Where are you guys going? Camping?'

She looked puzzled—and a bit hurt. 'You never told us,' she said, disembarking. 'We might have liked to come along. Mama's gone off for her training course in Scotland and we're on our own. Anyway, we wanted to call you guys for a bike ride.'

Duckling was scheming at about Mach 3. She leant over. 'We'll have to kidnap them,' she hissed. 'There's no way they can go back home now. They've seen us and they've been to the Villa. They'll guess where we've gone and tell Mama and Papa who will land up there with the cops by this evening to haul our asses back...'

'Kidnap them? Are you nuts?'

'It's simple: they need not know. We just take them along with us and tell them Paramvir will drop them back this evening. Their mom isn't here, so it's easy.' She looked at me. 'Turn on the charm, chick—you got to convince the dude!'

'What dude?'

'Arun, you ass! Get to work, Mata Hari! Flirt with him!'

'Duckling!'

I looked at Arun and smiled. 'Wanna do something crazy?' I asked all gung-ho. I raised my eyebrows. 'Something really whacko? Anyway Bhaiyya, you have to, because I dare you!'

He gave me one of his patronizing looks. 'What?'

'Hah, bet you won't. You're too chicken.'

He smiled at me as though I were three years old. 'What do you want me to do?'

'Okay, then I dare you and Sahiba to join us, rightaway. Put your bikes on the trailer and hop on.'

'What? Just like that? Without planning?'

'Chicken. Wakwakwak, chicken! Murgi, murgi, murgi!'

'Very amusing!'

'Then come on, what're you waiting for?'

Sahiba had put her hands on her hips and was frowning. 'Gosling, have you lost it?' she asked.

Duckling hopped out of the Woody and said something in her ear giggling. Sahiba's brow cleared.

'Oh,' she said faintly, 'oh, I see.'

'So, are you game?' I asked, my heart fluttering. Dammit if the dork and his sis were not willing we'd have to run them over or something. Otherwise our whole, beautiful plan would unravel.

'It's just for the day. Just hop on. Paramvir will drop you back home this evening if you like.'

Arun and Sahiba were eyeing each other speculatively. Their mom was out of the country... They were free. And we were good company.

Arun Bhaiyya nodded at last. 'Okay, so we'll join you.' He gulped. 'We could stay overnight too, if you don't mind—there's no one at home anyway.' Sahiba's eyes shone and she nodded eagerly.

'What are you waiting for then?'

They piled their bikes on the trailer and squashed in with us in the Woody as Nana beamed at them.

'We'll have to stop at our place so we can take some clothes and stuff,' Sahiba said. Can do, I thought, they lived just down the road.

'No problem, but pack quickly.'

'We'll be back in two ticks!' And they were, slamming the door of the Woody and beaming.

'Chalo,' I told a bemused Paramvir. 'Let's go.'

'Where are we going?' Nana asked.

'To the Rainbow Villa, Nana!' the twins chimed excitedly. They'd scrambled into the rear on top of the luggage to make room for Sahiba and Arun.

'Oh,' he said placidly. 'I see.' Then he eyed Arun who had squashed in beside me. Duckling and Sahiba were in the front with Paramvir.

'You interested in my Gosling, sir eh?' he asked.

I enjoyed the discomfiture on Arun Bhaiyya's face considerably.

The winter storms had devastated the roads and it took us

almost five hours of lurching and bumping along the narrow mountain track before we crossed the final stream and began the steep twisting ascent to the Villa. We had to stop on the way a couple of times for Nana to excuse himself—and for breakfast. By the time we reached, Nana was fast asleep, his head lolling on my shoulder (which was getting sore), his mouth open, snoring. At last the cars groaned up the last almost vertical hairpin bend and drew up outside the portico under the shade of the massive pines that towered over it. The sturdy stone structure seemed to have weathered the winter well, though there were leaves and twigs and pine needles strewn everywhere.

'We'll have lunch first and then settle down,' I said, glancing at my watch. It was one-thirty—at about this time, Mama and Papa would be driving into Shadow House...and the balloon would have gone up. The hell with them, I thought, dismissing them. And out here, in this mountain wilderness, it was so easy to forget them.

The first thing that I did after lunch was to round up everyone and order them to hand over their mobiles and switched them off. Though most of the time there was no signal, I knew the moment a signal came through our phones would begin to ring non-stop.

Now that we were here, we had to come clean with Sahiba and Arun Bhaiyya. They had to be told why their phones needed to be confiscated and switched off. We sat them down in the verandah.

'What?' Arun Bhaiyya asked me, 'Why do you want our phones? Mama will probably be calling us.'

'Get used to it then,' I barked, Nana-style. 'Sit down and be quiet and listen.' Sahiba's eyebrows shot up and Arun Bhaiyya looked scandalized; he had never been addressed like that before by what he considered to be a 'chit' of a girl!

'It's like this. We've run away and we've kidnapped you because you happened to be in the wrong place at the wrong time.'

'What?' Arun Bhaiyya gave a withering, disbelieving laugh. 'You've been seeing too many rubbish films.'

'It's true Arun Bhaiyya. Mama and Papa want to put Nana into a lunatic asylum and we're not having that.'

The whole story unraveled as their mouths and jaws dropped lower and lower.

'Ten days?' Arun said. 'You mean you expect to be here for ten days and not be found?'

'We need to be here just as long as it takes for a proper song and dance to start.'

'And us?' Sahiba asked. 'What about us?'

'You've been kidnapped, remember?' Duckling grinned. 'You have no say in the matter. You have to stay with us till the bitter end.'

'The bitter end? Which will be? We will be surrounded and then will rush out and blaze away with our last rounds while they shoot us to smithereens.' Sahiba rolled her eyes.

'That's Bonny and Clyde or Butch Cassidy you're thinking about,' I grinned, not feeling half as gung-ho as I might have sounded. 'But yeah, something like that.' I eyed Arun Bhaiyya keenly. He was the one big weak link in our chain. He had listened to our story quietly enough, but I was quite sure he would now get to his feet and pompously demand to be taken back home straight away. He was staring at me as if he had never seen me before, and as if I was some peculiar specimen from another planet. He could put the cat amongst the pigeons, good and proper.

'What?' I said, 'we'll take the blame for everything.'

'You can even say we tied you up and gagged you.'

'Can't you understand why we're doing this?' I asked fervently. 'I mean, you all know Nana almost as well as we do—you're over at Shadow House all the time, we've all had such fun with him,' I gulped. 'He's as much your Nana as he's ours.'

'Mama and Papa just can't dump him like that!' Duckling said explosively. 'They might as well just kill him outright.'

Arun Bhaiyya blinked and looked at his sister. Sahiba poor thing had tears in her eyes and was nodding.

At last, Arun Bhaiyya nodded slowly. 'Okay,' he said heavily. 'We'll go along with you.' I could have hugged him.

'Thanks,' I said. 'Thanks, so much.'

Then Duckling quietly removed the SIM from Nana's phone. The Chakrams' phones would still be active—because we couldn't tell them to switch off without saying why—that was now the only other chink in our armor. Fortunately, neither Mama nor Papa knew their numbers, though I daresay the police would eventually be able to track them and us down—but we'd worry about that when it happened. We settled Nana down in one of the two bedrooms and got down to sweeping and dusting the place thoroughly. The Villa had two cavernous bedrooms with adjoining dressing rooms opening into a large central living area, which combined as a drawing and dining room. The kitchen was a separate unit (quite ramshackle but with an ancient clay chulha which the Neerameerabais loved) outside.

'Nana will have one bedroom of course and maybe the twins can doss down in the dressing room alongside,' I said. 'One of the boys will sleep with him naturally.' I looked at Sahiba, 'You and Arun Bhaiyya could share the other bedroom and Duckling and I will camp in the dressing room alongside your room. We won't be all squashed one on top of another then. The Chakrams and Neerameerabais can camp in the living room.'

'Perfect!'

'Oh god!' Arun said gloomily, 'you mean I'll have to share a bathroom with three of you?'

'Well, maybe you can share the room with Dingaling, and Dumpling can share the room with me,' Sahiba suggested. 'Then we'll have boys in one wing and girls in the other.'

But Dumpling and Dingaling Enterprises Pvt Ltd refused to be separated, and Arun Bhaiyya perforce had to camp with us.

'This really is a good idea!' Nana said later that evening as we sat in front of the roaring log fire in the living room. (We'd been apprehensive about lighting a fire, but guessed that if we did it after dusk; no one would see the smoke.) Nana took a sip of his whisky and smacked his lips appreciatively. 'I just wish Shabby Aunty had been with us. Will you call her Duckling, sweetheart?'

'Nana, there seems to be a major network problem,' Duckling said, jabbing at his phone and frowning. 'We'll try tomorrow. One of the towers might be down, there's no signal.'

'Oh!' He sighed and stared silently at the fire, the drink golden in his hands.

It's funny how once it got dark the doubts and fears began flickering and stirring and magnifying a million-fold as the enormity of what we had done began to sink in:

We'd run away, bag and baggage, with an old man who was suffering from dementia. We'd taken him to a place where there was no medical help and communication was bad. Could we be arrested for kidnapping? Sure we had sort of 'kidnapped' Nana (without his knowledge), but at least we had taken him to a place where he was happy.

I couldn't help wondering what was happening at Shadow House. Mama and Papa would have driven in and…? Mama would have thrown an almighty tantrum—she liked everyone to be at her beck and call when she visited—as though she were royalty or something. We had hidden away Shabby Aunty's suitcases and stuff in the lofts and her bedroom was neat as a pin. But alas, Shabby Aunty was the other weak link in our chain and it got exposed all too soon. We didn't know of course, exactly what happened at Shadow House after Mama and Papa arrived, but we did later get to know (from Shabby Aunty) this:

That evening Aunty tried calling up Nana. Naturally she couldn't get through. So she tried us—me, Duckling and even the twins. No dice. A little anxious now, she called the landline at Shadow House.

Mama picked up and launched straight into her.

'Shabnam, where the hell are you all and what have you done with my father and children?' she shrilled. 'There's no one here! We're calling the police! The whole house is empty—even the wretched dog has gone. What is going on?'

Poor Shabby Aunty nearly flipped. 'I don't know what on earth you're talking about. I spoke to the kids and Nana yesterday. They were fine. What do you mean there's no one at Shadow House? Has it been ransacked?'

'Exactly that. It's empty. Even the servants have gone. It's not been ransacked; nothing is missing except them.'

'Oh my god.' But Shabby Aunty was no fool. 'Er...but how come you're at Shadow House?' she asked. (We hadn't told her of Mama and Papa's diabolical plan for Nana; she had enough problems of her own with that awful Raksha. Nor, thankfully had Mama.) 'The kids never told me you were visiting... Is Nana all right?'

'Didn't the children tell you? We decided it would be best if we moved Papa to a home in Delhi and sold the house. The kids will go to boarding school and Avantika will come back with us and go to university abroad—wherever she can get admission.'

Shabby Aunty nearly dropped her phone. 'What? A home? Are you serious?'

'Yes, one of those professional terminal care homes for the old and senile.'

'He's not senile.'

'He has dementia and probably Alzheimer's for god's sake. I don't want the kids to be exposed to that.'

'They've been getting along just fine…they've been marvelous!'

'Don't be silly Shabnam—this can't go on. Now where the hell are they? We can't get through to them on the phones. Do you have the servants' phone numbers?'

This is when Shabby Aunty really saved our bacon—and we owe her a million kisses for it. Of course she had the Chakrams' and Neerameerabais' phone numbers.

'No,' she told Mama, 'I don't have them. And I can't get through to the kids either.'

'We're calling the police. Enough is enough!' Mama said tearfully, 'and you better be available. They'll want to talk to you.' She banged down the phone.

Shabby Aunty looked at her phone. At eight o'clock that night, just as we had finished off with our first 'runaway' dinner, a very tasty chicken curry, Mahavir's phone rang.

Duckling and I froze.

'Hullo?' he said, going out of the room. He was back in a second. Nana was dozing by the fire so he handed the phone to me.

'Baby, Shabnam memsahib *baat karega*. She says all your phones are switched off.'

'Oh shoot… hello?' I barely whispered, as Duckling looked at me ashen faced.

Our great escape had already ended.

'Gosling? Baby where are you and everyone? What's going on?'

'Nothing Aunty!' I could see the twins and Sahiba and Arun eyeing me curiously. I walked out into the verandah and then into the ramshackle garden. It was a crystal clear and very cold night, the sky crammed with stars. A soft moon bathed the mountains in a silvery wash. The waterfall nearby sounded hushed and soothing. I sat down on the stone bench in the garden and huddled into my windcheater.

'Gosling, baby what's going on? You're all right, aren't you?'

'Yes, Aunty we're fine. All of us…'

'But where are you? Your Mama says there's no one at Shadow House. She wants to call the police.'

The tears just drowned my eyes; everything blurred suddenly. I got up and walked towards the waterfall.

'Aunty, they want to send Nana to a home,' I blubbered, and suddenly it all poured out. In a way it was such a relief. But I was still stubborn about one thing. 'I'm sorry Aunty but I can't tell you where we are. Please understand.'

She heard me out patiently.

'How long do you propose staying…er…wherever you are?'

'As long as they're here! As long as it takes for them to see sense, or until they go back and leave us in peace.'

'Baby that could be a very long time. How's Nana?'

'He's great. He's dozing by the fire.'

'Good. Give him my love. And sweetheart you can ring me anytime you want. You can always switch off afterwards if you don't want to talk to anyone else.'

'Thank you Aunty. Er, how's Raksha?'

'He's better than he would like everyone to believe.' She sounded exasperated. 'The doctors are saying he's one big con artist. They're recommending he be left to manage his own affairs on his own.'

'Oh. But he's on drugs—he'll just start taking them again.'

'Well, he knows what will happen if he does. They say he deliberately doesn't help himself half as much as he ought to or is able to.'

'Oh.'

'Have you taken all of Nana's medication?' she asked.

'Enough for a month.'

'And how are you for food? Or are you at a hotel?'

'Good!' I smiled through my tears. 'If we run short we'll have to hunt and forage.'

'Ah yes... Baby you know there will be search parties out for you by tomorrow. Why don't you come home and we could sort this out here?'

'No, Aunty. They don't care about him or us and they'll just go ahead and bung him in that place where he'll die in one week and...and...we'll...'

'Baby, no matter what happens you'll always have me,' Shabby Aunty said, evoking another flood of tears from me.

'Aunty, does the press know? The TV people?'

'The press?' She sounded surprised. 'I didn't imagine you would want that.'

'No, not like that. Just for them to splash the story about how a grand old man is being abandoned by his very own daughter in a loony bin and her kids are being sent away to boarding. Then they can grill her and ask, "So ma'am how does it feel to have dumped your beloved daddy into a loony bin, eh? Let us know! How would you like it if your own kids did that to you in twenty years' time?"'

'Easy now, don't upset yourself so!' But suddenly I had frozen. I had wandered a bit in the garden and was now just fifteen or twenty feet away from the waterfall. The water gushed down in a silvery plume, plunging into the glinting pool. The hushed roar was ever present… and then suddenly a whole damn orchestra of frogs began croaking. I looked at the falls and the phone.

'Aunty, I have to go,' I squeaked. 'Bye and lots love.'

I disconnected. What an ass I had been. I turned around. Arun Bhaiyya was standing a couple of feet away from me, his hands in his pockets.

'What were you doing? Eavesdropping?' I asked coldly. He was unfazed.

'Duckling's got her hands full keeping the others inside,' he said calmly. 'I came to warn you. But yes, I couldn't help but overhear your conversation—I'm sorry about that.'

'She'll know where we are,' I said dully. 'She'd have heard the waterfall and the frogs croaking in the background.'

He looked at me knowingly. 'You'll never be good at cloak and dagger stuff.'

'So tomorrow we pack up and run again.' I wasn't thinking straight.

'We can't keep running, Gosling. Besides, where to?'

'No, then we won't run! Why should we?' I said fiercely. 'What can they do? We've committed no crime. We've just come here for a holiday. We haven't kidnapped Nana or brought him here against his will. And this place—it was Nana's discovery after all and in the old days, when his Nana was the bada maharaja all this area was part of their kingdom. So in a sense it still is his. We'll just stay here till Mama and Papa have to go back to save the nation and forget about this lunatic asylum plan of theirs!'

'You sometimes say the funniest things, Gosling.'

'Now don't you talk down to me like you always do.'

He shrugged. 'I don't. But I do think you've done something very brave.'

I shot him a suspicious look. Brave? Did he mean that?

'Brave?' I repeated, 'or do you really mean foolish?'

A small ironic smile broke out on his face and he shrugged and walked back in.

9

$\mathcal{J}$t was strange waking up on a musty mattress on the floor in the Rainbow Villa's dressing room. As good hostesses we had given Sahiba and Arun Bhaiyya the main bedroom. The twins and De-Big Bazooka settled down quickest and were yelling and racing around all over the place by seven. The first thing that Duckling and I did was to go and check on Nana.

'How was he at night?' I asked Paramvir. Nana was sitting in his souped up Cadillac SUV wheelchair in the verandah, well wrapped up against the early morning chill, sipping his tea and smiling benignly at the world.

'He was okay,' Paramvir grinned, his gold teeth glinting. 'He likes it here.'

'General baby, where's Shabby Aunty?' Nana asked. He looked puzzled. 'My phone seems to be dead. Will you try and call her, please?'

'Good morning Nana!' I grinned and saluted him. 'Seems to be a problem with the network here,' I said. 'No one can get through. Shabby Aunty's in Delhi.' But an uneasy feeling in my gut told me she wouldn't be there very much longer.

'Oh well, then never mind,' he said mildly. 'But do keep trying.'

I could see that Paramvir was about to offer his phone. I beckoned to him urgently and drew him aside.

'Don't let him call Shabnam memsahib,' I said. 'That Raksha is not well and she can't speak to him. She's quite upset. She said she'll call him when she can.'

'It's okay,' he said and pocketed his phone.

'Put it on silent,' I instructed. 'If it rings he'll want to make a call after that. Tell him that you're not getting through to the network or something. Tell Mahavir to do the same thing.'

I shook my head. This was going to be one nerve-wracking 'holiday'. Duckling beckoned me out to near the falls. I had briefed her about Shabby Aunty's phone call the previous night.

'It's going to be tougher than we thought,' she said, shaking her head. 'There're just so many variables.' She looked up at the sky. 'You know, if they send helicopters over, Nana will want to go out and see them and wave and try to identify them.'

'Let's tackle the problem when it arises,' I said. 'Come on, let's help Meerabai with breakfast.'

There were more problems after breakfast. The Chakrams wanted to wash the cars and drove them down to the stream running next to the meadow. They were out in the open, the sunlight flashing off their windscreens—easily visible to any search party or helicopter.

'Oh god, we'll have to tell them why we've come here,' I told Duckling. 'We can't keep them in the dark anymore. They're going to freak.'

Duckling nodded. 'We have no choice.'

So we gathered them together and told them. The Chakrams' eyes flashed dangerously. They exchanged glances and then nodded.

'Baby aap bilkul phikir mat karo—hum sahibji ke paas rehenge, hamesha ke liye!' Mahavir said vehemently and Paramvir nodded in agreement. I could have hugged him.

'We won't let sahib and memsahib take him anywhere if he doesn't want to go!' Paramvir averred fingering his khukri. 'We will never leave him.' Thankfully they probably didn't realize the full implications of what we had done—and how they could also be held responsible. Or, they couldn't care less. Their beloved sahib was happy and that's all they wanted. The Neerameerabais looked worried but we knew they had little choice in the matter.

'Whew! What a relief. I was half expecting them to tell us to get into the cars and drive us back home.' Duckling wiped her brow.

'Now we can relax a bit, hopefully.'

We messed around all morning, (wondering all the while what was happening at Shadow House) while Nana dozed in the garden. In the afternoon, when it warmed up nicely, we paddled and fooled around in the pool. The twins tried fishing and actually succeeded (with Paramvir's help) in landing what they said was a couple of rainbow trout from the stream, which they tried to sell to us for dinner, for 'only ₹300 each!'

'Wonder what's happening at Shadow House,' Duckling said as we sat down by the pool and kept a watch on the sky. 'No copters as yet.'

'You know, maybe we should also keep watch on the stream, near the meadow. Anyone coming will have to drive or walk out of the forest from the other side, on that narrow path, cross the stream and then climb up here.'

'Maybe we can keep lookouts, do guard duty of two hours each or something.'

'There's that steep rocky ridge before the meadow on our side which will make a nice lookout point. We can climb up and lie down and get a clear view of the path as it leaves the forest on the other side and leads to the stream.'

'What do we do if we do see someone coming?' Duckling suddenly asked, stumping me. I shrugged.

'At least we'll know. We can lock ourselves in the house. They won't dare use force to get us out.'

Nana beckoned to me from the verandah.

'Baby, where is Shabby Aunty?' he asked. 'I haven't seen her all morning.'

'She's with Rakshas in Delhi, remember?'

'Useless bugger!' he said. 'Bloody fool good-for-nothing useless bugger.'

Then Mahavir came up to me. 'It's Shabnam memsahib on the line,' he said softly. I palmed the phone and walked quietly behind the house.

'Hi, how are you all doing?' she asked.

'We're great. Any news from Shadow House and Mama and Papa?' I asked.

'Gos, they're very upset but haven't yet informed the police. They think you've all just thrown a tantrum and will come back quietly when you're over it. Apparently they're ringing up all the hotels and resorts nearby to check if you're there. I'm driving back to Mahaparbatpur—I should reach late this evening.'

'What...oh...'

'It would seem odd if I were not there. I have been with your Nana for so many years.'

'Yes, but what about Raksha?'

'He can stew in his own juice for a while. A very long while... It'll do him good. I've washed my hands of him.' She sounded really pissed off.

'Oh.' It was then that I had yet another grand idea.

'Um Shabby Aunty, so you'll be going back to Shadow House now?'

She snorted sardonically. 'Sweetheart, I don't think your mother would approve of that. So I'll probably move into my old rooms in the hospital or stay in a hotel until this matter gets sorted out. By the way, what did you do with my things? Are they still in the guest bedroom?'

'Aunty, we hid them in the attic. But…um…please, can you…er spy for us?'

'What? What was that?'

'I mean can you keep us informed about what's happening at Shadow House—whether they've called the police or Air Force or whatever to look for us; or whether they've had a change of heart. Just so we can make our plans accordingly.'

I heard her chuckle. 'Baby, your Mama will kill me for that!' she said. 'But anyway I will be ringing you up frequently. How long do you propose staying where you are?'

'As long as it takes for them to understand and change their minds,' I said stubbornly.

'I wonder if they even realize why you've done what you've done!'

'They'd have to be very stupid not to know.'

'You'll be surprised.'

'There's one more thing. Arun Bhaiyya and Sahiba are with us. We…um…had to kind of kidnap them because they turned up at a bad moment, just as we were leaving.'

'You kids are rich! Really rich! Their mother must be frantic.'

'Their mom is in Calgary on a training course.'

Then it struck me what an ass I had been—that yesterday I had really gotten carried away by the melodrama of our 'escape' and all. No one but us knew that Arun and Sahiba were with us—they did not keep servants and were home alone at the time of their 'abduction'. So there was no reason why their phones had to be switched off. They could talk to their mom and reassure her that all was well. Also if their friends called and couldn't get through they might just go over to their house and that would mean trouble. If they took calls, they could reassure their friends that all was well and that they were busy or out of station. Of course when their mom returned after a fortnight and they weren't home the balloon would go up, but it would give us a whole fortnight time for our own escapade to end. If not, maybe one of the Chakrams could drive them back home in the dead of night and return here undetected so that no one would know that they'd been gone. Thank god that at the time I never realized that the police would be able to track down mobile phone calls and get a pretty good idea where they were coming from.

I buttonholed Sahiba. 'Call your mom and tell her everything's fine and that you're having a good time and being good children at home,' I said, handing back her phone.

'What? Are you nuts?'

'If she calls you and can't get through she'll freak.'

'Aah, yeah I guess so. Thanks.'

She duly called her mom and assured her that all was well and that she and Arun were being good and currently doing a load of washing.

Paramvir came up to us. 'Baby, sahib is calling you.'

'General, call up Shabby Aunty for me, will you? Something's wrong with my phone—it's dead. I haven't spoken to her this morning.'

'Nana, none of the phones are working here. Must be something about the networks.'

'When are we going back to Shadow House? I can call her from there. Let's go back.'

'Nana, the doctor said we should stay here at least for ten days. He said you need the change.'

'Ten days? Can we leave this afternoon? I want to speak to Shabby Aunty.'

'I'll keep trying,' I said, my heart sinking. I knew he wouldn't give up—he'd just go on and on until he spoke to her or drove us nuts. I would have to call Shabby Aunty and let him speak to her. But before I could borrow Paramvir's phone, she rang.

'Gosling, sweetie your parents are getting quite frantic,' she said, sounding worried. 'They've been to Arun and Sahiba's house—there was no one there naturally.'

'Oh!' My heart sank.

'I told them that they'd probably gone on holiday with their mother, but they're going to start searching seriously now. I think your father has been in touch with some top cop and told him to start a discreet search.'

'Oh, shoot!'

'And they want to talk to me too.' She chuckled. 'I think your Mama suspects I'm behind all this—the evil genius and I've spirited you all away somewhere.'

'Aunty, I'm so sorry. Do you think we should come back?'

I could hear Shabby Aunty take a deep, deep breath. There was silence for a moment. 'General, sweetheart,' she said at last, 'Don't worry! I'll deal with things at my end. You just look after Nana.'

'He wants to speak to you.'

'So let him,' she said, 'this is Paramvir's phone, isn't it?'

'Yes. Okay, wait a sec.'

I rushed up to Nana, my face red with excitement. 'Nana, it's Shabby Aunty. I got through at last—on Paramvir's phone!'

He was so delighted. He just lit right up.

But I was feeling quite terrible. We had really put Shabby Aunty in a spot. To defend us, she would have to lie her head off to Mama and Papa and the police; she understood why we (or well I really) had done what we had done and stood by us, but she also knew (as I do now) that we had taken a frail old man suffering from dementia to a back-of-beyond wilderness as a mark of protest and disobedience.

Nana handed back the phone to me and ten minutes later called me again.

'General, could you ring up Shabby Aunty please? I haven't spoken to her this morning.'

Shabby Aunty drove into Shadow House at about five that evening, just as Papa and Mama were meeting with the local police chief. (They had enough clout to have the police chief visit them rather than go to the thana to talk to him.) Mama apparently lit right into Shabby Aunty. As Duckling said, 'It must have been some catfight. I wish I'd been there!'

'What have you done with my family?' Mama almost screamed as Shabby Aunty got out of the car, having driven fourteen hours non-stop. 'Where have you spirited them away?'

I have to give it to Shabby Aunty—she takes no shit from anyone and gives it back straight from the shoulder. 'I think,' she told Mama coldly, 'that in the last twenty years or so, I have been more concerned about and certainly loved your family far more than you have!'

'How dare you!'

'Well, think about it. How many days have you spent here in the last twenty years? Two? Three? A week?'

'I will not be spoken to like that in my own home. My children and father are missing and you dare accuse me of being negligent?'

'What else would you call it?'

'You just want to get your hands on his money. That's why you've been all over him all these years. I want to see his will!'

The poor police chief tried calming things down. 'Madams we must not get excited like this. The doctor sahib and the minor children and servants are missing—we have to find them.' He turned to Shabby Aunty.

'Madam, do you have any idea where they might have gone?'

'The servants!' Mama pounced. 'They must have kidnapped them all. Those beady-eyed Gurkhas of Papa's with their horrible khukris. They might have even killed them by now!'

'You forget those same beady-eyed Gurkhas saved your Papa's life on more than one occasion—and were wounded for their trouble. And they don't have any village to go back to—it was destroyed in that landslide along with their children. Shadow House was their home.'

'Don't try to make it your home! That will never happen. Now, where are my children and father?'

Mama was clearly losing it (and I wonder how she had pulled off all those diplomatic coup-d'etats with this kind of attitude) and Papa had to calm her. He brought her a gin and tonic.

'I think, maybe more than wanting to know where they've gone, you should be wondering why they've gone,' Shabby Aunty said calmly. The police chief cocked an eyebrow. Another family tiff. Trust his luck! Not a kidnapping case with international terrorist ramifications—just a family quarrel: disgruntled children who had run away and taken their grandfather away with them.

'Madam, I do not think you should worry. It has been more than twenty-four hours since they disappeared and there's been no ransom call. So it is probably not a kidnapping. If they have simply run away they will return when their food or money finishes or the doctor sahib tells them to bring him home. It appears that they do not want to be contacted because all of their phones are switched off.' He saw the expression on Mama's face and added hastily. 'Of course, my men and my goodself will be searching high and low for them and we are monitoring their phones at all times. If there is a call we will be able to trace them. We will send word to all the hotels and guesthouses in the area.'

'I would suggest you track them down with all haste and all the means at your disposal,' Papa said. 'If there's anything you need in terms of support let me know—it will be organized. I'm talking to the Army and Air Force too for helicopters.'

'My family! My lovely family!' Mama collapsed in tears on the sofa. 'They've gone! What if I never see them again?'

The police chief leant forward. 'Madam, is there any reason why your children might have done this? Did you scold them? Did they fail their exams?'

'No,' Mama said with tears filling her eyes. 'We only loved them. We brought them presents when we met them.'

The chief frowned. 'Madam, what I don't understand is why they have taken the old man with them. You say he was ill—demented (unconsciously he pointed a forefinger at his forehead and twirled it and got a glare for his trouble). So why would children take someone like him away? He would only be a problem.'

'And they've taken the servants too,' Shabby Aunty said, sensing an opportunity. 'Kids wanting to run away would hardly take four servants along with them.'

'Unless the servants took them away,' Mama said again.

'But Madam I have known Paramvir and Mahavir for how many years,' the police chief said unexpectedly. 'They are brave, honest and very faithful men—old type of men, you don't find such men today. As memsahib said, they saved the doctor sahib's life at least twice. And they have no village to run away to, their wives have looked after the baba-babies like their own.'

'Just find them,' Mama sobbed as Shabby Aunty, ever the softie, sat down beside her and consoled her.

'I'm sure they're all right. They're just trying to tell you—us—something. The sooner we realize what the better.'

Papa sat down heavily and nodded slowly. 'How should we know what,' he said, 'we've been away too long—we don't even know them.'

'Just find them and bring them back, ' Mama wailed. She was pretty exhausted and jet-lagged, Shabby Aunty told us later.

'Madam, is there any place you think the children would have been likely to go?' the police chief asked Mama. She looked tearfully at him. 'Is there any place they particularly liked to go to?'

'How should I know?' she wailed. 'I don't live here! They're forever roaming around these mountains with Papa in those cars. They know the mountains here like the back of their hands. I don't know.'

Shabby Aunty discreetly excused herself and took refuge in the bathroom. When she returned, the police chief was taking his leave.

'Madam,' he was telling Mama, 'There may be pictures of the places they have visited. If you could look at the photographic albums or the computers, we will be able to get an idea of the places we could search. If you can do that tonight, then I will return tomorrow morning with some detectives and we'll begin to search at those places. Also, we would like pictures of the cars that are missing.'

Mama nodded. 'Okay, inspector, I'll do that,' she said, regaining her composure somewhat. 'We'll let you know. There should be pictures—Avantika was always asking for cameras and things.' Then she looked stricken again. 'I don't know what car or cars they've taken.'

'Madam,' the inspector said, 'we'll check all the pictures. If there are any cars that are not here, that should be here, we'll put out a lookout notice for them.'

'Thank you, inspector.'

And that is what Shabby Aunty told me when she called again, at around eight that night and gave me a detailed account of all that had happened.

'General, it won't be too long—there are albums full of our photographs at the Villa. That police chief is no idiot. He's asked your Mama to look through all the photograph albums and DVDs. And I can't smuggle all those out!'

'Shoot! You guessed where we are!'

'It was easy...'

'Aunty, what do we do?'

Shabby Aunty sighed. 'I really don't know. Maybe you should all just come home and fight it out.'

'Never, Aunty. Not until they promise that they're not going to send Nana away.'

'Baby, they'll just find you and bring you back.'

'No they won't!' I said stubbornly, the tears pricking my eyes. 'We won't let them! Let them come! We'll show them!'

Shabby Aunty sighed. 'Well, I'll keep you posted. My love to the other rascals.'

'Nana keeps asking after you,' I said. 'About every five minutes.'

'Goodnight, sweetheart!'

'Goodnight, Aunty. I'm so sorry we've put you into such a jam.'

It was a bigger jam than ever. When they saw the pictures, they'd see Shabby Aunty with us at the Villa and ask her where it was and why she hadn't told them that's where we could be.

I gathered the others around that night after dinner. Thanks to Nana's 'training' a routine had quickly been established at the Villa, and everything was already running like clockwork. Of course there were minor inconveniences—there was no electricity and the plumbing was primitive, so we had to fill buckets from the waterfall pool and haul them over (the Chakrams simply loaded up the Jeep's trailer with the drums and buckets from the pool and drove back and forth) and use candles and lanterns—which was rather romantic.

'We have a problem,' I said. 'It's likely that the cops will find us and haul our asses back by tomorrow. That's what Shabby Aunty thinks.'

'Shoot!' Duckling shook her head mutinously. 'But we'll never give Nana up to them!'

'Have you got handcuffs?' Arun Bhaiyya asked quite seriously.

'What?'

'If they come to take him one of you could handcuff yourself to him and say the verandah railing and throw away the key. That's how social activists protest.'

'Very funny. This is serious!'

'I know. If the press is here—especially TV networks can you imagine the publicity you'll get?'

'And who will inform the press?'

'I will.'

'Ah…but we don't have handcuffs.' I looked at the door as it opened. The twins (who had been presumed sleeping and excluded from the meeting) entered.

'We know everything,' Dumpling said nodding, 'so you don't have to deny anything. We know you've kidnapped Nana and are holding him to ransom from Mama and Papa.'

'And that the police will find us tomorrow.'

'We know how to throw them off the track. We thought of a plan. But it will cost you.'

'What? What plan? And we haven't kidnapped Nana.'

They looked at each other and shrugged. Duckling grinned suddenly.

'Babies, you've got it wrong. We've brought Nana here because we *don't* want him to be abducted!'

'What?'

'You remember, Mama and Papa want to send him to a home for loonies and throw you into boarding school? And we don't want that to happen. Do you?'

They shook their heads. 'No! Never! It's fun having a loony Nana.'

'Especially when he forgets he's given us pocket money. He might do the same with our birthday presents and give them to us twice. Or even three times!'

'And anyway we keep reminding him who he is and who we are every day, so he can't really forget us.'

'So that's why we brought him here.'

'But you said the police will come here tomorrow.'

'That's what Shabby Aunty thinks.'

'Well, we thought of a way of fooling them.'

'What way?'

They looked at each other and shook their heads. 'You'll have to pay us,' Dumpling said. 'Before we tell you our idea.'

'What?'

'Only two hundred rupees. Bas.'

'Two hundred rupees!'

'For Nana's freedom!'

Duckling nodded. 'Okay,' she said, 'we'll give you a hundred now and a hundred afterwards—if it works.'

'Done!' The twins' hands shot out and we shook. They knew a deal when they saw one.

'So what's the big idea?'

'You know where we cross the stream?'

'Yes.'

'There are big wobbly rocks on the cliffs beside the track on our side...'

'So?'

'We can roll down the rocks and block the track. So no one can come then.'

'They'll just push the rocks aside and come.'

'No,' the twins said. 'They'll simply think there's been a landslide and the path is blocked. So they'll go back.'

'That's a fifty-fifty chance.'

'Besides, I'm not sure we can roll down those rocks. It could be dangerous.'

'You have to dice with death for such things,' Dingaling said, shrugging.

'We'll have to rope the Chakrams into this,' I said. 'We can't do this by ourselves.'

'Yes, and we could use the Jeep to pull down the rocks if they're too heavy.'

'What do you think?' I asked the others.

'Worth a shot!' Arun said, looking at the twins with new respect.

'And,' the twins went on, their eyes shining, 'we can lie down at our lookout point and keep watch.'

Mahavir knocked and entered.

'Sahib is calling you to say goodnight.'

We went over. He was propped up in bed, his blankets up to his chin. The lamplight glowed softly on his ruddy face.

'Goodnight Nana,' we chorused, grinning and saluting him.

His eyes wandered around the strange bedroom with its flickering shadows of children on the walls.

'Goodnight troops!' he said. 'What ish this plashe and who are you all?' He looked puzzled.

We exchanged glances, and my heart sank. Paramvir stepped forward.

'Sahib had a big peg—he became a bit confused after that,' he said apologetically.

'Oh, I guess it's all right then. The whisky's confused him.'

'Nana, we're at the Rainbow Villa,' I said carefully. 'Remember?'

'And I'm Niharika and that's Nihal and we're your grandchildren!' Dumpling added quickly pointing at herself and Dingaling. 'We taught you only this morning who we were and you've forgotten! You don't pay attention!'

'Baby, General,' he called out as I headed to the door, 'call Shabby Aunty for me, will you? I haven't seen her today...'

10

Early next morning, we explained our plans to the Chakrams. 'They won't come here if they find the road blocked. They will think we didn't reach the Villa either. They'll go away,' I told them.

Paramvir looked a bit doubtful. 'It's dangerous work,' he said, eying the rocks we'd earmarked for our landslide. 'Anything can happen.'

'But we'll have to do it,' I insisted. 'It's the only way to keep them away.'

Paramvir nodded. He set off after breakfast as Mahavir stayed behind and swaddled Nana up in his coat and muffler—the weather had begun to change, and thin fleecy partridge-feather clouds were wafting over—promising rain. The Neerameerabais had got the kitchen organized—we'd carried industrial quantities of tinned stuff—milk, noodles, soups, biscuits, cake, kebabs, sausages besides sugar, salt, flour, tea, coffee, fruit, vegetables, cooking oil, butter—the works.

Shabby Aunty called a little after breakfast.

'General, good morning. How's Nana?' she asked.

'He's good, he keeps asking for you.'

'Oh, darling I spent the night at Shadow House with your parents. They went through the photo albums all night. Your Mama has been crying all the time. We're setting out for the Villa later this morning with the police. I've had to agree with them that it is very likely you all will be there. They saw all those pictures of us having a good time there. I'm sorry dear there was nothing I could do. I will have to show them the way.'

'Oh shoot!' My heart sank. I clung to the only straw we had left. 'Aunty, we have thought of a plan. You'll know what it is when you get here. Just say nothing. Just agree with whatever the others say, okay?'

She sighed. 'Okay dear, whatever you say!' she said. You know, that's what I liked so much about Shabby Aunty: she didn't talk down to us, she dealt with us as if we were normal people on equal terms and when she knew that we didn't understand something, she didn't say, 'oh, you'll understand when you grow up,' but tried explaining what she meant as simply as possible. She considered our views with as much seriousness and on an equal level as any adult's. I had put her between a rock and a hard place, but she wasn't squealing, she was standing by us. I loved her.

Fortunately Paramvir returned within the hour and he was grinning all over his face.

'It can be done,' he said, '*koi problem nahin.*'

'We'd better get on with it,' I said, rounding up the others. 'The search party from Shadow House must have set off. They'll be here in four hours.'

We accompanied the Chakrams up on to the ridge top, while the Neerameerabais remained at the Villa with Nana. It was cloudy and getting misty too, with spidery wisps of cloud wafting over the ridge.

'Those two big rocks—we push them down and they'll block the path nicely, and bring down some of those smaller rocks with them, which will make it look more natural,' Paramvir explained, pointing out the two enormous and somewhat precariously perched boulders. He and Mahavir were carrying long wooden staffs which they had cut from the forest. We helped the Chakrams wedge the staffs under the boulders. Then they lifted the ends up, one by one and levered the boulders off their perches.

'Dum lagake haisha! Jor lagake haisha!' they chanted and in spite of myself I blushed. The first boulder shifted, a gecko scuttled away from underneath. We watched, hardly daring to breathe. I was holding on to the twins tightly, Duckling was right behind me. Arun Bhaiyya and Sahiba were standing close by. The boulder rocked back and forth; cannily the Chakrams caught the rhythm of the movement and pushed in time. The boulder poised stock still for a second and then tumbled over the edge. It bounced down the steep slope with a terrifying rumble, unstoppable, taking along a rattling retinue of smaller boulders and rocks and kicking up a cloud of dust. The Chakrams peered over the edge of the ridge and grinned. The second boulder went down even easier. When I peered over the edge I saw that the twins' plans had succeeded beyond our wildest dreams. The track leading to the Villa was solidly blocked by the two big boulders and all the other smaller ones—it really looked like a natural landslide. Even better, they had settled right at the 'mouth' of the narrow gully; the track led steeply down into the stream and meadow here. From where they had settled it would be easy to push them over into the stream or meadow and open the track—by us. But it would be difficult to do this from the stream side without risking the boulders rolling backwards and crushing those doing so. I patted the twins on the head.

'Great idea kids,' I said, 'it's worked perfectly.'

'All our ideas work like this,' they said with dignity holding out their hands. 'Now pay up.' Dingaling looked down at the blocked path and then along the ridge at a job well done.

'You know there are those other rocks too, which we can tumble down—then the track will really be blocked properly.'

I nodded. 'Yes,' I said, 'so properly so that even we wouldn't be able to get out!'

'You kids are amazing!' Arun Bhaiyya had to admit. They bridled.

'It looks like it's going to rain,' Sahiba commented, eyeing the ivory sky. Far in the distance we heard the rumble of thunder.

'If they've left Shadow House at ten, they should be here around 2 or 3 o'clock,' Duckling said. She grinned. 'It might be fun to hunker down on the edge of the ridge and watch what happens when they arrive.'

'Fun or not, we have to do that,' I said. 'And keep our fingers crossed that they go back.'

It started to drizzle so we went back to the Villa. Nana beckoned me.

'Duckling, will you send Shabby Aunty over, I want to talk to her.'

'Nana, I'm Gosling.'

The twins heard this and quickly lined up in front of him.

'Nana, what is my name, rank and serial number, please, thank-you?' Dumpling barked parade ground style.

'Nana: minus seven from a hundred!' Dingaling snapped.

'Nana, what did you eat for breakfast this morning?'

But Nana was struggling to get out of his chair and was reaching for his walker. 'Where's Shabby Aunty? I have to see her right now, it's important...'

'Nana, she's in Delhi. We're here at the Villa.'

He settled back into his chair, looking bemused.

'Will you tell her to come here please? It's important.'

'Sure.'

'And General, the Studebaker's carburetor needs cleaning. The jets are blocked.'

'Nana, the Studebaker is at Shadow House, we're at the Villa, remember?'

'Where's Shabby Aunty? Will you call her please?'

'She went to look after Raksha, remember?'

'Bloody fool useless bugger.' He suddenly looked straight at me. 'Gosling, when did Shabby Aunty and I get married?'

I gulped. 'No Nana, you weren't married—she just came to live with us at Shadow House.'

'What? She never married me?'

I shook my head dumbly, wishing he would go off to sleep.

'I must ask her to,' he said and nodded firmly. 'Remind me to ask her, will you?'

'Sure, Nana!'

Paramvir came up with Nana's morning coffee and two ginger biscuits. But he wouldn't be sidetracked so easily.

'Gosling, for how many years have Shabby Aunty and I been married? What year were we married? Did...did we have any children?'

'Nana, she's been with us for as long as I can remember and I'm now seventeen. So you must have known her longer than that.' I swallowed. 'No, you didn't have any children.' Thankfully I knew for a fact that Raksha had been born before Shabby Aunty had met Nana!

'More than seventeen years? Yes, in what year were we married? Do you remember?'

'Nana, next year I'll be eighteen and you said you'd give me the Sunbeam.'

'The Sunbeam? Where is it? I used to take Shabby Aunty out on long drives in it...lovely car.'

'It's at Shadow House.'

He sipped his coffee and had his biscuits. Then he lay back

and closed his eyes. I breathed a sigh of relief and made my escape.

Arun Bhaiyya looked at me out of wondering eyes.

A little later the twins came up to me grumbling.

'Didi—that Nana's memory is totally kachara today. He didn't remember anything this morning. Who we were, where we were, what seven minus from a hundred is... He keeps saying Shabby Aunty, Shabby Aunty, Shabby Aunty, bas!' Dumpling blinked.

'Baby, you know he is like that sometimes. Maybe he'll be better tomorrow. You better keep testing him.'

'You bet we will. But we don't like it when he looks at us like that—like he's never seen us before. His eyes become like those of dead fish then, it's scary.'

I hugged her and Dingaling. And for the first time, a doubt nudged me.

'Babies, should we go back to Shadow House? Would you like it if Nana went to a home? We'd see him once in a while, and he'd be with people like himself,' I petered out weakly as the tears filled my eyes. The twins were looking shocked.

'Didi, he may be loco but he's our Nana. We don't want him to go anywhere! Put him with loonies and he'd only become more loony. And besides, who will look after us if he goes away? We'll be alone.'

'He's already spent much of his life with a bunch of loonies and he doesn't need to spend any more with worse ones,' Duckling chimed in, ruffling the twins on their heads.

'What?' Dumpling asked suspiciously. 'What?'

It had started raining by the afternoon; a soft whispery rain that slanted down and stung when suddenly pushed by gusts of wind. Duckling, Arun Bhaiyya and I set off to the ridge at around three, wrapped up in our raincoats—fortunately they were in camouflage colours—to keep watch on any arriving search parties.

Sahiba stayed behind and played Monopoly with the twins (one of their favorite games needless to say and she was going to be properly wiped out). We chose our spot carefully, peeping out from between two wobbly boulders, like snipers. Below, the track was blocked by our landslide, and ahead and below the stream rushed over its bed of pebbles as if late for an appointment. I rubbed the rain out of my eyes; it was cold and pretty miserable.

'You can go back,' Arun Bhaiyya offered, 'I'll keep watch.'

Duckling and I shook our heads. 'No way! This is our mess!'

'Yes,' he said in that infuriatingly serious manner of his. 'And Sahiba and I are collateral!'

'Too bad, Bhaiyya. You were in the wrong place at the wrong time.'

It was a chilly afternoon and we were soon stiff with cold. Paramvir and Mahavir had offered to do the stakeout, but I was adamant that we had to do it. They needed to be with Nana—he'd been a little more spaced out than usual this morning and I was wondering if he had had any more of those sly, silent mini-strokes of his. Or perhaps the altitude was making him light-headed. Or both.

I was jammed between Duckling and Arun Bhaiyya and we were lying packed so close that our heads often bumped together.

'They might go back because of the weather,' Duckling said, as the rain become steadily heavier. 'The roads will be a mess.'

'Nah…they might just take longer, but they'll come,' I said.

Duckling put her mouth to my ear. 'Should I go back, so you can be alone here with the dude?' she asked wickedly. 'We're pretty much jammed together here.'

'What?' I shrugged. 'If you're feeling uncomfortable, sure.'

She grinned. 'You look so beautiful with raindrops pearling your eyelashes and trickling off your chin and that aquiline nose,' she said sotto voce and rolled her eyes. 'Hasn't he told you that yet? What a moron.'

'Shhh...shut up and listen!' Arun Bhaiyya suddenly hissed. We cocked our ears. There over the deep throated roar and leaf-patter of the rain, came the grunt and stressed howl of an engine in low gear and high revs. I put my binoculars to my eyes and focused on the spot where the mountain path entered the stream on the far side.

'There!' Duckling whispered as smoky golden headlight beams speared out of the murk. A ghostly white Gypsy came around the mountain track, with red and blue lights flashing eerily on its roof. It was followed by a khaki Jeep. The vehicles stopped in front of the stream. Four paunchy policemen, followed by Mama, Papa and Shabby Aunty got out of the cars, unfurled umbrellas and peered across the stream at our 'landslide'.

I focused on Mama and nearly dropped the binoculars. Her complexion was white as parchment and haggard, her hair straggled in rivulets down her cheek and her eyes, small without their makeup, were red rimmed and puffy. She wore no lipstick. Gone was the perfectly made-up face, the heavy pearls and the even teeth in a perfect smile. She was an unrecognizable hag.

'Mama's aged about two hundred years,' I muttered with some satisfaction. She was leaning on poor Shabby Aunty—who was the only person I really felt bad and sorry for. Sure I did feel a pang when I looked at Mama again, but my heart hardened like Quickfix. It was all right for her to look like this now, but where had she (and equally Papa) been for all those holidays and birthday celebrations right through our lives? Surely they must have gone through all those albums and seen who was missing in most of the pictures? They'd missed the twins' tenth and Duckling and my thirteenth birthdays; they'd never even spent a single Diwali with us. And now she was crying because we'd run away? She needed to! But how weird was that!

I turned the binoculars on Papa. He was (as usual) trying to tell the policemen what to do, pointing out that it would be useless to cross because of the blocked road ahead. But he too looked gaunt and haggard as if someone had punched him very hard in the stomach. The cops were plainly flummoxed, scratching their heads and conferring. Papa looked worried and concerned too, and kept stroking his chin with his hands as if trying to think of a brilliant 'action plan' that would solve this nuisance of a problem in a jiffy.

Poor Shabby Aunty looked seriously worried. She knew where we were—would she tell the others or would she hold her counsel? She would have guessed that we had rolled the boulders on to the path deliberately, hoping that the searchers would go back. Then I stiffened.

The cops and Papa were examining the forest track leading into the stream. Obviously they were looking for tire marks that led into the stream. But fortunately the track itself was quite gravelly and stony so the tracks didn't really show and it would be impossible to say how fresh they were. But would they think of sending a constable on foot, make him wade across the stream and go ahead to check the Villa—in much the same way that Nana had made the twins do when we had come here for our picnics?

I think the rain saved us. It had got heavier and was now one of those steady downpours that could last an hour—or three days—and the stream was rushing over its bed quite wildly. Crossing on foot could be risky; it would be all too easy to lose your footing and be swept away. Furious mountain torrents were not to be trusted.

They folded their umbrellas and got back into the vehicles. Duckling suddenly wriggled backwards.

'I'm ggg…going back to the house,' she stuttered. 'I'm freezing. It looks like they'll go back. See you…' She slipped off into the mist, vanishing uncannily. Now it was just me and Arun Bhaiyya.

'We'll go back as soon as they leave,' I whispered, suddenly cold myself. I shivered.

'Are you cold or frightened?' he asked.

'A bit of both, I guess. Why don't they just pack up and go?' I said staring at the stationary jeeps. Their windscreens were fogging up.

'They're probably waiting for the rain to stop.'

'Shit…'

'Listen Gosling, for whatever it's worth—whatever happens I stand by you.' My god, that was the first time he had addressed me as an equal even though he made it sound as if he were doing me a favour! I didn't know whether to feel flattered or insulted.

'Thanks,' I squeaked.

But this whole thing had been my grand idea and it was not working out too well as far as I could see. Arun Bhaiyya, Sahiba, the Chakrams and Neerameerabais and Shabby Aunty would get into a whole lot of seriously hot water because of me.

'It's not going to work, is it?' I said brokenly. 'They'll just storm our bastion and haul us back and throw Nana into that hateful loony bin and dispatch the others into boarding school.'

'Maybe not,' he said, 'when they see how much your Nana means to you all.'

'I don't know whether they do, Arun Bhaiyya.'

Then he reached out and took my hand and patted it reassuringly. 'Don't worry, it'll be fine, you'll see,' he said and alas that patronizing tone was back.

We heard a faint sound behind us. I looked over my shoulder. Duckling.

'Sorry,' she said diffidently. 'I think you guys better come back. We have a problem. Nana took a whole lot of Piclin and well...' She rolled her eyes.

'What's that?' Arun Bhaiyya asked puzzled.

'Nana gets constipated and when he can't go when he's supposed to he gets very upset. So he's been given a laxative, except that sometimes it doesn't work like he would like it to, so he just takes a whole lot of it and then there's trouble.'

'Oh shoot.'

'It's not just that—he gets dehydrated and his sodium level falls and he faints.'

'Oh boy!'

'Look,' Duckling said as she squatted down beside us. 'I think they're going.'

We heard the sound of the engines start up and the lights came on again. One by one the vehicles turned around and bumped off back into the forest and vanished around the bend. The rain thrummed down unceasingly.

'Come on, let's go back.'

Both Arun Bhaiyya and I were chilled to the bone and shivering by the time we returned. The Neerameerabais fussed over us, dried us down and wrapped us up in blankets and gave us soup.

'*Aisa nahin karna chahiye baby!*' Meerabai clucked as she dried my hair. 'You'll fall ill.'

'How's sahib?' I asked Paramvir.

'Sleeping. He's okay.'

'And the potty?'

He grinned. 'It's all okay, but I've hidden his Piclin.' I screwed up my nose. Amazingly, they'd already washed the sheets and Nana's clothes but there was nowhere to hang them to dry but in the living room. It made the whole room smell dank and musty.

I eyed Paramvir's phone; it was on silent mode. I was dying to talk to Shabby Aunty and find out what had happened and what their next plan of action would be. Would they come back with bulldozers to clear the path and storm the house? Or had they assumed that we weren't here, that the landslide had probably happened before we had reached? Then something else struck me. Paramvir and Mahavir's phones would soon be out of battery. If we had to talk we would have to use one of ours. And the police would be waiting for the call.

I sat down with my head in my hands. It was all getting to be a bit too much. Had we bitten off more than we could chew? Should we just clear the road tomorrow and go back to Shadow House? But they couldn't, they just couldn't dump Nana like that.

Dumpling and Dingaling came and sat by me.

'Why are you crying, Didi?' Dumpling asked. 'What's wrong?'

'I'm not crying and everything is fine.' I smiled through my glimmering tears. 'We saw the hostiles off. Your plan worked beautifully, give me five!'

They did.

'Gosling Didi, Nana's awake and is asking for Shabby Aunty. We told him we'd look for her.'

Shabby Aunty called at around 10.30 that night. All evening I had been eyeing Paramvir's phone, dying to call her, but not daring to. It would have taken four if not five hours for them to get back to Shadow House, which made it 9 or 10 o'clock by my estimation. It was risky calling her even after that because I did not know whether she would be staying with Mama and Papa at Shadow House or would have gone back to her hospital quarters or hotel. I literally snatched the phone from Paramvir when he brought it.

'Hi Aunty, what happened?'

'Gosling, baby, they don't believe you all are there. They're going to search other places tomorrow, more hotels and rest-houses and dharamsalas and even temples and places like that, if the weather improves.'

'Great!'

'How did you get those boulders to plug the track like that?'

'That was Dumpling and Dingaling's brainwave. We rolled them down from the ridge top.'

'My god that must have been dangerous. How's Nana?'

I sighed. 'Not that great, Aunty—he was even more forgetful and absentminded today. And he took a whole lot of Piclin… And he's really missing you.'

'Baby, maybe I should tell them that I know you are at the Villa. This is becoming untenable and you're under a lot of stress. Maybe they'll see sense.'

I shook my head. 'Shabby Aunty, you can't do that. They'll blame you for the whole thing.'

'That doesn't matter.'

'It does, Aunty, to me it does!'

'Gos, your Mama is very upset. I've never seen her like this before. She's been wailing that she's lost her whole family and has no one and bitterly blames herself and your Papa—when she's not blaming me, that is.'

'Like one of those high-pitched filmy heroines,' I said sarcastically. 'Tears and sobs choking her voice all the time, I guess! Aunty, it's all natak. She doesn't care, nor does Papa. If we come back they'll just look grim and give us the silent treatment and shake their heads and go back to wherever they're posted after dispatching us to wherever they want to. I know them.'

Shabby Aunty took a deep breath. 'Okay darling. Now, would you be able to clear the track tomorrow? I thought I'd drive down and see you all. It might do Nana some good and if there's anything you need I could bring it along. I think your parents will be staying home tomorrow—they're completely fatigued—and let the police search.'

I brightened up. 'That would be great, Aunty. Nana will be thrilled.' Suddenly I frowned. 'You won't be thinking of bringing Mama and Papa along, will you?'

'Baby!'

'Just kidding, Aunty. Okay, we'll clear the track.'

'What can I get you?'

'Some fresh vegetables and fruit. And maybe half a dozen chickens and leg of lamb.'

She laughed. 'I just hope the weather clears though. The roads are terrible. All right, goodnight sweetheart and my love to everyone.'

'Goodnight, Aunty.'

I put the phone down and told the others, clustered around agog. I was also relieved that we'd be opening up the track again tomorrow; I didn't quite like the feeling that we were trapped here in the Villa, because the only other way out of here would involve an overnight, two-day trek through boulder-strewn forested terrain. We had done it with Nana in the past, but there was no way he'd be able to do it now. Besides, I wasn't quite sure I remembered the route. There was no place for a helicopter to land here either—we really were stranded up on a mountain ridge. Well, until tomorrow morning at least.

It was still raining steadily by the time we decided to turn in at 11.30 p.m.; this really seemed like some kind of freak cloudburst.

What was worse, was that Nana had begun coughing—and he could shake the plaster off the walls and shatter window panes with the violence of his coughs.

'It's as though he's trying to turn himself inside out like a sock!' Dumpling grumbled as she and Dingaling turned up in our room clutching their pillows. 'We can't sleep in the room next to him—can we sleep here?'

I padded over to Nana's room. Paramvir was on duty, sitting by the bed. A fat white candle wavered as I entered.

'I've given him his medicine, but it doesn't stop,' he said worriedly.

'Shabby Aunty is coming tomorrow,' I said. 'We have to clear the road in the morning. She'll know what to do—I'll tell her he has this cough. She can bring more medicine.'

Paramvir looked relieved. 'Very good, baby,' he said, as Nana erupted in a fresh paroxysm of coughing.

I must have barely nodded off when we were all shaken out of our beds by an almighty rumble. The floor trembled slightly and then was still. The rumble died down. De-Big Bazooka leapt up and began barking.

'Earthquake!' Duckling screamed, sitting upright with a jolt. 'Get out, get out everyone!'

Arun Bhaiyya and Sahiba were up too as were the twins, all white and scared.

'What the heck was that? It seemed like an earthquake.'

Mahavir and the Neerameerabais came into the room, looking stricken.

'Are you all right?'

We nodded. 'Should we get out?'

They shook their heads. 'It's a landslide,' they said.

'I'll check,' Mahavir said, picking up his long brass torch.

From his room we could hear Nana cough almost continuously.

Mahavir returned in about fifteen minutes looking grim. 'The house is safe,' he said, 'but the track is completely blocked. More boulders have fallen from the ridge top. It will require bulldozers to clear the road. But we'll know better tomorrow morning.'

I went pale. We were trapped. Good and proper. And Nana seemed to be heading for pneumonia.

What had I done?

11

$\mathcal{T}$he rain stopped some time early the next morning, but everything dripped and gurgled. I set out with Mahavir to check the damage the landslide had done. All too soon it became amply clear: the track was solidly blocked by a huge pile of earth, rock and rubble. I glanced up at the ridge top: the two rocks behind which we had hidden and had looked out were gone. We had been sitting on top of a potential landslide site. There was no way of driving out of here.

I called Shabby Aunty and told her. She'd been getting into her Innova to begin her drive to the Villa.

'The path's completely blocked, we won't be able to clear it. Nana's been coughing like anything all night. Aunty, what do we do?' I was very near tears.

'Baby, I'll have to tell your parents. They'll be able to organize a proper search and rescue operation.'

'Aunty, I'll tell them. Right now!'

She took a deep breath. 'Okay sweetie, I'm on my way to Shadow House.'

I took a deep breath as the others clustered around me again. 'I'm ringing home for help,' I said. 'Papa will be able to organize something. We have to get Nana out of here.'

I punched the landline number at Shadow House. Miraculously the bell rang.

'Yes?' Mama said in a quivering voice. 'Who is this?'

'Mama, it's me Gosling...Avantika.'

'What? Is this some kind of joke? What Avantika...where?' She started blubbering and her voice climbed to a hysterical pitch. 'Have you been kidnapped?'

'Mama, we're all right but Nana's not well. He's got a terrible cough.'

'Where are you?'

'At Rainbow Villa. But we're trapped. There was a landslide.'

And then, alas Mama's nasty, suspicious 'govmant of India rubber-stamp' (as Nana had called it) mind kicked into gear. 'What? That waterfall place? Don't be ridiculous. How can you be there? We were there yesterday, the track was blocked. Of course there was a landslide. So where are you really now? Tell me the truth.'

'Mama we're at the Villa. Please ask Papa to organize a rescue.' The voice faded in and out, and then the phone went dead. It still had a bit of battery, but the call wouldn't get through.

'Mahavir, can I have your phone, please?'

It was no use. None of our phones could get through to anyone. The networks were properly down. And all our phones were very, very low on battery. In the high mountains the batteries sometimes just discharged at a rapid pace, whether the phones were being used or not.

'Maybe Shabby Aunty will be able to persuade them,' I told the others hopefully.

'So we just wait here?' Arun Bhaiyya asked.

'What choice do we have?'

'Is there a way out on foot?'

'There is, but it'll be risky and anyway you'll have to cross the stream at some point to get to the other side and civilization is a two-day overnight march.' We had done this 'march' with Nana on one of our stays at the Villa during holidays. It had been a memorable 'character-building' camping trip.

'Oh.' His face fell.

In his bed, Nana coughed and coughed. We lined up before him to say good morning as usual, feeling awful.

'Good morning, sir!' we chorused.

He opened his watery eyes, a handkerchief at his mouth, and nodded. He was exhausted. He must have slept very little.

'Where's Shabby Aunty?' he asked hoarsely. 'Will you send her in please?' Then he started coughing again.

After breakfast we walked down the track up to the point where it had been blocked.

'Wow, it looks like someone had cut a huge wedge out of the mountain side and it's fallen over on to the path,' Sahiba commented, eyeing the rubble.

'Children come back,' Paramvir said uneasily, eying the raw ripped out mountainside. '*Aur gir sakta hain.*'

Then Mahavir came running up holding his phone like a banner. 'Memsahib ka phone…' he said, 'the signal is weak.'

'Gosling,' Shabby Aunty sounded very upset. 'Gosling, I told your parents where you were and they didn't believe me. They said you had just rung up and told them the same thing. They think we're all conspiring against them. Your Mama threatened to have me arrested. Darling, I don't know what to do. I told the police that I knew where you were but they didn't believe me either—they too think there's some hanky panky going on.' She sounded angry, 'They accused me of leading them on a wild goose chase.' Then she laughed. 'What else can you expect from them?'

'Aunty, don't worry,' Duckling said, taking the phone from me. The phone had been on speakerphone and she'd been listening avidly, 'Mama and Papa see monsters everywhere except in the mirror!'

'Yes, darlings now listen...'

But the line went dead again and didn't come back.

At the Villa, the twins, indefatigable as ever, grilled Nana—who had thankfully begun feeling a little better. (The Neerameerabais had concocted something soothing out of roots and herbs they had gathered in the surrounding forests and given it to him.)

'Nana, identify me!' Dumpling ordered, and Nana merely smiled and ran his finger down her cheek.

'And me? Who am I?'

'And do you know who all these people are?'

Nana beamed at them toothlessly.

'Paramvir please give him his teeth. Then he will be able to talk properly.'

'So who are we? Uff Nana, it's such an easy question!'

Nana pointed a forefinger at me. 'She was born on board a 747—the Empress Noor Jehan while the whole plane cheered,' he said. 'Her mother was very angry with me. She never forgave me.'

Duckling turned to me. 'Wow! He remembers!'

'What's your name, darling?' he asked me kindly.

Dumpling crossed her arms and tapped her foot firmly on the floor. 'She's your eldest grand-daughter Colonel Gosling. That is Major Duckling. I am Private Dumpling and that is Private Dingaling. You should remember because you only gave us those names, ranks and serial numbers. And those are our friends, Arun Bhaiyya and Sahiba Didi. And those are Paramvir and Mahavir who looked after you in the battlefield.'

Nana saluted us all. He seemed a little more cheerful. Outside a mountain bulbul began to whistle melodiously.

But the twins hadn't finished. 'Nana, how many cars do you have?' Dingaling asked.

'Eh, now run away.'

'You have ten cars, repeat after me Nana: "I have ten cars. A Packard, a Rolls Royce, a Mercedes, a Sunbeam, a Woody, a Jeep, a Rover, a Bel-air, a Thunderbird, a Studebaker." Come on Nana, you can do it!'

He smiled. 'I made you all push the Rolls-Royce outside your school one day,' he said wagging a finger. And then, 'Where's Shabby Aunty? Will you call her for me?'

'Uff oh, Nana, Shabby Aunty is with that rascal Raksha…'

'And the phones here are dead!' Dingaling quickly added.

But that afternoon, Nana's cough came back with a vengeance. He coughed and coughed and lay back on his pillows exhausted as Paramvir and Mahavir tended to him.

'He's getting very weak,' they said worriedly. We knew they wouldn't leave his side no matter what. The poor Neerameerabais had their hands full running our bivouac and looking after us all. Worst of all, there was no sign of any rescue. It looked as though no one believed that we were here. Poor Shabby Aunty was so much of a persona non grata that nothing she said counted. That evening I made up my mind. If there was no sign of help—and if the phones still remained dead—I would set out on foot first thing tomorrow morning.

'What!' the others chorused 'Are you nuts?'

'Look, the weather's cleared up and I don't think it'll rain anymore. No one believes we're here. It'll take me a couple of days, but I'll be able to get help. We can't just stay here and do nothing…not with Nana so unwell.'

'You can't trek alone in the forest for two days!' Duckling was appalled. 'You'll be eaten by a bear!'

'I'll take De-Big Bazooka. He'll look after me,' I said.

Arun Bhaiyya shook his head. 'Nonsense! Don't be silly, I'll come along with you,' he said in that ponderous way that always got my goat. 'Of course you can't go alone. You might twist your ankle or something,' he said, as if I had learned to walk just yesterday.

'Okay,' I glared at him, but was secretly relieved. 'Thanks.' I swallowed. 'If you hear and see nothing after two days, Duckling and Sahiba will have to set off.'

'Sure. Do you know the way?'

'I guess—we just have to basically walk upstream and then cross over and walk through the forest until it meets the track on the other side. We're sure to meet villagers there; they're always taking their goats and cows to graze. Remember we trekked with Nana?'

'Yes, but we don't have tents, we didn't bring any,' Duckling pointed out.

'We've got sleeping bags, we'll take those.'

I informed Paramvir and Mahavir of our plans fully expecting them to raise objections. But they didn't. Nana had got fever now and they were getting seriously worried. But they wouldn't leave him for a second and with a lurching pang I suddenly realized why: If anything…if anything bad happened to Nana, they just had to be by his side till the end. To put it brutally, if he died they both would be at his side when it happened. That was their duty. Anything else for them would amount to desertion, dereliction and sacrilege.

'Be careful,' Paramvir said heavily and put a hand on my head, his eyes full of concern. 'You know the way? And good baba is going with you.' They had come with us the last time we had done the trek and knew the route; I hoped I would still remember it correctly.

I suppose the worst part was that the stupid phones were dead—that and the huge boulder of guilt that had anchored in my stomach. All of this was my doing, if anything happened to Nana it would be my fault. And what had I achieved? Zilch.

I didn't think for a second that Mama or Papa had a clue as to why I had planned what we had done. When we finally got back to 'civilization', there would simply be that deathly, accusing silence, and we'd be sent on our way to all our private hells so that they could carry on just as before as if nothing had happened. They hadn't called the press and there would be no big international scandal about their treatment of Nana and us.

Our nutcase Nana would be left in a nut house to die and would forget us forever.

Arun Bhaiyya and I set off early next morning armed with our stout staves and bulging knapsacks. It would have been quite a heroic departure except that I was not feeling heroic at all, just hugely guilty and very apprehensive. Nana had coughed all night again. He needed serious medication and quickly. Worse, for the first time ever, he had snapped impatiently at Paramvir, who was shocked. But then I explained to him that it was only the illness that was responsible and hoped he'd understood.

We'd taken enough food and water for three days, torches, a nifty little gas stove, our sleeping bags, towels, insect repellent, matches, first-aid, penknives, energy bars, windcheaters, spare socks and sandals, a set of clothes...whew! If all went well, we ought to reach the nearest village by tomorrow late afternoon.

Arun Bhaiyya too was quiet as he checked his stuff. The only one who seemed to be enjoying the whole thing immensely was De-Big Bazooka who was dashing around excitedly.

'Okay, so we're off!' I said diffidently as the twins nodded. 'Keep giving Nana his tests when he seems better. We'll be back with help as soon as we can.'

'Be careful, Gos,' Duckling said, wiping a sudden tear. She hugged me. Arun Bhaiyya was hugging Sahiba. Then I hugged the twins and the Neerameerabais who were looking completely stressed out, poor things.

'May god be with you,' they said, embracing me.

'What about Nana?' I said suddenly. 'I haven't said bye to him.'

He was sleeping and we didn't want to wake him.

'He doesn't know we're trapped here,' Duckling said. 'He doesn't know any of it. So you just go. If he asks for you we'll make some excuse or the other.'

I tiptoed into his room and looked at him. He was fast asleep, his mouth open, snoring. His breathing was guttural. But at least he wasn't coughing.

It was a chilly but clear late spring morning. Normally there would have been so many things to stop and stare at and wonder about, but we couldn't do that today. The path meandering along the torrent was muddy and gluey and it wasn't long before we were up to our calves in the mud. Both of us had quickly discarded our shoes and socks and slipped on sandals. There was a danger of leeches, but we had to risk that. Hiking boots gummed up with clayey mud became very heavy indeed. All we really had to do was to work our way eastwards upstream up to the place where it met a confluence of three other streams, rather like a roundabout. There was an island in the middle of the 'roundabout' and we had to get on to this and then cross to the southern side and then walk along the stream that met the roundabout from this side. It really wasn't all that great a distance, but the terrain was rough. We had to clamber over boulders, take long diversions into the forest away from the stream and then backtrack to it again, cross several rather rapid but smaller streams and go up and down steep rocky ridges. Big Bazooka, ever the lazy bum, found it hard going and every now and then just sat down on his fat bottom for a rest and refused to budge.

'Come on boy, this is what happens when you keep taking rides in Packards and Studebakers,' I said. Arun Bhaiyya for most of the part remained quiet.

'You okay?' I asked at last, wondering if he were having second thoughts and wanted to go back.

'Yes, I'm good,' he said. 'How about you?'

'I'll survive,' I said with more confidence than I felt. 'Want to take a break? We've been going non-stop for three hours.'

'Yeah and that fat dog is pooped!'

We munched our energy bars in silence, while De-Big Bazooka wolfed down a couple of biscuits and then thirstily lapped up water from a rock puddle.

'My parents…they're…' I choked off. It sounded so strange saying 'my parents' when I didn't feel one iota that that's what they were. I shook my head. 'They're not like that—they're not like normal parents, they're just two interfering busybodies bent on buggering up our lives because it suits theirs.'

'Take it easy. We have a long way to go. You can't break down already!'

'Who's breaking down?' I snapped.

He just raised his eyebrows and pursed his lips.

'Come on, let's move on.'

'Um, where do we camp for the night?' he asked. 'Do we have to find a spot, or do you know a place? You said you've done this trek before.'

I nodded. 'There's a lovely spot some distance ahead—it's an island in the middle of the stream. We should be there by about four o'clock. We pitch camp early, because it gets dark very quickly here.'

'An island?'

'Yes, maybe thirty feet long, in the middle of the stream. The stream broadens out where it meets three other streams and becomes shallow. We wade across to the southern side; on the island there's a deep rocky overhang which we can sleep under.'

'Will it be safe? What if the water's high? Or there's a tidal wave in the middle of the night?'

'Then we get swept away, happy?' I smiled sarcastically.

'Do you know, that's the first time you've smiled all day,' he said, raising a laconic eyebrow.

'It is not!'

'Is too...Listen, it'll work out, you'll see.'

'Thanks,' I said in a small voice.

But it wouldn't. I was quite sure of that.

'Oh shoot!' I said staring at the rushing water in front of us, a couple of hours later. 'How are we going to cross that?' We had reached the place from where we normally crossed over to the 'island' where we camped. Usually, the stream was shallow and benign here, but because of the recent rain, it was now an angry, swift-flowing torrent flecked with white and brown. 'And we absolutely have to get across—the village is on the other side.'

'How long is the rope we brought?' Arun asked. 'If it's long enough, we could anchor it on this side, I could tie it around me and hold on to it and cross. If I lose my footing, I'd still be able to haul myself back.'

'Too risky! You might just let go.'

'I won't. I'll wrap it around my waist. Otherwise we're stuck here.' He pointed to a pine tree, growing crookedly almost right on the bank. 'That's a good tree we can tie the rope around. Once I get across, I'll fasten the rope at my end and you can untie it from the tree truck and tie it around your waist. Then I'll haul you over.'

I had to give it to him; it was a good, if risky plan and really the only way we could get across.

'Okay, but let me go first,' I said. 'This is my mess.'

'You're too light—you'd get swept away easily. I'm heavier than you.'

'Just be careful of rope burn.'

'Um,' he frowned. 'What about De-Big Bazooka? How does he get across?'

'Shoot!' We looked at the dog who was sitting there, grinning all over his face.

'Okay,' Arun said, 'here's what we do. I go across, you harness the rope around him and I'll haul him over, then tie a stone around one end of the rope and throw it over to you. Then you can proceed as we planned.'

'Okay, you sure you'll be able to throw the stone so far, with the rope attached to it?'

He shrugged. 'Otherwise you'll be left here to fend for yourself!'

'Very funny!'

It was pretty hairy. The water reared up around Arun Bhaiyya as he stepped gingerly into it. Luckily he (and I) was further weighed down by our (thankfully waterproof) knapsacks. He lost his footing once, but didn't let go of the rope, which anyway was wound around his waist. A few long minutes later, he was standing on the little sandy beach of the island. He waved. Then I untied the rope from the pine tree.

'Here, boy,' I called De-Big Bazooka and tied the rope to the fellow's harness.

'Go,' I told him, 'go to Arun Bhaiyya. He's got biscuits!'

'Here boy,' Arun yelled from the island. 'Come here! Good dog.'

But De-Big Bazooka was having none of it. He was quite happy being with me at my end. I dragged him by the collar to the water's edge and he looked at me questioningly.

'Yank him in the water, then he'll have to swim!' I yelled at Arun. He gave a mighty tug and with a yelp of surprise, De-Big Bazooka suddenly found himself in the water. The idiot started paddling, but heading back towards me.

'Pull him Arun!' I yelled, not knowing whether to laugh or cry.

Arun gave another mighty tug and suddenly the dog realized it might be easier to swim towards Arun instead of me. He paddled furiously and was soon up alongside Arun Bhaiyya, shaking himself dry and looked towards me and barked. Arun untied him and then tied the rope to a rock and threw it over. It landed near my feet.

Now it was my turn.

'Tie it firmly around your waist and shoulders like a harness,' he yelled. 'I'll pull you over.'

'Yikes, the water's freezing cold,' I squealed as I entered and braced myself against the rough current. It was like rappelling along a very slippery horizontal surface. Twice I lost my balance and was floundering in the water, screaming and spluttering and being carried downstream.

I felt Arun tug and pull at the rope and found my footing. A few moments later (that seemed like an age) I stumbled ashore and he just pulled me out by the arms.

'Whew! Are you okay?'

'Cccold, but fine,' I stuttered clutching on to him. 'I don't want to do that again.'

'We'd better change or we'll catch pneumonia,' he said, letting me go and unzipping his knapsack. 'Thank god we've got a set of dry clothes.'

'Ch...change? You mean here?' I looked around. The island consisted of a pebbly beach and the low cave-like overhang, which had space enough for two maybe three sleeping bags placed side by side like cigars in a box. You could sit up in your bag, but if you tried to stand up, you'd bump your head.

'Well, I don't see a changing room anywhere...do you?' Arun grimaced.

He'd taken out his rolled up jeans and T-shirt and shorts from the knapsack.

'All right, you look away, I'll change first.'

I stared blankly at the running water my face turned away.

'I'm done,' he said a little later, 'now, you'd better change, you're shivering!'

'Wh...wh...what ccan I ddo about that?' I asked irritably, trying to open my knapsack.

'Here,' he said, taking it from me and opening it. He took out my clothes, which Meerabai, bless her soul had wrapped up in a towel. 'Now get out of those wet things, dry yourself down and change quickly. I'm going to light the stove.'

I stripped off my clothes and rubbed myself down vigorously with my back firmly to him. 'Don't you dare peek,' I warned. I'd put my change on top of my knapsack and dropped my wet clothes on the rocks. And then De-Big Bazooka decided to play games. He darted in, grabbed my change from the bag and leapt away with a triumphant if muffled 'woof!'

'Bazooka! Get back here!' I squealed, turning around in horror. Bent over the stove, with his back to me, Arun swiveled around and looked straight at me

'Oops!' he looked away scandalized. 'Hey, Bazooka here's a biscuit, drop those clothes boy!' The stupid dog dropped the clothes and snarfed up the biscuit as Arun retrieved them and handed them over. 'Here you are!'

'Thanks,' I squeaked, clutching the towel to myself with one hand and reaching out with the other.

'Sure you can manage?' he asked.

Somehow I struggled into my clothes, after which Arun insisted that I get into my sleeping bag to get warm. 'You'll get hypothermia, get inside and warm up.'

He scrabbled around the island and made a small fire out of driftwood. Then he opened up a tin of mackerel and baked beans and heated them on the stove. We ate them straight out of the tin, using the small plastic forks and spoons that Meerabai had packed. It tasted divine.

'You know, I've never eaten with a knife and fork while camping rough!' Arun said seriously. 'Are you warm now?'

I nodded. 'Yes, thanks.' I was cocooned up in my sleeping bag, and now with a bit of food inside me feeling considerably better.

My hair was still sopping wet and I tried drying it with the towel.

'Here,' Arun Bhaiyya said, 'I'll do it for you.' I was touched. Very professionally he began vigorously rubbing my hair dry as I sat up and watched the small orange flames flicker. De-Big Bazooka snoozed near us—we'd given him some of his dog food (Meerabai again) and he was happy. It was an indigo evening, getting darker by the second and suddenly a whole chorus of frogs started up, startling us.

'Music,' Arun said looking at me. Wow! Maybe he was beginning to thaw!

'I wonder how Nana's been today,' I said, staring at the fire.

Arun checked the phones. Nearly dead, no signal… Useless.

'They can't just cart him away to a home. He'll just die there, alone and miserable.'

Arun didn't say anything and I gulped. Maybe now they wouldn't have to take Nana to a home to die because...

'It's okay,' he said. 'Let's just get help first and we'll take things from there.'

'I guess.'

'You know, not many kids would have dared to do what you've done for your Nana.'

'Yeah, like nearly kill him.'

'Like spirit him and his whole household away because you don't want him carted off to a loony bin. That takes guts.'

'Well, it doesn't look as if it's going to work.'

It was inky dark now, but the sky shimmered with stars. 'You know, he'd make us look at the stars every night and at the mountains every morning before we went to school,' I said. All that now seemed so far away and remote, as if it had happened in another lifetime. 'And his cars; how he doted over them.'

'Dotes,' Arun said succinctly. 'You mean dotes over them.'

I nodded dumbly. 'I guess,' I squeaked. 'You know I was with him when we discovered the Packard. I was six years old and Nana had gone to see this old curmudgeon of an ex-general who'd been looking for a doctor who would tell him to go on sitting on his ass and watch TV all day and drink rum.' I smiled, 'At least that's what Nana said.'

'And?'

'Well we drove up to the fellow's house—a good five hour drive, and Nana saw him and told him that if he didn't get off his ass right away and be active, his heart would just slow down and stop and fill up his lungs with fluid, so he would drown slowly. Really read him the riot act and scared the shit out of him by telling him what a heart and lung transplant would be like. Anyway, he actually started walking and exercising and three months later, we went up again and he was in the pink of health. Duckling had come along with us and she was a really wild three-year-old, poking her nose all over the place. She opened the door to this shed at the back of the garden—and there was the car, with chickens roosting in its seats and creepers growing through its wheels and grille. We hotfooted back to Nana.

"'Nana, old car!" she said and I told him what we had found. The general smiled.

"'Yes," he said, "I have this old khatara—it was given to me by my father, who said it had packed up," he told Nana. "I've never started it and don't even know what it is. You can have it for ten grand if you think it's worth that much, otherwise I'll sell it to the kabaadiwalla."

'And there, like some ravaged and banished beauty queen was the Packard. Nana did a double take. One of the chickens furiously chased Duckling around the shed. Needless to add, Nana bought the car on the spot.'

'Wow! A chicken chasing a duckling around a classic Packard!'

'Nana spent the next five years restoring the car. I think the Packard and the other cars helped him get over Nani's death and the way Mama treated him.'

'And when he wanted respite from you guys...' He was deadpan-serious.

'Very funny!'

Arun Bhaiyya crawled into his sleeping bag. The fire was dying down. De-Big Bazooka, ever the big baby had wriggled between both our bags, and was trying to lay his big heavy head on my tummy, his soft brown eyes on me.

'Do you think we need to keep the fire going all night?' I asked.

'No, we'll have to feed it every half hour. Let it be.'

'What if a leopard comes calling?'

'We have Big Bazooka as bait.'

'Funny!'

'Goodnight.'

'Goodnight, Arun Bhaiyya. And thanks again.'

I lay on my back and looked up at the low roof of the overhang. Above, the stars winked and shimmered. Suddenly I wondered what I was doing in this cave in the middle of the night, with Big Bazooka's head on my tummy and Arun Bhaiyya in his sleeping bag next to me. It was just unreal. In a few moments, I would suddenly wake up as Nana blared Colonel Bogey on his trumpet, with his deep baritone ringing out joyously, '*Hitler! He only had one…!*'

As for tomorrow…what would tomorrow bring? Well, for a start we'd have to get all soaked and shivering again when we crossed over from the island to the other side of the stream before we set off towards civilization and help. And we wouldn't have dry clothes to change into. Not good.

And would we be in time? Or would have I, with my foolishness and headstrong manner, have gone and killed the person I loved the most in the whole world?

12

'Would you like breakfast in bed?'

'Wha…ugh…Bazooka gerrof!' I sat up spluttering and pushed my hair out of my face. Big Bazooka looked lovingly at me and licked me. Just outside the cavern, Arun peered in, his hands around a steaming mug into which he dipped a tea bag. 'Bed tea?'

'Look who's in a good mood! What time is it?'

'Six-thirty.'

'Brrr…it's cold…'

'Your windcheater.' He held it out.

'Will you stop patronizing me,' I said irritably, 'And stop serving me bed tea! I can get it myself.'

'Very well.'

I wriggled out of the sleeping bag and glared at him, snatching the windcheater.

'How did you sleep?' I asked, sipping my tea, grateful for its warmth.

'All right, under the circumstances.'

'I'm going for a pee,' I said, scrambling off to the far end of the island. 'Turn around!'

When I got back, he'd got the fire going again and had opened a tin of sausages.

'We're eating well,' he said. He tossed a couple to a pleading De-Big Bazooka. I had to admit, this might have been fun if it hadn't been for the nature and purpose of our 'assignment' and

Arun Bhaiyya wasn't such a total wet blanket. Again, I wondered uneasily how Nana had been during the night. The phones were still dodo dead.

'Look, the water's gone down during the night, we can easily wade across to the other side,' Arun said.

'Thank god, we don't have any more dry clothes.'

'How soon before we reach civilization?'

'We should be at the nearest village by four this afternoon. But hopefully we'll meet someone with a functioning phone before that.'

We spread our sopping clothes from yesterday, and tied them to our knapsacks to dry, packed up and set forth. The stream had reverted to its usual benign self, and at no place was it more than knee deep. We rolled up our jeans and waded across. Hopefully now we would meet shepherds or villagers or even trekkers and be able to summon help quickly.

'You sure you know the way?' Arun asked, as I paused when the path forked in two. Both the tracks that led away from the fork were faint and not too frequented and I wasn't quite sure which one to take. Hopefully both would eventually lead to the village.

'This one,' I said with more confidence than I felt, pointing to the left fork. 'We go this way.'

We did...and we kept going. The path went up and down and wound back and forth and sometimes disappeared altogether. Then it came to a second stream, a much smaller one that I remembered.

'We're on the right track!' I exulted and Arun merely grunted.

But then I missed a turn-off. It really wasn't my fault because the villagers had stopped using that path and it had become overgrown with disuse. We came to a third stream—which I didn't remember and then suddenly got confused. Was the small second stream the right one or was it merely a result of the recent rain? Was this the correct one? It could be—all these mountain streams looked the same. So the turn-off towards the village ought to be ahead.

'This is the original stream we needed to cross,' I told Arun Bhaiyya. 'That earlier one was a decoy—all this rain...' He just raised his infernal eyebrows. 'The turn-off should be ahead.'

To put it succinctly, within a couple of hours of crossing the third stream, we were lost. There was no turn-off and we just plodded on hoping to come to it. For a long time, I just kept going, pretending I knew what I was doing. But then, at around midday I knew I had to come clean. If anything, we seemed to be going deeper into the mountains, the gullies we crossed were steeper and wilder, and we were hacking our way through the pine and fir forests now as woodpeckers cackled mockingly at us from the trees.

Arun Bhaiyya kept looking at me questioningly from time to time and I just smiled bravely at him and nodded—and kept going. Then at last I sat down on a mossy rock and looked at him.

'Let's take a break.'

'Sure!'

De-Big Bazooka flopped gratefully down at our feet.

'Arun Bhaiyya...'

'Yes?'

'I...er...I have a confession to make. We're lost. I have no idea where we are.'

He blinked, took off his cap, looked at it and then all around.

'Oh.'

'I'm sorry. All the paths look just the same and we came on this trek a long time ago and we don't have GPS or anything.'

'Can we retrace our steps and go back to the stream? We

seemed to have left it way back.'

'I don't know. It just seemed to vanish suddenly. Anyway we could try going back.'

'It's okay,' he said, sardonically, 'There are 1.2 billion people in the country; we're sure to bump into one of them.'

'Hopefully one with a functioning mobile phone.'

'That would be nice.'

'We have enough food for today and tomorrow, don't we?'

'Yeah, but we better fill up water at the next stream.'

'I'm sorry to get you into this mess.'

'Let's try to figure which direction we should head in. Now where's north? Umm maybe we should just go on ahead, this trail must lead somewhere. There could be a village around the next bend.'

'Okay.'

'Listen, if we want to get back to the main island stream, let's just follow the next stream we come to. It'll hopefully lead us to it—they all join together in the end, don't they?'

'I don't know,' I said very near tears again. 'I guess so.'

We took a break and then set off along the narrow overgrown trail. It meandered back and forth, up and down, vanished into gullies which we had to climb into and out of again. Then, hey presto, it plunged into a stream again. We crossed this but couldn't follow it because of the steep, rocky terrain on both sides of it, so plunged on into the forest and wonder of wonders, some distance ahead found ourselves alongside it again (or so we thought at the time), and were able to follow it from here on! But it just went on and on, between and over rocks and boulders and grimly we kept to it, scrambling, scrabbling and determined not to lose it.

But by three that afternoon, we were thoroughly lost and tuckered out—say nothing of De-Big Bazooka, who kept giving us martyred looks as if to say, 'Take me home now, will you?' I distracted myself by stopping to take photographs.

Sometimes I would brighten up with hope as certain places suddenly appeared familiar, but then fir and pine and deodar trees everywhere look the same. So do a forest and fern filled gullies and ditches and mossy earth banks. By five, the sun had gone behind the mountains and we were trekking in a deep moth-dark gloom that matched my mood perfectly.

'We'd better look for a place to camp,' Arun said, 'it'll be dark soon.' He looked around. We plodded on through the endless trees, clambering over lichen and moss-covered rocks and boulders, keeping the stream in sight. I was completely confused by now, and had no idea where we were. We plunged our way through a dense copse and emerged in a small grassy meadow, speckled with wild flowers, with a tiny trickle of a brook running through it—this baby stream probably joined the one we were currently following.

'This looks good,' Arun Bhaiyya said, uneasily eyeing the dark brooding forest that surrounded us. 'Come on, let's gather pine cones and twigs and light a fire.'

I looked at him gratefully. 'I don't know what I would have done without you,' I said in a small voice.

He shrugged.

We got a small fire going and crouched around it gratefully. It had become chilly and the temperature at night would drop more.

'What a mess!' I said, opening another can of sausages and emptying them into our little saucepan. 'We could be lost here forever.'

'Yes,' he said completely seriously, 'and a hundred years from now, they'll find our bleached skeletons grinning up at them and say, "Hey these must be those two kids who ran away on a rescue mission and got lost."'

I eyed him stonily and stroked De-Big Bazooka who was lying beside me.

'You don't seem to know it, but you have a great talent for wisecracking in critical situations,' I said acidly.

He nodded.

'I hope Nana's better,' I said, staring at the fire. 'I hope he's still alive. I would never forgive myself...'

He just looked steadily at me. 'Listen, don't beat yourself up over it. You know why you did what you did.'

'But do you think it was the right thing?'

'I guess it was. No one was to know that we'd end up getting trapped and now lost.'

We cleared a little patch of stones and pebbles, between a set of looming boulders that formed a sort of cul-de-sac and would protect us from the wind, and lay down our sleeping bags. De-Big Bazooka curled up next to the fire, one eye on us, his ears flicking this way and that at the unusual forest sounds.

'Arun, do you think there are wolves here?' I asked tremulously, staring up at the sky, where the first stars had begun to tremble.

'I guess Bazooka will warn us if there are.'

We were both so tired that we passed out almost as soon as we lay down. When I awoke, everything around me was grey. A dense fog had snuffed out our camp and I could barely see the end of my nose. But it wasn't as cold as I feared it would be, and I was actually sweating in my windcheater and down sleeping bag. I sat up as Big Bazooka came up to me and nuzzled me.

'Hi boy!' I said and wrapped my arms around his damp coat. 'Oh, you poor fellow, you're soaking with dew.'

'Who's that?' Arun said sephulchrally, sitting up with a start.

'Arun!'

He scrambled out of his bag. 'I'm going for a leak,' he said.

'Hey, don't wander off and get lost,' I said unzipping my bag. 'You can't see anything in this stuff.'

'I won't.'

I switched on my torch. 'Make sure you can see the light.'

'I'm just going beyond the boulders!'

The fog was a mischievous one, shifting and moving like lace curtains being blown back and forth in a breeze. At times I could see the vague shapes of the rocks surrounding us, and within seconds, nothing but soft dove greyness everywhere. I quickly put De-Big Bazooka on the leash. I didn't want him wandering off and vanishing. And then of course, Arun disappeared.

'Arun Bhaiyya?' I called querulously, waving the torch about. 'Can you see the torch? Where are you?'

There was just the muffled silence of the fog in reply. 'Arun?' Big Bazooka whined and wagged his tail and looked up at me. 'Arun, don't do this to me! I'm not in the mood for games!' I took a couple of steps in the direction he had gone, holding on to Big Bazooka. 'Arun!'

Nothing. Just silence. And then a faint scrabbling—but that could have been Big Bazooka. 'Arun!' my voice was shrill. 'Can you see the light?'

'Yes!' he suddenly said, almost in my ear, making me jump as De-Big Bazooka's tail thumped against my legs.

'Yikes, you…you don't do such things!'

'Sorry,' he said, his face inches from mine. 'I dropped the cap of the toothpaste tube and was trying to find it.'

Dropped the freaking toothpaste tube cap? I hit him with both hands. He caught them easily. 'Hey, take it easy, it'll be all right.'

'It won't, it won't, it won't! How can it be all right?'

'Like this?' he asked and with heart-stopping gentleness

enfolded his arms around me. 'You've got tiny pearls of dew beading your eyelashes.'

I nearly passed out. He had actually touched me, dared to hug me and said something nice, no not just nice but actually romantic to me! Needless to say, he disengaged in a jiffy and hid his embarrassment in the fog.

The fog cleared enough for us to safely resume our trek to nowhere at about eleven o'clock. 'Which way?' he asked, looking up at a clear blue sky that had suddenly emerged from the gloom.

'Your guess is good as mine. I have no idea in which direction we ought to head, but we'll continue along the stream. It has to reach somewhere.'

'Should we just stay here and light another fire and hope someone sees our smoke?'

'No, let's carry on. I can't bear to not do anything.'

We left the pretty little meadow and plunged into the gloom of the forest, making sure we were either in sight or earshot of that tumultuous little stream. Mushrooms glowed enticingly from the forest floor—bright yellow, day-glo orange, scarlet and white and caramel brown. The stream just seemed to plunge happily, deeper and deeper into the mountains. Needless to add we'd seen not a single soul all morning in this country of 1.2 billion people.

'Where are they all?' I asked irritably.

'Who?' Arun asked.

'The 1.2 billion…'

'Well, I know where two of them are.' Wow—wonders would never cease! He was joking again!

The path suddenly went straight down to the stream and ran alongside it. At times we had to enter the water and rock-hop as it vanished and then reappeared downstream.

'All these stupid ridges and streams and mountains look the

same!' I grumbled as we hopped and stepped like herons from boulder to boulder for the next half hour. 'Hope this leads us somewhere.' Dusk would be falling in a couple of hours and it looked like we'd be spending our third night out in the open. I was ragged and very tired. It was also getting nippy and we had both put on our windcheaters. Our clothes from yesterday's dunking were still clammy and cold, even though we had tied them to the straps of our rucksacks so they could get some sun and breeze and dry off.

'Just be careful,' Arun said warningly and promptly put his foot on a wobbly rock.

'Gaaah!' he yelled, grabbing my hand to save himself, and we both landed straight in the water spread-eagled on our backs. Luckily, the bed was sandy and our knapsacks cushioned our fall, and thank god we didn't hit our heads on the rocks. We spluttered to a sitting position, gasping with cold. Arun's face was going white. 'Oh shit, I think I've busted my ankle!'

I sat up, spluttering, and stared in horror as he hoisted himself up onto a boulder, with the water streaming off him. Gingerly, he removed his boot; already the left ankle was swelling and his face was drawn with pain.

'Now what do we do?' I said the panic rising. I pushed my dripping hair out of my eyes.

'I'll be fine in a bit,' he said, blinking. 'We'll just rest here a bit.'

'How are you?' I asked anxiously after five minutes. He had closed his eyes.

'Umm...okay...' But he wasn't because he couldn't put any weight on that leg; he tried standing up and just crumpled up.

'Shit!'

We were stuck in a boulder-strewn section of the stream. Ahead, the stream curved around a bend and disappeared from view. Where we were stranded, it was impossible to even lie down.

'I'll just check around the bend,' I said. 'We can't stay here at night, on these boulders. Be back in a jiffy.'

I made my way carefully around the bend, wading through knee deep water again. Thankfully there was a small sandy beach on the left bank—we could camp here, if Arun could make it. I went back.

'There's a spot we can camp in around the bend,' I said. 'I'll help you. Do you think you can manage to get there?'

I handed him his stave. 'Now hoist yourself up with the stick and put your arm around my shoulder.' He looked at me for a long moment, and took a deep breath.

'Okay,' he said at last. It was there in his eyes and written all over his face; he had never put his arm around a girl before (well maybe except me that morning in the fog) and certainly not asked one for help; it was not meant to be like that. I staggered under his weight, but at least he was upright, his bad leg dangling.

'Now one step forward—mind that rock...' It was slow, painful going and once Arun grunted with pain when his ankle accidentally bumped against a boulder. De-Big Bazooka eyed us quizzically and whined, wondering if this was some strange new game we were playing. Dripping, we staggered around the bend and finally made it to the sandy bank, Arun clutching tightly on to me. Gently I lowered him down. He sat with his back against a boulder, his face white with pain.

'Whew! Are you all right?'

He nodded. 'Guess so,' he whispered. 'Thanks.' He looked around. The brooding forest crouched down right up to the little beach, beyond it the stream rippled musically over its bed of white and grey and maroon rocks and disappeared into the mauve gloom.

'Come on, we'd better get out of these wet things.' I rummaged in my knapsack and took out the first-aid kit. Then I paled. Our only set of spare clothes which had been tied to our rucksacks to dry were now also soaking. 'We have nothing dry to change into.' I yanked out our towels (and blessed the Neerameerabais for insisting we take them). They were full size and dry, rolled up at the bottom of my rucksack. 'At least we have these!'

Arun Bhaiyya took off his windcheater and shirt and rubbed down vigorously with the towel. I wrung out his windcheater and shirt as best I could and spread them on a rock.

'Let me see your ankle,' I said taking out the first-aid kit from my rucksack.

'There's some Iodex and bandages here. We should bind up that ankle.' Gently I removed his sock as he lay back ashen faced. I applied the ointment, and then wrapped the bandage around it firmly. He winced and grunted a couple of times.

'I think you shouldn't move the foot,' I told him.

'Hold on, I'll just retrieve your knapsack,' I said getting to my feet and wiping the water out of my eyes. We had left it on the rocks where we had fallen. Thank god again, it was waterproof. Our sleeping bags were in it and would hopefully be dry zipped up tight. I retrieved it. The sleeping bags were dry.

'Come on you'd better get into your sleeping bag,' I said, 'you've got practically nothing on and will freeze to death.'

'Can you give me an empty bottle first, please?' he asked hoarsely, his eyes eloquent.

'Oh,' I said, comprehension dawning, 'Yeah, sure—here!'

A few minutes later, deadpan, I emptied the bottle into the stream and rinsed it thoroughly, wondering how many times I'd be doing this before we were rescued. It was bizarre: we had set out to get help for Nana, now we needed to be rescued ourselves. Arun Bhaiyya, who prided himself in micro-managing his sister, was now completely dependent on me, and our prospect seemed dismal. We were stranded on a tiny beach, surrounded by thick forest, and I had no idea where we were. We were running out of food. Water, thankfully we had plenty of.

'Will you be able to get into your sleeping bag?' I laid it out.

He looked at his slick jeans. 'In these? They'll soak the sleeping bag.'

And that would be surefire pneumonia.

'Okay, I'll help you out of them—then you get in and zip up good!'

He firmly tied the towel around his waist and I helped him peel off his jeans. His black eyes had become expressionless.

'It's okay Arun Bhaiyya, it doesn't matter.'

'I'm sorry,' he mumbled, 'I was careless.' His stiff upper-lip pride had taken a hammering and part of me was gloating while another part felt bad for him.

'It's okay,' I said again. 'You're hurt and I'm just helping you like I do the kids at Nana's hospital. That's all.'

He just nodded. I helped him into the sleeping bag, though he jolted his ankle a couple of times and grimaced and went pale. At last he was snugly zipped up inside.

It was almost dark now, and the forest was full of night sounds; the cicadas' high-pitched violins, the mysterious sussuring and hushing of pine needles, dry leaves whispering secretively as they were chased in circles by the breeze, the invisible gurgling of the stream, frogs suddenly breaking out in chorus, the scream of a wildcat somewhere upstream, the yodeling maniacal calls of jackals somewhere down on a mountain ridge, and then the big booming hoots of that most magnificent of birds, the great horned owl. It made the hair on the back of your neck prickle. Again I wondered uneasily about wolves.

'Build a fire,' Arun bhhaiyya said. 'See if you can find any driftwood.'

What I found instead was a large dead branch from a pine tree, lying partially in the water. I yanked it out and propped it up between a couple of rocks and lit the dry end. Then I strung up our sopping clothes around it and parked myself right next to it to warm up.

'Good!' Arun said. 'We'll have to think of a way out of here tomorrow.'

'I wonder how Nana's doing,' I said, opening up our last tin of tuna. 'I wonder if he's even alive.' Suddenly, all that—the Villa and everyone else trapped in it, seemed so utterly remote and yet that was why Arun Bhaiyya and I were where we were.

We ate hungrily. 'Now try and sleep. Goodnight!'

At our feet, De-Big Bazooka curled up. He was getting used to this.

Shivering, I wriggled out of my wet clothes, wrapping the towel around me. I propped up our staves, strung our rope between them and hung up our clothes to dry in front of the fire. Then I slipped quickly into my sleeping bag.

'I just hope monkeys don't steal our clothes tonight,' I said, snuggling deep into my bag. I lay awake looking at the fire and then up at the stars, remembering how Nana had told us that all space aliens knew Morse. Well, I did, and on a whim I began flashing the good old dot-dot-dot, dash-dash-dash, dot-dot-dot, SOS signal.

'What are you doing?' Arun asked sleepily.

'I'm flashing an SOS hoping a Martian will see my signal and inform everyone where we are,' I said. 'Nana says that all space aliens know Morse.'

It was a restless night for both of us. For a long time I watched the fire sputter and flare, then die down, and then crackle as the resin in the wood caught. We had spent many nights under the stars with Nana and I would have really enjoyed this if it hadn't been for the circumstances. I remembered the fun song sessions we had had around campfires with Nana, with him having all of us in splits as he marched around playing the Colonel Bogey on his trumpet and singing that rude version and reading us Spike Milligan (which was his all-time favourite). And suddenly I felt terrible and sorry for Mama—that she had missed out on all these wonderful things during her childhood—she had really been the orphan, not us. No wonder that she had turned out to be the way she had. Even so, Nana had made up for his sin of omission by the way he had brought up all of us. If only Mama could see that.

I guess I must have eventually dozed off because when I glanced at my watch again it was five-thirty: still about half an hour to sunrise. At our feet De-Big Bazooka stirred, got up, went round and round and flopped down again. I glanced at the fire: it was low, but still flickering. I glanced sideways at Arun—he seemed to be asleep. I quickly wriggled out of my bag and padded to the line where I had hung our clothes to dry; they were still damp but wearable. The chill gave me goose pimples. I stirred the fire and looked across it at Arun. He was awake now, and looking at me.

'How's the ankle?'

'Stiff. It hurts when I move it. I could hardly move all night.'

'Unzip your sleeping bag—here's the bottle...' I said matter-of-factly. He looked like a little boy as he propped himself up.

'Thank you,' he whispered, going red. I turned away and began rummaging in my rucksack.

It wasn't easy helping him with his jeans; they were still

clammy and tended to stick. As carefully as possible I eased the narrow trouser leg over his bad ankle. At one point he grunted with pain and clutched at me dizzily. Involuntarily, I held on to him.

'Ssorry...' he whispered, his face pale, disengaging from me.

At last we were 'dressed', and ready for the day. By now, a faint peach glow in the eastern sky signaled the arriving day. Above, the sky was pale powder blue; it promised to be a clear sunny morning but I knew how quickly it could change. Arun propped himself up against a rock and I looked at his ankle. It was swollen and he still couldn't put any weight on it. I wondered if he had broken it.

We could go nowhere; we were trapped here until help came.

The only food we had left was half a dozen energy bars and some of Bazooka's dog food. I gave him some and he gobbled it up.

'Now what?' I asked him. 'Any ideas?'

'Did Nana teach you to hunt and fish?' Arun asked sardonically. 'It might be useful now if he did.'

'Very funny!'

'I'm serious. But still, we've been gone three nights, someone should be looking for us. I suppose they'll find us.'

I sat down. 'Mama and Papa have to leave in a few days,' I snorted. 'At any rate we've gone and upset their plans for Nana properly.'

But Nana...when I thought of him coughing, my heart just sank. What had I done?

'Maybe you should go and look for help,' Arun suggested. 'Just continue to walk downstream and don't leave it, so you won't get lost. You might meet a herder or shepherd or someone.'

'Fat chance.' But I knew I would have to do that. I got to my feet. 'Come on Bazooka!' I looked at Arun. 'You'll be all right here by yourself?'

'I guess,' he said.

'See you in a bit...'

'Take care.' I waved and entered the water and with Bazooka jumping gaily by my side, started hopping and stepping across the rocks like a heron.

13

Jt can be terrifying when you're alone in the wilderness, looking for help. You have only your thoughts to keep you company and in my case, in my present situation, those were not pleasant at all. Would I ever find help? Or would Arun and I just die here of exposure or hunger or a broken ankle or be eaten by wolves or whatever... Was Nana still alive, or had I killed him? What were Duckling and Sahiba and the twins doing at this moment? Surely the Chakrams would have figured some way of getting out of this mess—they were resourceful and had been in dangerous situations with Nana many times before. And all this was my fault. I, who was the most steady, sensible, logical, level-headed one of the lot. I had gone and done something extraordinarily stupid. By now, there was probably a price on my head.

'What do you think, Bazooka?' I said glumly, as the fellow frolicked happily by my side. 'I'm probably wanted dead or alive! There must be bounty hunters out looking for me, with shoot at sight orders.' I sniffed and then bit my lip. But still, whatever, Mama and Papa could NOT simply pack Nana off to a loony bin, just like that. I, we, all of us, wouldn't let them. They had no right! (Of course they did, but they also didn't!)

'Do you think top-shot bureaucrats have consciences?' I asked Bazooka bitterly, who plunged on ahead with a joyful bark. He was getting used to being active and liking it. 'Or do they behave like blocks of wood and lumps of granite all the time?'

I decided to walk downstream for an hour or so, hopeful of meeting someone, and then back again, till I reached our camp. I crossed over to the other bank, because it seemed easier to walk along that than the one where we had set up camp. Even if I had to wade through the water, I would not leave this stream as it seemed like a fairly major stream, unlike many of the others, it didn't plunge into some anonymous gully or gorge and disappear. I had to be careful and watch my footing—the current was deceptively strong and to fall and twist my ankle would be fatal. At times, bits and pieces of the scenery did appear vaguely familiar, though then again, all mountain streams running through deep rocky gorges and forested valleys look pretty similar. After about an hour or so I was hungry again, and nibbled at an energy bar. We would have to ration our food or forage. I stared at the water—maybe we could fish? With what? Dip our saucepan into the stream and hope a fish would obligingly swim into it? I brushed the hair out of my eyes—I was getting light-headed, staring at the rushing water all the time.

Suddenly I cocked my head. Above the musical gurgle of the stream, I could hear a muted low roar. It was the sound of a waterfall. Eagerly I walked on; the stream suddenly broadened out and then, just disappeared over the edge of a cliff—it was a waterfall. I scrambled over to the very edge, and peered over it. I was pretty sure it was the same ridge the stream near the Villa fell over... because right there up ahead in the distance were very familiar mountain peaks. Now at last, I had a vague idea of where we were—and in which direction I needed to head. If I followed the ridge, I should eventually come to the waterfall at the Villa—and be home! I shook my head. For three days all we had done was to trek in one enormous circle!

Now, to walk on, along the ridge or to go back and let Arun

know? I'd been gone over an hour and had no idea how much further I'd have to go; probably another hour or so. He'd get frantic if I wasn't back soon. I walked slowly upstream, wondering what to do when Bazooka suddenly stood stock still, his ears pricked, staring at the opposite bank. The fur on the back of his neck began to bristle and a growl rose in his throat.

'What is it, boy?' I barely dared whisper, going up to him and holding him by the collar. I stared at the trees crowding the bank, and then between the tree trunks saw swiftly moving dog-like shadows slipping by, heading upstream.

Wolves!

I had left Arun upstream, an hour's hike away. Alone and helpless and marooned with a busted ankle! I headed back. 'Come on Bazooka, let's go back!'

We splashed our way back. Occasionally I would stand still and stare at the bank, my heart thudding rapidly, wondering if the wolves were following us, eyeing us balefully across the water. Or had they run on ahead and were tearing Arun to pieces... Once, a bird screamed high up in the sky: a falcon. The tears flooded easily into my eyes as I remembered Nana lining us up in the gazebo and pointing out falcons to us. Did he now even know what a falcon was?

I returned to our 'camp' forty-five minutes later, exhausted and panting and got the shock of my life. There was no sign of Arun. His sleeping bag lay alongside mine. His stave was gone too. I looked hard at the ground but couldn't make out if there were signs of a struggle or not. Thankfully there was no blood anywhere. His rucksack lay nearby.

'Arun Bhaiyya!' I yelled, 'where are you?' Desperately I looked up into the trees, thinking the wolves might have chased him up there. Could they have just dragged him away silently, into the forest? Would I stumble over his mangled remains? Oh god, just what had I gone and done? Everything was spiraling right out of control. This was like a nuclear reaction gone hooligan...

'Find him, Bazooka!' I said grabbing Bazooka by the collar and stuffing his muzzle into Arun's sleeping bag. 'Find Arun!'

The silly fellow hadn't been trained to find anything and didn't know what the heck to do. He just looked up at me, his tongue hanging out and wagged his tail.

'Big help you are!' Okay, I'd have to calm down first and think. Obviously, Arun had either managed to get up on his own and limp off (for which I would never forgive him), or had been rescued but then where were the rescuers because surely they would have wanted to rescue me too (I hoped). I refused to consider other nastier possibilities at the moment. If he had walked off on his own, there would have to be a path somewhere here and his stick would have left distinct marks on the ground. I scoured around the camp and hey presto found a narrow trail disappearing into the gloom of the forest. There were indentations and holes where obviously he had pushed his stick, as well as a faint footprint. With my eyes glued to the path I followed. To my right, yet another stream rushed downstream and yet again I got the uncanny feeling that I had been here before. Bazooka plunged on ahead, excitedly.

'Hey not so fast, come back here!' I yelled as the wretched dog bounded off down the track. Arun must have taken off almost as soon as I had left him, which meant he would have gone around two hours. But with that busted ankle he couldn't really go too far. Three quarters of an hour later I had still not caught up with him and was getting seriously worried. The path mercifully, was quite even and seemed tantalizingly familiar in parts, but I knew that was just my imagination and tired mind playing tricks. In spite of his ankle Arun appeared to be doing a brisk clip.

And then suddenly I'd just had enough and couldn't go any further. I sat down on a rock, put my face in my hands and bawled as my heart broke and broke. Dimly I heard Bazooka bark joyfully and then there was a scuffling sound close by.

'Hey are you all right?' Tearfully, I looked up. Propped up with his stick, Arun stood in front of me, a hand reaching out to my cheek.

If it hadn't been for his busted ankle and that sad sack face I would have knocked him flat. I just stared at him, clenching and unclenching my fists, my mouth opening and shutting, gulping back sobs. Then I really freaked out.

'Where...where...how dare you go...?' I sobbed, 'wolves... did you see...'

'Get up,' he said gently and held me with his one free arm. 'Are you all right?'

He smiled wanly.

'Come along, there's something I need to show you,' he went on in that superior manner. He turned and began limping off in the direction he had come, using his stick as a crutch and not letting his bad ankle touch the ground.

'Wha...what...?' I spluttered.

I followed him, blind with anger. I hoped his ankle hurt like hell.

'Do you know there are wolves in this forest?' I shrilled at his back, 'and they were heading this way and I thought they'd got you and it would be my fault and I would never see you again except torn up in bloody shreds.'

He stopped. 'That would have made you happy?'

'You...you...you always do this to me! Yes very happy!'

'Of course I like to make you happy too.' He took my arm. 'Look,' he said, 'doesn't that make you happy?' He pointed.

I followed his indication. There maybe two hundred yards away, halfway up a hillock was a pine tree, its trunk split down from the top by lightning. It was the pine tree where Nana had hidden one of the clues of a treasure hunt a long time ago. We were just twenty minutes away from the Villa! We had roamed around lost, for three days and had in spectacular fashion, gone around in one huge circle and virtually returned home without realizing it. I had spent most of the morning trekking in entirely the wrong direction, getting further away rather than closer to 'home'. Our last camp had been just an hour's trek away from Rainbow Villa and we hadn't a clue. That's what the ruddy mountains can do to your sense of direction. If we walked along this path for fifteen or twenty minutes or so, we'd reach the tributary of the stream that led to the waterfall just behind the Villa.

'Well, we're back to square one...'

'I just hope Nana is still alive.' I choked back a sob.

We staggered towards the waterfall hearing its muted roar through the trees.

'We'll come to the top of the waterfall, we'll have to make our way back down then and across the pool. Then we can shout, or you just wait and I'll call the others.' Carefully I helped Arun down the steep path from the top of the waterfall to the far side of the pool.

'Now we wade across,' I said and looked at the far bank.

The twins were there, skimming stones across the water. They spotted us immediately and their mouths fell open. Arun was limping and I was weaving from side to side from exhaustion.

'Gosling Didi! Arun Bhaiyya!' Dumpling shrieked and came charging up, splashing through the pool as Bazooka bounded up to them barking madly. Duckling and Sahiba, who had been sitting on the bench in the garden looked up and rushed towards us, their faces incredulous. They helped us across the pool and escorted us towards the house like returning prodigals.

'How's Nana?' I asked clutching on to Duckling, who was crying, her arm tightly around my waist.

'He's much better,' she gulped. 'What happened to both of you? They're sending helicopters up to look for you.'

Sahiba and Dingaling helped Arun up the verandah steps. Hearing the commotion, the Chakrams and Neerameerabais emerged and bore down on us with beaming smiles.

'Nana?' I asked Paramvir. 'How is he?'

He smiled. '*Theek ho raha hain baby...*,' he said, 'he's getting better.'

'But...but how...'

We walked into the main living room and suddenly my legs gave way and I collapsed into one of the rexine covered sofas.

'Gosling Didi, Shabby Aunty is here!' Dumpling chimed, and sure enough, Shabby Aunty, neat and trim as ever emerged from Nana's room, her arms open wide in welcome, relief all over her smiling face.

'*She's* here too,' Duckling warned and I glanced at her. Her face was set, her eyes flinty, she clenched her fists.

'How...who?' And then I stopped. Stepping out from the room and behind Shabby Aunty, was Mama. She gave me one look and shrieked, 'Avantika!'

I passed out gracefully.

On the slanting roof, the first pitter-patter of a drizzle began.

I was lying on the sofa when I came to, and Shabby Aunty was at my side with a cup of hot chicken soup and a tired smile. Mama was with Nana in his bedroom. Duckling and the twins stood around in an anxious semi-circle.

'What happened here while we were away?' I asked weakly.

I could see Arun Bhaiyya sitting at the dining table eating, as Sahiba hovered anxiously around him and stuffed food into him. It looked as if she too had been crying. Then I heard Arun Bhaiyya give Mahavir directions to our last camp where our things still were so he could retrieve them.

'What happened here?' I asked again.

'Paramvir's phone suddenly got a signal and he called Shabby Aunty. He tried both of you too, to call you back, but you had switched off. Anyway, he told her where we were and she told Mama and since the police were out looking everywhere else, they came on their own and managed to cross the stream on foot. They've left the Innova on the other side. Papa had to go back to Delhi—he got a call from the Prime Minister's Office, of course.' Duckling's shrugged. 'What can you expect?'

'But Mama didn't go?'

'No. I haven't spoken to her and don't want to. She's been sitting with Nana all the time, crying. All natak.' She looked at me. 'They're sending helicopters up to look for you guys—as well as search parties on foot.'

Shabby Aunty looked at me. 'Feeling better sweetheart?' She smiled and stroked back my hair.

I nodded and stared glumly at the rain that had begun falling in earnest again. Thank god we were indoors! 'How's Nana—I want to see him.'

'He's good. Shabby Aunty brought a whole attaché case full of medicines and injections and stuff. He's much better, his cough has almost stopped.' I got to my feet.

The curtains were open in Nana's room. He was lying in bed staring at the rain and mist outside. Mama sat by his side, her eyes red rimmed and puffy. Shabby Aunty had set up a makeshift IV line and went to check it.

'Hi Nana, how're you doing?' I said softly. He turned and his face lit up.

'General sweetheart! Where have you been? You never told me your Mama was coming here.'

'Um, yeah it was a surprise for me too.'

I glanced again at Mama. She was looking a little better than she had been when I had seen her last from across the stream. But the thin line of her mouth was not promising. She looked at me.

'We're thinking of having Nana air-lifted out of here. He really needs to be in hospital. They'll be picking him up later in the afternoon. Then they'll pick us up, or we'll all have to clamber across that landslide as I and Shabnam Aunty had to.' She looked at me. 'Avantika, do you have any idea about how…?'

I walked out of the room. I had every idea about what I had done and how much inconvenience and trouble I had caused the entire world blah, blah, blah… And now I had lost. She was here. She would air-lift our beloved Nana to hospital and from there to a loony bin and we would probably never see him ever again, because either they wouldn't allow children to visit or he'd die in one week flat or both. It was over. I went back to the drawing room and sat down. Duckling looked at me questioningly. Then the twins marched into Nana's room, their eyes bright.

'Right Nana!' I heard Dumpling say briskly, 'Please identify me! Who am I and what is my name and rank and serial number?' Then, 'Paramvir, his teeth please—I've told you, he can't talk properly without them!'

'What cars do you have, Nana?'

'What did you eat for breakfast?'

I shuddered. It was hopeless. A few minutes later the twins marched out.

'He got six and a half out of ten today,' Dumpling said nodding in satisfaction and glancing at the clipboard she carried.

'Yesterday he got just three out of ten.'

'So how was your hike with Arun Bhaiyya?' Duckling asked me, her eyebrows up. I shrugged.

'Like trekking with a log of wood.' I smiled tiredly. 'Until he busted his ankle and needed the help of a mere girl!' Arun was resting in the other bedroom. Shabby Aunty had checked his ankle; he'd maybe torn a ligament, she thought. She had bound it up properly and he was more comfortable, as Sahiba (poor kid) fussed over him.

'You did a good job with his ankle,' Shabby Aunty told me, giving me a hug. She looked at me. 'It's all right Gosling, but at some point you and Duckling will have to talk to your Mama.'

'What's the point, Aunty? She'll just do what they planned to do. Besides, they'll be taking him away in an hour or so!' Duckling had told me that the helicopter was scheduled for four o'clock, before it got dark.

But then at three-thirty the call came that the weather had deteriorated too much—there was no way they could air-lift Nana this evening. They would have to wait for it to clear up and for the wind to drop before trying anything like that. They were now thinking of air-dropping a crew of men the next day who would clear the blocked track from our side so we could drive across as usual. But all of us would have to spend another night at the Villa. It wasn't really an issue as additional supplies of food and water and medicines had been dropped, but it would mean, that for the first time in god knows how many years, Mama would be spending the night under the same roof as all of us.

And this was our roof, not hers.

You think that would make the slightest difference to her? I doubted it and so I (and Duckling) avoided her all evening.

We sat with Arun and Sahiba as he recounted in his drip-dry manner, our three-day adventure.

'Were you scared?' Dumpling asked her black eyes wide. 'Spending the night in the dark forest?'

I nodded. 'When I saw the wolves, I was.'

'And Bazooka? Was he scared?'

'He was angry.'

'He would have fought them and killed them.'

'And Arun Bhaiyya? Was he scared?'

'I don't know, but I thought the wolves had eaten him when I got back to the camp and he was not there.' I looked at Arun. 'You should have at least left a note.'

'Sorry, I didn't think. I was concentrating so hard on just trying to stand up without falling down again.' He had the grace to smile sheepishly.

Duckling looked at me. 'You know, Mama wants to talk to us,' she said. 'She's been saying that over and over again. Has she spoken to you?'

I clammed up. 'No, and I don't want to talk to her. There's nothing to talk about. You know Mama, she'll just go and do what she wants to anyway.'

'I know. I haven't talked to her at all either. But she…she seems different. It's probably all natak,' Duckling began. 'She was crying like anything after she crossed over with Shabby Aunty and hugged and kissed us all—even Nana—all the time and wouldn't let us go and…'

'Well, I haven't let her hug me so far and she's not going to because I'm not going to let her, so there!'

They looked at me in silence and Duckling just nodded gently.

14

$\mathcal{J}$t was wonderful eating a properly cooked hot dinner (chicken biryani no less!) after three rough nights and I might have enjoyed it more had I not been thinking about what was surely going to follow. Well, I'd try and dodge the bullet, I thought. I finished quickly and pushed my chair back.

'I'm going to bed,' I said, 'I'm pooped.'

They all looked at me. Mama was sitting at the head of the table, Shabby Aunty at the other end; a couple of spare chairs had been drawn up for the twins. Duckling sat beside me and Arun across, next to Sahiba. 'I'll just say goodnight to Nana.'

'Darling, you and Harshita will be sleeping with me in Nana's room,' Mama said matter-of-factly. 'Shabby Aunty will be using the adjacent room and the twins will sleep in the dressing room next to Arun and Sahiba's room.'

'What? But I sleep with Duckling and the twins.'

I knew what she wanted: a catfight, one to one, tooth and nail, over Nana. It was a fight we could never win and she knew that. Okay, I thought suddenly, we would stand and fight. We'd tear her to shreds even if we died in the attempt!

I shrugged. 'Fine Mama, no problem, if that's what you want.'

I changed and lay down on one of the two mattresses that had been put on the floor. Duckling settled down beside me, silently, her face set. Nana was fast asleep. I guess I could have easily pretended to have gone to sleep and we could have avoided the battle, but I was far too worked up now, and was spoiling for a fight. It was time to clear the air. Half an hour after dinner, Mama and Shabby Aunty came in, followed by Mahavir to do a last check on Nana.

'Mahavir, will you please take one mattress to the other room?' Mama coolly ordered. 'The two babies and I will sleep there and Shabnam memsahib will be with sahibji here.'

'Wha…' I stared at the door that led to the dressing room: Solid teak, two inches thick, soundproof as a vault. So when the shrieking and killing started Nana would not be disturbed. Mama too was preparing for battle.

'Avantika and Harshita, come along darlings,' she said. We sat up, exchanging glances. I got up and walked mutinously into the room, followed by Duckling as Mahavir lugged my mattress across. And then at last it was just Mama and Duckling and I in the killing room. I sat on my mattress with my knees drawn up, glaring at Mama as she brushed her hair. Duckling looked from me to Mama and back. Attack was the best form of defence, so I lit right in, my voice pitched unnaturally high.

'Don't say anything to us; we don't want to hear your voice. But do you and Papa have any idea, even the tiniest iota of an idea, of what you're doing? Not only to us, but to Nana? You've hated him ever since he got that planeload of passengers to chant *dum lagake* when I was born and you've been taking your revenge ever since! What kind of people are you both? He did everything—do you hear—*everything* for us. He braided my hair and changed Duckling's diapers and taught her to read at age two, he gave the twins their bottles and taught them profit and loss while you… you and Papa junketed around the world on government money! And now you want to dump him in an asylum, just because he can't remember what he ate for breakfast? You make me sick! You make us both sick. You make us all sick!'

'Avantika...' Clearly she had been taken by surprise. I launched back into her, all my pent up rage exploding; I glared and wagged my finger in her face.

'Just you try to do that and see what we'll do. We'll go to the press, you hear? We'll tell them what a doting, loving mother and father you've been to us, how you missed out nearly all our birthdays and Diwalis and dumped us on Nana just because he'd put you in boarding school. See if you like being hounded by shrill women stuffing mikes into your face asking you if you really love your children.'

Her eyebrows were arched. 'And Shabnam Aunty said that you were the sound, sensible, stable one in the family,' she said mildly.

'And yes, talking about Shabby Aunty—she's been more a mother to us than you'd ever be...in a million years!'

Duckling gulped back sobs but then it became all too much for her. 'Yes,' she hiccupped, 'we hate you both! You've never been our real parents and will never be. Never, never, never!' she wailed. I put my arms around my sister and rocked her back and forth. I know all this seems hugely filmy and embarrassing but the poor kid was just fourteen then and I had just been through a hugely traumatic time.

Mama looked at us as I glared accusingly at her and held my fiery little sister close. She looked sort of introspective, grave even and nodded. 'Baby, while we were at Shadow House, Papa and I spent the entire night leafing through your photo-albums and watching the DVDs you had made. We know what we've missed, the price we have paid and will regret that for the rest of our lives.' She smiled wanly. 'I never thought I was capable of crying so much.'

Hello? What was this? Capitulation? Already? Not a chance.

She was just lulling us into a false sense of security—then wham, wham, wham—she'd launch her missiles! That's how these diplomat types worked. I nodded sarcastically.

'Yes, I'm sure you have been crying your eyes out over everything you missed: every crazy birthday party we had, every nutty treasure hunt Nana sent us on so he could have a cuddle with Shabby Aunty, every little business swindle the twins tried to pull—sure you regret that!' I shook my head witheringly. 'Mama, it's so easy to do what you want to and trample all over everyone else and then shrug and shed a few tears and say, oops, so sorry. But it doesn't undo anything!'

I looked towards the solid door; behind it in the other room, Nana would be asleep, his mouth open, snoring gutturally. 'Do you know how he used to wake all of us up every morning?' I asked, choking back tears. 'He used to clomp up and down in his big, fat army boots, and play the Colonel Bogey March on his trumpet and sing, *Hitler! He only had one ball...!*'

Her eyebrows shot up and she put a hand to her mouth, obviously shocked. 'And he would come to each of us and say goodnight to us separately, making us feel special. He made us look at the mountains every morning and point out things to us, and he'd inspect our uniforms and...' I was weeping now, because I knew that these were the things Nana would never do again... and Mama and Papa didn't care two hoots about them. Mama had settled down beside me and tentatively put her arm around me and Duckling.

'Don't!' I said, jerking away. 'Don't do that! Just go away! You've never been here when you were needed so why are you here now? We don't need you! We'll never need you! You're... you're redundant!'

'We're not going to go away, baby,' she said softly. 'So you are going to have to get used to having us around.'

'What? What are you talking about?' Was she setting yet another devious trap?

She looked at us steadily. 'I'll tell you but now that you've had your say, you can listen to me, it's my turn. For a start, I—and your father—did not "dump" all of you on Nana because I wanted revenge or anything like that. Nana just wanted me to excel in my career—he was hugely proud of what I'd done. And I knew that I didn't want the four of you to go through what I had been through while I was growing up, traipsing around like a gypsy during the holidays, with no place I recognized as home. That's when I decided to leave you with him, and he was delighted.' Her face was neutral as she went on. 'It hurt us a lot when we had to deposit you at Shadow House and go away, and the only way we could survive was to plunge into our careers completely.' She nodded. 'I know you kids paid the price for that—because we must have come across as cold and unfeeling. But babies, it's cost us too—more than we ever imagined.'

'But...' I interrupted, 'remember that time in Delhi? Nana said that you should never have had children?'

She nodded. 'Yes, because he knew what I—and your Papa—were missing by not being with all of you as you grew up and was sad because of that.' She paused and then went on. 'Now, do you realize what Nana might become like in the future? We know what he's done for you—and you do too, all too well. We want you to remember that—not what's likely to happen. In time, he may not recognize you at all, he may even hate you and shout at you and we don't want you to be subject to all that.'

'He won't forget us. The twins won't let him.'

She smiled. 'Yes, they're hammering away at him aren't they?'

'So just because you think we won't be able to handle it you want to dump him out like he was garbage.'

She shook her head. 'No, Avantika, we thought that he'd get better, professional care in that place—and it would be a burden off your shoulders.' She looked at her long tapering fingers. 'But when we came to Shadow House and saw those albums and DVDs and now that I've spent a couple of nights here, with Harshita and the twins and Shabnam, I think maybe you all might do a better job at keeping him happy.'

'What are you saying, Mama?'

'You'll have to learn to accept him the way he is. You'll have to give him the love and affection you've always been giving him, but not expect anything in return. You may even get cursed and be yelled at, he might say horrible things to you, he may not recognize you and treat you like a hostile stranger, he may even try to hit you.'

'But that's just the disease, isn't it; it's not really him.'

'Yes. Papa and I just doubted if you'd realize that and be able to handle it. It's not easy for *anyone* to handle that sort of thing, least of all those who have been closest and most loving.' She looked thoughtful. 'But in a way I think Niharika and Nihal have learned how to handle the situation remarkably—the way they give him his memory tests! They shake their heads and cluck when he does badly, and cheer when he does well, but they don't take it to heart. They just carry on normally with the rest of their lives...swindling everyone they can, I suppose!'

I pinched myself. I was actually having a rational conversation with Mama! What had happened? By now we ought to have been throwing things at each other. But I was still wary.

'So, what does this mean?'

'It means that your Papa has gone to the Prime Minister's Office to submit our resignation. We'll be living in Shadow House, henceforth.'

'What?'

She smiled dryly. 'If that's all right with you.'

'Do...do you know Shabby Aunty has moved in? She was in the guest bedroom.'

'She told me. She'll stay on of course.'

No cow! 'But...but...where will?'

'We're not going to upset your arrangement. There are plenty of unused rooms in Shadow House—we'll move into one of those. Shabby Aunty can stay on in the guest bedroom.'

To be sure that this was happening I fired a final salvo.

'You sounded very different on the phone when you spoke to us from London or wherever you were. You said things like "don't be silly...don't be ridiculous". You were angry and cold and didn't want to listen.'

'I'm sorry about that, and frankly we have no excuses. I was impatient and distant—and then Harshita lost her temper and was rude. I think we had just been apart for too long, living completely separate lives. Distances and silences can build terrible, hostile walls between people—that's what happened I think. Then I saw your photographs, the things and life we missed, all of you growing up, the crazy things your Nana did with you, Shabby Aunty, this place.'

'Do you think your career was worth it?' I asked brutally, still not believing I was having a one-to-one civilized dialogue with Mama. 'I mean giving up all that?'

'It was worth a lot—and your Papa and I were very good at what we did. We just didn't know how to combine the both of them, to multitask as it were and maybe we all paid the price.' She frowned and then suddenly smiled. 'Actually I think you guys had a pretty good time with Nana, don't you? It wouldn't have been half as much fun with Papa and me, I can tell you that!'

I nodded. 'Yes, we did—and we still do.'

She put her arms around us and embraced us and this time we did not back off. 'So let me get this straight Mama,' I whispered, still not fully believing what had happened. 'You and Papa will be shifting to Shadow House and living there permanently.'

'Yes. And probably Papa will drive you to school in the Woody and...'

'I'm done with school, Mama...'

'Well, the others then.'

'And Nana will remain at home?'

'Yes.'

She hugged me again and I hugged her back. Then she kissed my cheek. 'There's one more thing I want to ask you,' she said.

Oh god, oh my god, she was going to ask me if she could call me Gosling or better General Gosling! I nodded eagerly in anticipation.

'Anything Mama!'

'Baby, you were alone in the mountains and forests with that boy, Arun for three whole nights. Did... did he...you...did anything happen that shouldn't have?'

'*Mama!*'

Epilogue

It's been four years since our epic 'escape caper' to Rainbow Villa and I'm still teased about it by everyone. Sure it was a crazy thing to do, and now that I'm older and wiser, I wonder how I summoned the courage to actually put the plan into action. But I still believe that it worked.

Much to Duckling's and my surprise, Mama and Papa settled down in Shadow House quite easily (possibly because of their training as diplomats!). They both help out at the hospital in administrative matters. Knowing them, they're probably running the show and the permanent staff members don't even realize it. They've also done a lot of 'home-work catching up' (that's the twins' description) with us; we've spent hours with them with the photo-albums on our laps or watching slide shows, explaining and re-living the pictures so they get a good idea of what daily life was like with Nana. This has really broken down the wall that had come up between us and it made us relive all those wonderful times without hurting too much, because now we had our parents with us to comfort and sympathize. Papa especially virtually 'interviews' us about every event or outing—I wouldn't be surprised if he's writing a book on Nana—he doesn't admit as much, but these diplomat types love secrets, don't they! Mama and Shabby Aunty after that prickly start to their relationship became friends and take turns at being with Nana (Paramvir and Mahavir look after him, as usual)—as do we for that matter—so he's hardly ever left alone.

I'll be joining medical college soon here in Mahaparbatpur where a swanky brand new campus has come up, staffed with hotshot doctors and faculty. Shabby Aunty says there's no place like India to get brutal, bloody, hands-on training in medicine and surgery And yes, I drive my lovely yellow Sunbeam all over the mountains and love the sound of its raspy little exhaust bouncing off the sheer rock faces.

Shabby Aunty continues to work at the hospital and live with us and is as madly in love with Nana as ever. She's (thankfully) given up on Raksha and, as Duckling rather prosaically puts it, while rolling her eyes, 'has found everlasting love and happiness here, in the warm bosom of our family.'

Sahiba and Arun Bhaiyya still live just down the road. Sahiba wants to become a journalist and Arun is doing automobile engineering. This has made the twins very suspicious.

'Be careful, Didi!' Dumpling warned me direly. 'He thinks that if he becomes a car mechanic Nana and Papa will allow him to marry you. All he really wants are Nana's cars!' All I am willing to admit to is that I still can't put my bicycle together and Arun Bhaiyya is still trying valiantly and exasperatedly to teach me how to.

Duckling's buckling down for her Boards and seems torn between her desire to become an astronaut or museum curator. She's taken over the attics at Shadow House for her collections and has started specializing in antique silver animals. The twins call her museum, 'Attic Antics.'

Dumpling and Dingaling Enterprises Pvt Ltd. continue with their nefarious business activities. They've emotionally blackmailed Duckling and me into continuing with our daily 'rituals' with Nana—the Colonel Bogey good mornings, the goodnights and inspections, standing out on the gazebo, staring at the mountains and sky. They continue to give Nana memory tests and ask him to subtract seven from a hundred. I think Mama was right: while they take their 'student's' performance very seriously they don't take any of it to heart. They cluck and mutter and shake their heads when he does badly, and cheer when he does well, but after that they sort of detach and just carry on normally with the rest of their notorious little lives.

Nana for the most part spends his days in his armchair or the 'Cadillac' SUV wheelchair, dozing or watching Paramvir and Mahavir wax and polish his beloved cars, with De-Big Bazooka snoozing at his feet and either Mama or Shabby Aunty keeping an eye on him and chatting away to him as they go about their household chores. He doesn't say very much but beams happily when the twins march up to him, salute and jerk their chins towards the Packard and bark: 'Nana sir, what car is that?' Paramvir and Mahavir occasionally give him some car part to fix—sometimes he gets it all wrong, but sometimes he does the job with precision and perfection and it's wonderful to see the concentration on his face as he uses a screwdriver or spanner. Sometimes of course, he seems very sad and depressed, but the twins organize some entertainment to distract him; they might just blare some music and begin to dance or generally play the fool. We like to think that he still recognizes us all because though he's mostly silent, he's usually beaming when we're around and sometimes gives us a slow salute. Just the other evening, he smiled at me, his eyes twinkling and said softly: 'Sweetheart, do you know you were born on the Empress Noor Jehan, a Boeing 747, somewhere between London and Bombay, 30,000 feet above sea level?' Of course he repeated that about thirty times for the rest of the evening—and I answered him patiently every time, blushing:

'Yes, Nana, *dum lagake haisha…!* Remember?'

And every time he gave a throaty chortle. Then he closed his eyes and went back to snooze before waking up and asking again.